HURDA

Advance praise for *Hurda*

'A remarkable debut—compassionate, polished, unsparing, technically adept. The multifarious voices together create a haunting melody of rural India. Read this right away.'

Prayaag Akbar, author of *Leila*

'*Hurda* is a stunning debut. Atharva Pandit's masterful storytelling voice left me spellbound.'

Sonia Faleiro, author of *The Good Girls*

'I feel like I know what a murder investigation in rural India must be like. This is more an experience than a book; beware, you might end up haunted.'

Jerry Pinto, author of *Em and the Big Hoom*

'Reminiscent of Bolaño's polyphonous whirlpools, Pandit's novel deftly inverts the adage that it takes a village to raise a child. A remarkable debut.'

Tanuj Solanki, author of *Manjhi's Mayhem*

HURDA

ATHARVA PANDIT

BLOOMSBURY
NEW DELHI • LONDON • OXFORD • NEW YORK • SYDNEY

BLOOMSBURY INDIA
Bloomsbury Publishing India Pvt. Ltd
Second Floor, LSC Building No. 4, DDA Complex, Pocket C – 6 & 7,
Vasant Kunj, New Delhi 110070

BLOOMSBURY, BLOOMSBURY INDIA and the Diana logo
are trademarks of Bloomsbury Publishing Plc

First published in India 2023
This edition published 2023

This is a work of fiction. All names, characters, organisations and events portrayed in this novel are either products of the author's imagination or are used fictitiously.

ISBN: PB: 978-93-56402-28-7; e-Book: 978-93-56402-21-8
2 4 6 8 10 9 7 5 3 1

Typeset in Fournier MT Std by Manipal Technologies Limited
Printed and bound in India by Thomson Press India Ltd

FSC www.fsc.org
MIX
Paper from responsible sources
FSC® C010615

To find out more about our authors and books, visit www.bloomsbury.com and sign up for our newsletters

To my parents
for everything

CONTENTS

Part One

EMERGENCY

14–15 February 2013
Murwani, Maharashtra

Anisha

Everything in front of her was blue and green, golden and bright. The air was pleasant and crisp except for the whiff of cow dung, which did not bother Anisha all that much, not as much as the cow dung itself—splattered on the road, there for the entire day until the cleaners arrived late in the evening and scooped it up.

Anisha, eldest of three sisters, always wanted everything to be clean, tip-top clean. Flick a speck of dust here, clean a line of grime there. It bothered her when she couldn't do that. When she noticed a stain, a smear, something soiled, it bothered her when she couldn't pick it up, when she couldn't clean it up, when she couldn't make it look right again.

Perhaps that's why she went away, her mother would say later, because she could feel the dirt roiling inside her house but couldn't clean it. She could scrub the walls and scrape the floor, but how could she clean the muck that filled her with disgust but couldn't be seen?

So she went away, said her mother. She went away. And along with her went her sisters, because they couldn't stand to live inside that shithole either.

That day, on 14 February 2013, Anisha was out and about because she was supposed to go to school; she was supposed to be in school, but she carried no school bag and she wasn't wearing her uniform. Instead, she sported a watermelon-green top. There was a hint of a smile on her lips and her eyes sparkled with anticipation.

That day, she was a happy girl, all of fourteen, wearing her favourite top. She knew it could attract attention, of course, a girl wearing anything attracts attention, but at that time of the morning, at around quarter past seven, people didn't really care about who was wearing what, because such people—people who would have noticed—were yet to step out of their houses.

Or so Anisha believed.

Anisha: tall and jumpy, looking a little bit older than her fourteen years. She never walked, she always hopped. Left foot in the air and right foot on the ground; then right foot in the air and left foot on the ground. Plaits wrapped up tightly: a school requirement. A mischievous smile hanging on the edge of her lips, always.

A man Anisha didn't know rode on a bike from the opposite direction. He wasn't fully awake yet, but his eyes widened as he leered at Anisha, from head to toe, his tongue out of his mouth, licking his lower lip: good morning, indeed.

She noticed the man, she saw him do all that he did, she saw his eyes move up and down and up again, but she had conditioned herself to ignore such things, so she ignored it and continued on her way.

From her home Anisha hopped away in the direction of Shivaji Putala, Murwani's main square. But she did not enter the square or the market adjoining it. Instead, after taking a right that led to the market, she slipped into a narrow lane that circumvented the market and the main square and walked through Futane Wadi, past Rafiq's Biryani and a line of repair shops she knew would still be shuttered. She emerged fifteen minutes later, on the main village road snaking towards the national highway, abutting a line of paddy fields. She crossed the road and disappeared into the fields right opposite Sugandha Fast Food Centre.

Later, the owner of Sugandha Fast Food Centre would claim that he had seen Anisha, the eldest sister, in a green top, crossing into the paddy fields and disappearing inside them. He would also claim that he had spotted her as she emerged on the temple side. She had made her way towards the temple, he said, or perhaps somewhere further.

Then the discussion about the direction Anisha took that morning would cease, at this little bit of information: that she was spotted on the main village road, that she had walked into the paddy fields adjoining it, that she had walked towards the temple and then disappeared beyond. Then the discussion, for the time being, would circle around the facts about the top, specifically the colour and the make of it. Everyone seems to remember how tight this green top was. How it was something that decent girls from Murwani wouldn't have known existed, let alone thought of wearing out on the streets. The other point of concern was the question of how: how was it that she had managed to change into it—this top—during the hustle and bustle of that morning?

Anisha's mother didn't know which green top they were talking about, she had never known her daughter to own a green top. Then again, who knows? Everyone knew everything about her daughters and no one knew anything about her daughters. That was how it had always been.

The matter at the heart of everything, then, was that Anisha had been spotted wearing a green top. For days and months after, it was at the periphery of discussion wherever the people of Murwani met or gathered: it might be true, they said, that she had walked out of the gate wearing her uniform, which is what her mother claims, though what her mother claims is as good as what the police claim, which is not to say much, so it might be true, who knows, but what is known, what is known for sure, they said, is that Anisha had waited for her mother to head out of their shack to fetch water. Then—listen to this—then, silent as a cat's paw, she had sneaked in through the back door, changed out of her uniform into the said top and then slipped away. Nods and hmms.

No, no, others said, maybe what you said is true, yes, it does seem possible, yes, but what we heard was different. What we heard was that she had made her way out of the shack wearing her uniform, like her mother says she did. But she had changed into the green top and dumped her school bag—listen to this—inside that granary five minutes from her home. Which granary? That granary re, on the way to Shivaji Putala. Aangle's granary? Haan, that one. Daring baaz that girl, dumping her stuff into Aangle chi granary. Nods and hmms. Now listen to this: once she had changed into her green top, that tight green top, one would expect that she would make her way towards wherever it is that she wanted to go wearing that green top, yes? And wherever it is that she wanted to go wearing that green top would most certainly not be her school, yes? But that's exactly what happened: she changed out of her uniform, dumped her school bag inside that granary and then, to ensure that nobody noticed her, she chose to walk through the long line of paddy fields to her school, Murwani Vidya Sadan.

That is what happened, they said, those who said it.

It is possible, however, that they didn't know shit. Because the fact of the matter was that Anisha's home had neither a back door nor a gate—it was a shack—and perhaps she hadn't made her way to the school through the paddy fields, because there were people claiming to have seen her on the main road.

At this point the discussion would twist back to the topic of the direction. Someone would say that Anisha was wearing this green top until late afternoon, which is when she had been spotted near the petrol pump. The main source of this information was Raju Bokle, a paanpatti-wala. Said Raju Bokle: 'I saw her leaning against a petrol pump pillar at around three o'clock. She was wearing a green top. I don't know why she was wearing that instead of her uniform . . . I don't think she ever went to school that day.'

Four others said that Anisha was wearing a green top; two more said that she never went to school that day. At least two children claimed that they had seen her in school. A teacher, her class teacher, said that Anisha had never made it to school, if we are to believe that day's attendance sheet.

But her mother said that Anisha had left for school that morning, and that when she left, she had been wearing her school uniform, just like her sisters Priyanka and Sanchita, who had left a little earlier. As far as their mother was concerned, on that morning, the morning of 14 February 2013, everything had been business as usual. Things would turn unusual only much, much later in the day.

Priyanka

They said that of the three sisters Priyanka was the brightest. She was also the youngest. In photos of the sisters, she beams without the worries that seem to restrict the other two sisters' smiles. It is perhaps her age, an age of innocence and of ignorance.

Though perhaps not. Because, despite being the youngest, Priyanka, her grandfather said, was the most mature among the sisters. All of nine, she already knew that there was no future in Murwani and that her eventual life would be somewhere else, preferably in some city. Besides, she had told Ajoba that she did not like the village and she did not like the way the people of the village treated them.

And how did the people of the village treat them?

The family wasn't exactly shunned, but the rumours about them were too many to be ignored. What made it worse was that no one from the family had bothered to address those rumours or clear the air about them, so for years everybody with the exception of a few had accepted them as true. While some of the rumours—that the mother, for example, was a madwoman, and that Aaji and the mother did not get along, and that the mother hit poor Aaji every night to let out her frustration—were more or less typical, the one thing people consistently repeated was that the mother had killed her husband. What had killed her husband was a disease, some kind of fatal illness; they said that these days one never knows about illnesses and diseases, there are so many, but this one was rather strange, because the husband, the father of the three sisters, had been sucked dry. Yes. Imagine a mango being squeezed, bitten and sucked: that's how he had died. And who knows anything about such diseases?

So they said that the sisters' father, an alcoholic who used to work at the car factory on the edge of the village, had died due to a 'mysterious illness'. There are people who believe that his wife had sucked the soul out of his body because she no longer loved him. At any rate, they said, she wasn't exactly a devoted wife, so it was not surprising at all. It was Aaji, some say, who had started the rumour that persists even today: that the mother had indulged in jadoo tona to kill her husband. And now, they said, those who said it, now the mother was teaching her daughters this black art, the art of sucking souls. It figures, they said, those who said it, because look at the unruly behaviour of that elder sister, Anisha, look at the awkward manner in which that middle sister, Sanchita, carries herself, look at the way the youngest, Priyanka, is so proud of her brains, as if she is the only shaani around here. Do you think all this is normal? Three sisters is never a good omen, to begin with. And now this.

This reputation was the reason Priyanka wanted to get out of the village as soon as it was possible for her—and Janhavi knew that she would. One fine day her best friend would leave forever.

What Janhavi remembers of that day is that it had begun with her cowering behind Swapnil, a dhippad fellow with a broad enough back to conceal the tiny tot Janhavi. That's the image that comes to her mind when someone asks her about that day. The fourteenth of February 2013. Priyanka taking notes, Ganpule Sir, their English teacher, reading out something from their Balbharati textbook and Janhavi hiding herself, hoping against hope that Ganpule Sir wouldn't notice her. Because when Ganpule Sir noticed her, or some unfortunate student like her, weak in studies, weak, especially, in English, he liked to lob a trick question or two at them, and he liked it when they shifted in their seats, uncomfortable in their lack of knowledge, unlucky in their lack of intelligence. 'Haan tar, Janhavi, I hold a *dash* of flowers in my hand . . . What of flowers am I holding in my hands, Janhavi?' he would ask and then he would watch her, in excruciating silence, a moment he would stretch as far as he thought was sufficient. Then he would click his tongue and shake his head and deliver his favourite line: 'English. You need it in the outside world, children.'

Then came the punishment: he would make Janhavi stand in front of the classroom, which meant enduring the mocking stares and the sneery giggles of her classmates as she fiddled with her uniform and tried to control her tears. It had happened thrice before, and by this time everyone was convinced that Janhavi was dumb; they said as much, behind her back, but also, increasingly, to her face.

So Janhavi was cowering and trying to hide from certain humiliation, while Priyanka was still in the classroom. This must have been at around eleven-thirty, two periods before school ended, when everything was normal.

But then Janhavi spotted Anisha in her green top.

Quiet as a lizard on the wall, Anisha tiptoed to the door of the classroom and stopped just below the 'Honesty Is the Best Policy' sticker. Then she peeped in and extended her hand, as if any moment now she would ask Ganpule Sir: 'May I come in, sir?'

But she didn't *ask* anything. When Ganpule Sir did not pay her any attention, she cleared her throat and said: 'Sir . . . there's an emergency, sir, I need to take my sister home.'

Ganpule Sir continued to read out aloud.

Anisha repeated: 'Sir, I need to take Priyanka home. It's an emergency, sir.'

Now Ganpule Sir, his spectacles on the edge of his sharp nose, looked at Anisha.

'What is it?'

'It's an emergency, sir . . .'

'What?'

'I need to take my sister home. It's an emergency, sir.'

Ganpule Sir's gaze shifted back to his textbook. He grunted and then continued with his reading, which was signal enough for Anisha to look at Priyanka, smile and nod. Then Priyanka got up and scuttled out of the classroom with her sister, into freedom. As they walked out, hand in hand, they whispered something to each other, those two sisters, but Janhavi couldn't figure out what. All she heard one of them say was 'hurda'. Something to do with hurda.

What hurda? What emergency? Maybe something had happened with either their Aaji or their Ajoba. But in that case why was Anisha smiling and looking happy? And what had an emergency got to do with hurda?

Then Janhavi spotted the bag. Priyanka's bag. A tomato-red rectangular school bag with a smiling duck and a smiling mouse plastered over the back-flap, just above the silver latch that locked with a *click* sound. It was Priyanka's most prized possession, and it had attracted appropriate attention when Priyanka brought it to school for the first time, about three weeks ago. Almost everyone in the classroom wanted to touch it, sling it over their shoulders, feel it over their backs.

But Priyanka had clutched it tightly and told everyone to keep away.

'My sister said, "Don't let anyone touch it." Don't touch it, it's expensive,' Priyanka had announced to a group of girls and boys on that first day. Then she pointed at Janhavi. 'Only Janhavi is allowed to touch it,' she declared, elevating her best friend's standing in the classroom.

Before they were best friends, they had been classmates, Janhavi and Priyanka. Eventually they had become bench mates. Then in November last year their class teacher Sugandha Miss had decided to separate them to teach them a lesson for all the giggling and whispering they did during the class. Go and giggle with someone else, find new friends, she told them. So they were seated a row apart now, Priyanka on the second bench from the door and Janhavi on the fifth. Of course, that did not stop them from exchanging wry looks across the classroom and smiling at each other and making faces and giggling.

When she recalls that day, however, all Janhavi remembers is her friend walking out of the classroom with her sister. No knowing glances, no wry smiles. Priyanka was gone before anyone could ask her anything, before anyone could even start wondering what emergency could have befallen those three sisters.

Sanchita

The third sister, the middle one, was the quietest. Ask about her, and a lot of people wouldn't know what to say: we don't know much about her, she wasn't very talkative, she always trailed behind Anisha, she was devoted to Anisha, she was always trying to copy Anisha . . . They spoke about Sanchita in the same breath as Anisha and in contrast to Priyanka—that Priyanka was intelligent and Sanchita had no opinion of her own. She did what Anisha did, or what Anisha asked her to do, and that was that.

A girl with short, unevenly cut hair and curious, watery eyes. Sanchita was twelve, and she had a bubbling inner life. One only needed to probe a little and striking details would emerge. For example, while Sanchita did not speak very often, and while she was always considered extremely shy, someone who averted her eyes and chose silence, she was also an enthusiastic dancer, an avid watcher of television and a girl with a lifelong fascination for history.

They say that the middle ones are always the most ignored, but Sanchita was her Ajoba's favourite. Theirs was a meeting of souls, a recognition of each in the other.

Said her Ajoba: 'Sanchita wasn't very bright, she wasn't very good at her studies, but she was just . . . she was just very observant. My daughter-in-law used to say that Priyanka would make the family proud, but I personally felt that Sanchita would be the one to get out of this village first and make a name for herself. She was a good dancer. They used to have these little dance competitions among themselves, and she always used to win. I remember the fun we had one time in that kitchen. The girls made a trophy out of cardboard, and because I had nothing to do, they asked me to judge their competition. They sang and danced well, all three of them. They used to dance to all the Hindi songs and some Marathi songs, but mostly Hindi songs. On the radio. They danced and I clapped, and I remember watching them and thinking: these girls are so talented! They are going to make us all proud one day . . .'

On one of the walls of their kitchen—the only concrete wall—Sanchita had scrawled a number with green chalk. This was the number from a teleshopping network that Sanchita used to watch every night, after dinner. That was the only time the sisters were allowed to watch television. In any case, that teleshopping network was the only channel on their TV. Like many teleshopping networks, the channel repeated the same things throughout the day. Mostly it advertised machines to reduce weight or colourful stones set in rings to help you get lucky. But what caught Sanchita's attention one day was the Katrina Kaif sticker pasted on one of the weight-reducing machines being advertised.

Sanchita had been obsessed with the actress ever since, and she believed that the number displayed on the ticker on the TV was Katrina Kaif's—so the little girl had mugged up the number and scribbled it on the wall to remember it for when she was given a phone. Not that she would receive a phone anytime soon, she was aware enough to know that, but she believed Anisha would jugaad something. She always did. One day Sanchita had asked her elder sister about it, about a phone, because she had heard people talk about it, about a phone that Anisha carried. Can I make a call, Anisha Tai? I know you have a phone, can I make a call? Instead of dismissing Sanchita and pushing her away, Anisha had simply laughed. Who do you want to call, Sanchita? Who is this friend you want to call?

Katrina Kaif.

That had made her sister laugh even more.

'Don't be stupid, Sanchita.'

Katrina Kaif. 0087668 . . .

But it wasn't just Katrina Kaif. There was also Rani Laxmibai. And Ahilyabai Holkar. And Hirkani. Sanchita especially liked Hirkani's story, set in the time of Shivaji Maharaj's reign. Once, during a school play, she had even played the part of the milkmaid who, according to legend, scaled down a steep cliff surrounding the Raigad Fort in the dead of the night to be with her infant daughter. The story had struck a chord with Sanchita.

The girls always wanted to listen to those stories, of Rani Laxmibai and Hirkani and Ahilyabai Holkar, and while their Ajoba was a willing participant who ensured that he knew all the historical details, their Aaji disapproved of these storytelling sessions.

'Girls don't need to know all this. They become unnecessarily bold.'

What better example of this unnecessary boldness than Anisha?

That's what Prateek Shende thought that day, on 14 February, as he watched Anisha stand by the door and scan the classroom. He had always known that the three sisters were strange—he had been told enough times to stay away from them—but he found the elder sister, Anisha, to be the strangest. Why? He didn't know why. Perhaps because she was unlike all the other girls—she was unnecessarily bold; she was known to do whatever she wanted, whenever she wanted and however she wanted, and that, Prateek had been told, was no way for a girl to behave.

'Emergency . . . there is an emergency, sir . . .'

Prateek looked on with envy as his classmate Sanchita followed her sister Anisha out into the corridor and down the stairs. What could be the emergency? Then, immediately: there's no emergency. The girls are kidding, fooling around. There's no emergency. Prateek thought about his elder brother, Pranil. Would he come looking for Prateek to tell him about an 'emergency' like Anisha had? If he ever did, Prateek thought, he should come during Danish Sir's Hindi class, since Danish Sir was always trying to cough and speak at the same time, with the result that he could manage neither to his satisfaction. That was exactly how Sanchita had managed to slip out: by the time Danish Sir had controlled his coughing, *zoop*, the sisters were gone.

'They are gone.'

Danish Sir was also in the habit of repeating obvious things. Yes, Danish Sir, they are gone. Poor Danish Sir: years of being around chalk and dusters had weakened his lungs, made him prone to respiratory troubles. Naturally, he was prone to being taken advantage of, as the sisters quite clearly had. But it didn't seem to matter to Danish Sir much, the fact that Sanchita was gone. He snapped his fingers, coughed for a little bit longer and asked the class to concentrate.

But who could concentrate after something like that? Everybody was thinking about the emergency. About the sisters. It had brought a sense of excitement to a boring classroom on a dull day. Prateek knew the element of mystery would remain, and he knew that the thoughts inside the classroom would revolve around Sanchita, which was a rare thing because no one really noticed the girl. She was shy, and it seemed as if she had some kind of problem speaking. Prateek had never seen her having a conversation with anyone: she had always remained in her corner; alone, aloof, morose.

Prateek's bench was by the window. He looked outside and spotted the youngest sister, Priyanka, standing all by herself on the school ground, fidgeting, looking around, nervous—until Anisha and Sanchita joined her and Anisha began telling them something excitedly.

Lucky, these sisters, Prateek thought. No emergency-vemergency, they are just skipping classes to have a fun day out. Though what if it *is* an emergency? What if Anisha had been called home first, because it was a genuine emergency, and then she had been told to bring her sisters along? What if something had happened to their grandparents?

But it was way more believable that the sisters were bunking school. Prateek wasn't sure why he was thinking along those lines. Perhaps it had something to do with the fact that he had been fantasizing about doing something similar: the watchman was on leave for fifteen days, and the school hadn't bothered to find a replacement for such a short period of time. This was their only chance to bunk school without anyone noticing. Pranil could come in, panting and sweaty, as if he had had to run to reach the classroom, and call out for his younger brother because they needed to be home for an 'emergency'. Then they could go out and have a gola and a plate of Chinese rice each near the petrol pump and go back home as if nothing had happened. Oh, the thrill of it!

Prateek smiled at that thought and looked outside again, just in time to spot the three sisters slink out of the school premises, take a right turn and disappear behind the crumbling wall.

Didn't the sisters live in Sakhare Kinara? That was on the left, not on the right, and Prateek knew this for sure because he knew where the sisters lived—he was their neighbour.

Well, in a way.

The house where the sisters lived was the only sad and isolated building in a close-knit wadi, and it abutted Prateek's uncle Datta Mama's paddy field. In fact, their uncle sometimes claimed that the Gudadhes had encroached upon his land to build their 'sorry shack', but mostly he complained about those daughters-of-bitches sisters and the way the family carried itself in general. Not the best of neighbours in Datta Mama's book, but what to do? What he *could* do was instruct his nephews to stay away from them, which he did incessantly.

'Gone case people. All six of them. Gone case. One of the sisters is your classmate na re, Prateek? What is her name you said?'

'Sanchita.'

'Sanchita. And how is she? Behaviour wise?'

'Fine.'

'Chappal maru ka be? What does that mean? Fine. What does that mean?'

'She is quiet. And she is a little dumb.'

'Is she your friend?'

'No.'

'Good. Waste of space. Is she the intelligent one?'

'No.'

'Waste of money, too, in that case. Is she your friend?'

'No.'

'Good. Your friends must all aspire to be doctors and engineers. Not these daughters-of-bitches and slackers. You know what their father did for a living?'

'No.'

'That's because he did nothing. A total slacker. Drunkard. Died that way, too. You stay away from them.'

So, like ideal nephews, Prateek and Pranil had always stayed away from the sisters. The brothers had a bright future, everyone agreed on that: the elder one, Pranil, was going to be an engineer, and Prateek was going to be a doctor. They were the ideal brothers and the girls were the whorish sisters.

And see, there's the proof. There was no emergency, the sisters went away to make merry, that's all. Prateek didn't feel disgusted about that, though. He thought: why can't Pranil and I do something like that sometime? What are we so scared of?

Long after the sisters had disappeared, Prateek kept looking in the direction they had vanished, longingly.

Janhavi

After Ganpule Sir's English class, Kerkar Sir, the man who taught them geography and history and science, all three of which he sometimes combined in his seemingly never-ending enthusiasm, had walked into the classroom and announced the next two periods as 'free' on account of his 'back-to-back meetings'.

Janhavi remembers that the boys had hooted and the girls had cheered. But Kerkar Sir had shushed everyone. 'That doesn't mean you get to go outside. Sugandha Miss will come and monitor the class. You do whatever you want to do, but inside the classroom.'

Who cares? As long as there were back-to-back free periods! And yet, Janhavi's excitement was momentary. Because who was she supposed to spend her free periods with? Priyanka was already gone.

That day Janhavi looked at the branches and the crows and the sparrows a little more than she normally did. Thinking: where did Priyanka go? Anisha was always bunking school and whiling time, and no one really bothered about her. Now she had taken Priyanka along, and Janhavi had no other friend to speak of. There was Manisha, and there was Ahilya, but Janhavi didn't really enjoy their company. They bored her. So she yawned and placed her head on the desk and started imagining what it would be like to live in a world without parents, where there was nothing but chocolate and talking birds and animals.

She woke up when it was already five minutes past the final bell and Sugandha Miss was asking her to go home. Janhavi rubbed her eyes and nodded, dazed and confused. She looked towards Priyanka's bench and saw Ahilya standing beside it, and she had . . . whose bag was that? Was that Priyanka's bag?

'Ahilya! You cannot touch—give me that bag. It's not yours.'

Ahilya was startled but she managed a smile. Then she stuck her tongue out.

'It's not yours either, Janhavi.'

'Only I am allowed to touch it. You know that. Priyanka said so herself. Give me the bag.'

'No. Let me—'

'Ahilya,' Sugandha Miss scolded. 'Stop this nonsense. Give Janhavi the bag. And Janhavi, where is Priyanka actually? Why did she leave her bag here? Take the bag and go find her. Ahilya, don't make me ask twice, haan, you will regret it actually. Strange girls . . .'

Ahilya held the bag by its strap and offered it to Janhavi. When Janhavi tried to take it from her, Ahilya pulled back the bag and stuck out her tongue again: 'Take the bag, na!' Then, as if suddenly losing interest, she dropped the bag on the floor, sniggered and said: 'It's not *that* shiny.'

Then she was gone, and so was Sugandha Miss, leaving Janhavi alone inside the classroom.

Janhavi decided to drop the bag at Priyanka's home. She had done that before, so there was no reason why she shouldn't do it again. She picked up the bag and tried to sling it over her shoulder while balancing her own cloth bag, torn along the edges. Once she had managed to balance both the bags, she walked out of the classroom and down the stairs on to the school ground. She thought: maybe Priyanka is waiting for me in the playground, and maybe she'll instruct me to drop the bag at home and come back to play.

But Priyanka wasn't anywhere on the playground.

Janhavi looked around for a bit, hoping to find her friend, hoping to ask her whether she wanted her to drop the bag home, whether they were still meeting in the afternoon and whether they were still going to watch that cricket match in the evening. Janhavi had no interest in cricket matches, but Priyanka loved them. She loved the atmosphere of those matches, played under the bright glare of orange and yellow lights, procured specially for the local tournament which was to begin next week: this was a practice match, but according to Priyanka even practice matches were terrific fun, although Janhavi didn't enjoy them as much since they did not have the jatra-like atmosphere of the actual tournament.

But Priyanka was nowhere to be found. Not on the playground, or anywhere around the school.

Janhavi sighed, walked out of Murwani Vidya Sadan, turned left and continued down the macadam road, towards where the three sisters lived.

Anisha, the eldest, Priyanka, the youngest, and Sanchita, the quietest, lived with their grandparents and their mother, who used to accompany the girls to the school earlier but had stopped about two years ago.

Now the sisters walked to the school all by themselves: Anisha leading them, sometimes walking between them, holding their hands, but often right in front, not really caring about them—or about anything in the world.

The Mother

(Excerpts from an interview transcript. Interview conducted on 23 February 2019.)

'As always, I was at home during lunchtime, trying to clean the house, trying to keep it tidy, trying to make it look like a house instead of the shithole that it was . . . and it was around lunchtime, in the afternoon, that the little girl Janhavi came to me and said: Kaku, bag. All she said was: Kaku, bag. She is a little slow, that girl Janhavi, but she was a good friend of my Priyanka. Or at least she was a very helpful friend, I could see that because she was always helping Priyanka with things.

Like bringing her bag home while she went and played with her sisters. I told Janhavi a number of times: Look, Janhavi beta, you are Priyanka's friend, but if she treats you like you are her servant, that's not a good thing. You shouldn't let her treat you like a servant. It's as simple as that. Have some dignity. Don't let my daughter treat you like you are a rag. I told Janhavi that, but Janhavi, like I said, is a little dumb. She was a little dumb, I don't know what her situation is now, but I remember her face: poor little thing, just trying to help. Just trying to be of use somehow, because otherwise she was a dumb child, that's what Priyanka used to say. That she needs to do all her homework because Janhavi is dumb, but then I told Priyanka: Well, if you treat her like a servant, the least you can do is use your brains and help her out. That's what she did, my Priyanka, she helped her out, and they were friends. Very good friends.

'Now that I think about it, I don't think the sisters had any other friends apart from Janhavi. I don't remember any other friends. The three of them were enough for each other, I think. They didn't really need anybody else. But they accepted Janhavi, probably because they felt bad for her. Some girls are like that, they have one friend and no one else, and I think Janhavi was like that—all she had was my Priyanka. And she was devoted to her. She came that day while I was washing the house. The walls of the house. Now me washing the walls of that house was a matter of speculation, as everything in that village was. Why does this woman wash the house so much? What is it to you if I wash the house ten times or fifty times a day? It's my house, I will wash it the way I want and as many times as I want to. What's it to them? But they used to gossip about it behind my back, I know that. That I wash the house because the odour is unbearable. What odour? The odour of death, they said. They said: When we step out of our shack, we carry that smell with us, the smell of death. As if these people know what death smells like, these tuchhyas. These bitches. As if they have ever known death the way I have. As if they know what it is like to live with death. As if they know what it is like to realize that someone is going to die and yet take care of him day in and day out, as if they know what it feels like to be awake at night because your husband is in pain and howling . . . not one of them came to sit by my side during those days; not one of them told me: Strength to you, Mai, Mauli will make everything all right. They don't know anything about this house, about what happened to us, about the way we suffered, the pain we know, the pain we saw . . . My daughters, they witnessed the agony of their father and they tried to forget it, but they don't let us forget, how can they let us forget? No, they pass judgements, they have a lot of time to pass judgements, they wouldn't let us forget the pain, even though they don't know how it feels, and I really hope to Mauli they never know how it feels, actual pain, the pain that pierces your bosom and never goes away . . .

'Anyway, I was washing the house when she came, Janhavi, and she handed me that bag. Red bag with cartoons. Now that bag was another matter of speculation. Where did the girls get such shiny bags? What's it to you where the girls got their shiny bags? They got it because I gave them the money for it. They got it because I had a windfall, because the company had provided me with some benefits—but what's it to anybody where the bags had come from? I don't need to explain to anyone where the bags had come from and where the money for the bags had come from. It was nobody's business what I did with my house and what my daughters did with their money. They bought those bags with honest money, that's all anyone needs to know. So Janhavi brought back the bag and I thanked her, but I also asked her: Where is she? Your friend? I don't remember what Janhavi said, but I do remember what I thought at that time: must be on the playground, trying to get a glimpse of the game. Cricket was Priyanka's favourite sport, for some reason. She loved watching it, and there was this night cricket tournament that was being held at that time . . . and I thought, maybe she is on the playground, on the petrol pump side . . .'

Bhushan

The moment Bhushan opened his eyes, he felt the pain gather in his muscles. It had been that way for three days now. Fever and fatigue, incomplete sleep and terrible nightmares.

It was 6.30 a.m. School began in an hour, and Bhushan didn't want to miss another day. He was sick, but he had always been sick. A mere nine years of age, Bhushan's short life had been a series of fevers and aches and doctors and tantriks. At least in school he was with other people, people who didn't care much about him but who were forced to share a bench with him or to make small conversations: a day in school rejuvenated Bhushan, made him feel as if he was actually a part of something other than worries and fallen faces and the sourness of the nightly kadhas.

Today, however, his cough was terrible, he could tell. He stood up on his mattress and felt dizzy. Bhushan closed his eyes and balled up his fists and retched. He felt nauseous, and he decided that it was better to sit down again. His Aai came rushing from the kitchen.

'Bhushan beta, sleep. You need rest.'

'But all I have done is rest. I want to go to school.'

Going to school was important if he wanted to become a pilot, and he had decided to become a pilot the day he had spotted that thin white line in the clear blue skies. His parents knew their unfortunate child's dream was impossible; impossible not because he didn't have it in him but because they didn't expect him to survive beyond ten or eleven. That's what his patrika had said. That he would die before he turned fifteen. His mother had cried for days after they were told that. His father felt sad, but he had reasoned that it was, one, God's will and, two, it was merciful: it meant that Bhushan wouldn't have to suffer for long, and God knows the boy had already suffered enough in his life. High fevers that left him weak for weeks; breathing problems, vomiting blood, backaches, a perennial cold and cough, sometimes spots of blood with mucus . . . It was hard to witness, for Bhushan's parents and also for his elder brother, whose agony for his brother's condition had slowly turned into apathy.

Ravi, the brother, smacked Bhushan on his head and laughed. 'No school today either? Rawaas na ekdum. Fucking lazy bum.' He nudged his younger brother gently with his foot. But then their mother slapped him on his back and pointed at the door. 'Ravi, go and bring some water from the well. Do you want your breakfast?'

'Yes.'

'Then go and bring that water. Two buckets. And stop bothering your brother.'

'Why does *he* get to sleep?'

'Because he is sick.'

'But he is always sick. Make him work at home, na! I have to go to school.'

After breakfast, Ravi left for school, and Bhushan went back to the mattress. Not that he wanted to, but he could feel the fever rise again: he felt the chills as he dipped his bhakri into his tea. He felt a shiver and then another—until he was shaking and crawling into his smelly blanket.

He dreamt of water. That he was floating on water, or that he was deep inside some waterbody: a lake, an ocean, some kind of sea, a well? Bhushan was floating, he wasn't drowning; but Bhushan didn't know how to swim. The local boys went for a swim in that huge well by the edge of Futane Wadi, but Bhushan had been told to keep away from water. Not that he wanted anything to do with any waterbody. He preferred the silence of the paddy fields and the gentle whispering of the forest trees . . . and yet, the fields and forests never made it to his dreams. Water, for some reason, often did.

When he woke up three hours later, Bhushan felt refreshed. This was new, this was rare. He wanted to jump, which is what he did. And he didn't feel dizzy at all. There was no headache and there was no muscle pain. It was as if the three hours of sleep had led him into a magical world, a world where he was fit and fine and ready to shine! For the first time in a long while, he smiled without feeling any pain. It felt good to be good.

Bhushan wanted to go out. He knew he had been wearing the same clothes for the past many days, that they were sickness clothes, that they were smelly clothes, but it didn't matter: he wanted to go to the playground and watch Ravi play cricket. He wanted to stand on the edge of the highway and watch the heavy trucks and the shiny cars pass by, he wanted to go into one of those rice fields and stare at the slim white line in the blue sky: that's where he wanted to be, in the skies, far, far away from here, looking on from above.

Soon after he woke up, his mother went to deliver his father's lunch at the factory and Bhushan knew she would be gone for an hour.

That's when he stepped out.

Anisha, Priyanka, Sanchita

Anisha was seen in her green top. She wasn't wearing her uniform.

Priyanka was wearing her uniform, but she didn't have her bag with her.

Ditto Sanchita, who was seen holding Anisha and Priyanka's hands.

They were seen at several places, at the same time.

Said Keshavrao Bhalavi: 'This must be at around eleven-fifteen. I remember this, bhau. Very clearly I remember this, bhau. Anisha, that eldest sister, she was wearing a green top, very sexy top, you know, between you and me, a top through which we can see things. We don't need our imagination kay? And she was going towards the petrol pump. I don't know whether she was going *to* the petrol pump, but she was going in that direction. What you need to understand, bhau, what you need to understand about Murwani is that there are two points here: a temple side and a petrol pump side. Opposite. Completely opposite to each other, bhau, so that is how we see it: we are either going towards the petrol pump side or we are going towards the temple side, even if we are not *actually* going to the petrol pump or to the temple, do you understand this, bhau? Haan, so that sister, Anisha, I saw her going towards the petrol pump side, but I am not sure . . .'

Said Prabodhan Lanjewar: 'Do you see that Sone Taran Karja Mukti Kendra wall? Haan, that wall, rao, everyone calls it Sone Taran wall. Actually Sone Taran Karja Mukti Kendra is in Dhupal, two hours from here by my Sumo. I have a transport business, so I know chappa chappa of this area. But that wall, that is where I saw the three sisters. Haan. In the morning, bhau. Hmm . . . must be around eleven, bhau. Yes, near Sone Taran wall. What—I don't remember what they were doing exactly. Walking, I suppose. But I am not—no, they were standing actually. Yes, rao, they were standing, rao. But not all the three sisters, rao, not all three of them. Two of them. Hmm. Eldest I think . . . or maybe the youngest—I don't remember, rao, but two sisters were standing and one of them was missing. I don't remember exactly, but . . .'

Said Meenakshi Ramteke: 'I saw the sisters talking to a man. Actually I saw a couple of other children also talking to the man. And I *think* the sisters were among the children. But I am not sure. I *think* they were among the children talking to the man. Haan? The man . . . I know the man, yes, I have seen him around quite a few times in Murwani. Yes. Quite a few times. His name . . . hmm . . . I am not sure—'

Said Bhagwan Badole: 'They called him Mullah Chacha. I don't know what his actual name is, and I don't know whether he spoke with the sisters or what the entire issue is. All you asked me was what he was called and he was called Mullah Chacha. That is all I know.'

Bhushan

He stepped out on to an empty road, which was a relief. There were shouts and laughter from somewhere close by, but he couldn't see who was shouting and laughing, and it didn't matter, as long as they didn't see him and as long as they weren't his neighbours, who would most definitely tell on him. He began walking, but as soon as he came to the end of the dirt road that joined the main road, Bhushan felt the dizziness return. He felt as if he was being weighed down, and he knew that the fever was coming back, that his temperature was rising. So when he reached the Public Health Centre right in front of the Sone Taran wall, he sat down.

By the time Mullah Chacha offered him two Parle Kismi toffees, Bhushan had no idea how much time had passed and how he had passed it. He had never met old Mullah Chacha before, but he had seen him from a distance once and heard about him plenty. People spoke about the uncle from Rajasthan who distributed chocolates among children and played cricket with them and insisted that he bowl while the others bat. Ravi had told him about Mullah Chacha. Everyone knew him, everyone but Bhushan.

That day, as Bhushan sat in front of the Sone Taran wall, at the edge of one of the paddy fields, disoriented and hungry and thirsty and angry and confused all at the same time, Mullah Chacha had walked up to him and pulled Bhushan's hands towards him and asked him to open up his fist. Then he had placed two Parle Kismi toffees, one on each palm, and smiled.

'You look sick. Are you sick?'

Bhushan had stared wide-eyed at Mullah Chacha's chubby face, unable to come up with an answer.

'This will make you feel better. But don't eat them alone. Share them with your brothers and sisters, haan?'

Then Mullah Chacha was gone, but not quite. For Bhushan would later, much later, claim that after Mullah Chacha had offered him those toffees, he had met with the three sisters right in front of the PHC and offered them some as well.

Said Bhushan: 'I saw all the three sisters. I was outside. I was going to the . . . to the paddy fields. I liked going to the paddy fields. I was going to the paddy fields and I saw them. Not in the paddy fields. I saw them on the road. The three sisters. They were walking. They were walking hand in hand. They always walked hand in hand. They were laughing and they were talking, but I wasn't interested because . . . because I wanted to go to the paddy fields quickly. I knew if Aai returned home and did not see me in my bed she would be worried. She would cry and go out and shout. I knew it would worry her. So I had to be back on time. But I saw the three sisters, and before I saw the three sisters, I met him. I met him, Mullah Chacha. And the three sisters met him, too. Mullah Chacha. They met Mullah Chacha and Mullah Chacha gave them chocolates. In front of the kirana shop. Babulal Kirana shop, in front of that na, they stopped and Mullah Chacha gave them each a chocolate. I love chocolates, but Mullah Chacha had already given me two so I didn't ask for another one. I wanted another one, but I didn't ask for it. He gave them . . . I think he gave the sisters the chocolates. I love chocolates, but I didn't ask for another one from him.'

Janhavi

Janhavi wasn't exactly enthused to be on the playground in the sweltering late-afternoon heat. Especially since she was surrounded by the sweaty boys on their bikes and bicycles, weighing their bats and wiping their faces with their caps and making empty gestures of hitting every ball out into the paddy fields. But she had to be there, she had no other option.

Because she knew something was wrong.

Priyanka had not turned up to finish their homework together, and apparently Priyanka was not home either.

Janhavi had kept an hour-long vigil outside that shack of theirs and had not seen anyone enter or exit the house. Finally, she had walked up to the tin door of the shack and knocked on it lightly. Their grandfather had opened the door. Janhavi had always found Ajoba an intimidating man, although that wasn't saying much because Janhavi found almost everyone intimidating: she had muttered something and Ajoba had stared at her for quite some time before asking: 'Janhavi na tu?'

Janhavi had nodded.

'Priyanka's friend. But Priyanka isn't home.'

'Where is she, Ajoba?'

'Mahakal knows.'

'When did she go out, Ajoba?'

'Mahakal knows, pori.'

Ajoba had scratched his armpits and stared at Janhavi for some more time.

'I will search for her then.'

'Hmm.'

Janhavi had spent some more time around the shack, hoping to see Priyanka come back or go out, presuming that Ajoba had lied. But she had seen no one and she had seen nothing.

As afternoon gave way to evening, Janhavi decided to make her way to the playground, where they were supposed to go and eat berries while watching the cricket game. Maybe Priyanka had gone to fetch the berries without Janhavi and maybe she would surprise her at the playground, Janhavi thought, although even then her young mind told her that something like that had never happened before and there was no reason why it would happen now.

'Ae Ganya, laav ki gloves.'

'Na na, no gloves and all. I don't need gloves and all.'

'Cream? Anyone wants this cream?'

'Mulgi ahe ka be tu? Cream. Bhokat das jaun, bhai. Pussy.'

'He *is* a pussy, rao. He doesn't wear a Macho, he wears a maxi, bhai.'

Their laughter disturbed Janhavi. The way they laughed. Then the way they asked one of the younger boys to spread his legs and the way they smashed their bats between his legs. She had squirmed when the boy had squirmed, and she had screamed when the boy had screamed. Then they had looked at her and sniggered as she fiddled with the edge of her skirt with her trembling fingers. One of them had smiled and acted as if she were a ball and he was hitting her with a bat, and the others had laughed, but then fortunately an uncle arrived and slapped the boy with the bat and asked him to concentrate on his game.

'Bhankas you want to do next week? If you are not serious about this, you can get lost and never show me your face again and I won't care. Leave that girl alone and focus on the game. M.S. Dhoni, M.S. Dhoni! Get out of your pants first, chutiyas.'

That had given Janhavi some relief because the boys' attention was now completely on the uncle and the playground and this ball and that ball and that shot and this shot. Things Janhavi didn't understand and wasn't interested in—although she did recognize one or two terms, cover drive and bouncer and spin, because Priyanka discussed these things. Pointing her finger at a player and saying things like, 'See, he is good at bouncers.' 'See, he is good at pulling the ball.' Priyanka. Interested in everything.

Where was she?

Janhavi waited until the boys argued about the toss, until the boys placed their fielding and discussed their strategies, until the boys began their match and hooted and shouted and made a ruckus, those boys on the field and those boys watching the game sitting on their scooters and bikes, commenting about who should have done what; until the floodlights lit the fading evening. Janhavi waited and sobbed. She didn't know why she was sobbing: there wasn't any particular reason. Except perhaps the fact that she was missing Priyanka and the fact that she didn't know what had happened to her friend, where she had disappeared.

Then it began to drizzle and the boys stopped play. When they started fighting about whether to continue with the game or postpone the match or declare it a draw, Janhavi decided to go home. It was already dark, and she didn't like the way it felt when it rained: damp, muggy and depressing. As if auguring some kind of bad news.

The Mother

(Excerpts from an interview transcript. Interview conducted on 23 February 2019.)

'And then I said: enough of this waiting. I am going to look for them. Because it had rained and it was already nine by that time, or after nine, and the girls were never out and about for that long. Eight, yes. Eight-thirty, yes. But not nine. Actually, it is possible that they had stayed out after nine, it is possible that had happened in the past and it is possible that I don't remember it, but that night I think it was Mauli who told me: Go out and search for your daughters. Now is the time. Go out and search for them. There is still time.

'That is what I did, I swear on my Mauli. We had been waiting together inside our shack, all three of us, waiting for the girls to return so that we could have our dinner together. We always had our dinner together, I don't know why that was, there was no particular meaning to it, it was just that Ajoba always insisted on having his dinner with the girls, and he always watched them as they ate, and he always had this thing . . . I don't know how he did it, but he always understood which one of them wanted more food, which one of them was hungrier, and then he always gave away his share of chapati or rice or dal to one of the girls. That is why he waited for them, although he never said it like that. He never told us: You can eat while I wait. He never asked us: Why do you want to wait? Eat your dinner if you are hungry. He never said all that because Aaji would have been scandalized by the mere thought of eating before the man of the house had his food. That is not possible. She would wait for my daughters to come back, but she would grumble and groan when I served all of us together. That is not how it should be, she would mutter, this is not the way; this is not proper conduct. To hell with proper conduct, because by the time those girls returned from wherever they had been, I would have been hungry for hours. For hours. It's not an easy thing to stand there in that kitchen at the factory all day and cook meals for the workers and then not think of food when I get back home. So I would serve everyone and I would start eating while Aaji sat there, muttering under her breath, rolling those beads in her hands, her eyes half-closed . . . But I didn't care. And as far as I could see neither did Ajoba or my daughters. So Ajoba and I waited, patiently, looking forward to sitting together as a family, or what remained of our family, and having a peaceful dinner together.

'But that day they didn't return home, my daughters, and I decided to go out and look for them, which is easier said than done. Most of this cursed village has no streetlights. I took a torch and I told Ajoba that I was going out to look for my girls and ask around, and Ajoba insisted that he come along. That won't be necessary, Ajoba, I said. It's Murwani, it's our village. No one is going to harm me in this village. But he kept on repeating: No, no, it's my responsibility. It's my responsibility. I remember he said: What will they say? Letting a woman out alone at night. What will they say? Then Aaji, that heptali, she said: Let her go. She is not going out to look for her daughters, she said, she wants to go and fuck around, which is why she doesn't want you to come. Because she wants to go into the fields to fuck another man. Then she called me a rakhel. That rakhel doesn't care about her daughters, all she wants is to go and fuck around like the randi that she is, Aaji said. I didn't respond. I got up and left. I walked out of the house and on to the road that led us into the village. I heard Ajoba shouting. He was following me. Mauli knows the man doesn't listen and the man doesn't understand. He started following me. Did you lock the door? I asked him. No, he said, how can I lock the door when she is inside? What's the need to lock the door? Precisely because she is inside, I thought, but I didn't say that. I simply went back to the shack and I locked the door from outside. I heard a whimper from inside, but I ignored it.'

PI Dighole

Police Inspector Sanjay Dighole licked his fingers and stared at the oily yellow spatter his potato bhaaji had left on the report he was preparing. He wondered how he was going to explain that little stain, since the report was supposed to be submitted to the Superintendent of Police. And SP Madam was a . . . how to put it? She wasn't exactly a pain in the ass as much as she was a strict disciplinarian whom Dighole had come to hold in high regard. She never depended on her PA, always pointed out mistakes, never bantered, and always corrected those little errors in reports herself.

The report Dighole was writing wasn't just any other report, though. This one was about the alleged murder of Head Constable Gangadharrao Patle, his colleague, and it needed to be perfect, or at least more or less sincere. It was a high-profile case, after all; micromanaged, media-managed, a topic for local gossip, a case being honed for election rallies. But no worries. A whitener would do the trick, although of course SP Madam would notice that too.

Dighole sighed and was about to yawn when he realized that he also needed to burp. So he stifled the yawn and burped instead. Then he squeezed his eyes in disgust. A late dinner, Dighole knew, messed up his gut and forced him to burp every five minutes. Although the burping helped relieve the burning inside his chest for a short while, it left a hint of a bad taste in his mouth—an hour of that and Dighole knew that his mouth would begin to smell like the bottom of a vertical mortuary. If something like that even existed.

It wasn't murder, Dighole thought as he picked on his teeth with the elongated nail of his forefinger and peered at the report. Head Constable Patle was obviously disturbed. His eldest son was a drunkard, his youngest had not performed well in his class ten board exams, his wife was always ill and the bills were mounting. Patle's salary as a Head Constable could not take care of both his wife's and his mother's illnesses, which were many and frequent. Behenchod, Dighole thought as he dug deeper into his yellowed teeth, the SP couldn't take care of her husband's medical expenses with just her salary if it came to that, let alone Patle. Not that there was anything wrong with the SP's husband, at least not medically.

They had discussed this, PI Dighole and Assistant Police Inspector Sangere, how the salary they were paid was so pitiable that the people in the village did not consider their profession respectable anymore, despite the possibility of a pension.

'How is that pension helping Patle, ask na, Dighole Saheb.'

'Behenchod. Pension pan saala mungigat.'

'He was taking too much up his ass, Dighole Saheb, that's my opinion about all this.'

'He kept saying, na, remember? He kept saying this is too much, this is too much, I can't take it anymore, I can't take it anymore. I am too tired. I am too tired.'

'It was all too much up his gaand, Dighole Saheb, take it from me.'

'If only he had fucked his wife up her gaand, problem would have solved itself automatically,' Dighole had said, and then they had sniggered, like teenagers sharing a lewd joke.

Patle had fashioned a noose out of the leg of his khaki trousers, which Dighole thought was a symbolic gesture on Patle's part. They had found his body on the outskirts of Murwani, and the first thing Dighole thought when he saw Patle's body was that this was just an update. Patle looked the way he had always looked: dead man walking. Now he was just a dead man hanging. What the fuck do these journalists know about Patle to scream murder? But the higher-ups know better, don't they? We open our mouths and they start fingering our lubricated assholes with their long and smooth fingers, ahe ka nay, Sangere had said, laughing as he demonstrated what he meant with his middle finger. 'Eh, Dighole Saheb, you fuck your wife like that, don't you?'

'Bhosadichya Sangere, you will be the next one up there on that tree if you don't stop about me and my wife,' Dighole had replied, letting out a noisy burp. 'And I assure you *that* won't be a suicide.'

'It isn't a suicide now, Dighole Saheb, it isn't a suicide,' Sangere had said, looking at the outline of Patle's body spread out under the white sheet. 'Eh, Dighole Saheb, do you think Patle ever took our advice?'

'What advice?'

'Fucking his wife like that, up her ass?'

Dighole closed his tiffin, probed his mouth with his tongue for pieces he could chew on for some more time—potato was his favourite bhaaji—and walked up to the pot for a glass of water. The tumbler was there, but the pot was empty and Dighole closed his eyes and tried to control the frustration building up in his belly and making its way up to his throat.

'Aai chi gaand,' he muttered and hurled the empty steel tumbler.

The Mother

(Excerpts from an interview transcript. Interview conducted on 23 February 2019.)

'We tried looking everywhere. The school and the playground, especially. While we were walking from the school to the playground, which is at least a fifteen-minute walk, Ajoba was perspiring and constantly stopping to catch his breath, which scared me because it was a February night and nobody sweats on a February night. So I said: Ajoba, listen, please, let's go back, you be with Aaji, try to sleep and I will search for them . . . but he wasn't ready to listen. At one point he told me that *I* should head back home and he would search for them, which is when I decided that the better thing would be to go to the police and ask for their help.

'When I reached the police station I thought: What a mess. I had never been inside one before. Why would I? I had never had the misfortune of going to a police station before that night. I had passed by it sometimes, but never bothered to peep inside; I had never even bothered about its existence. There was no reason why I would have seen a police station from inside, I had never done anything . . . but all that changed that night. That night when we reached the police station and saw that Inspector . . . Inspector Dighole, haan barobar, Inspector Dighole for the first time. He was a burly and round fellow, that Inspector, your typical police-wala, and he was staring at the floor when we went in. I don't remember much about what happened inside the police station, but I remember this: the policeman staring at the floor of the police station, as if he was trying to search for something, but I knew he wasn't searching for anything because I also remember that his eyes weren't moving. He was simply staring at the floor, that Inspector, his eyes empty and hollow . . .

'Don't get me started about that bhosadichya. That chodhichya. He did nothing. You know what he did that night? He sat at his desk and he dug with his fingers deeper into his disgusting mouth. We were telling him: Inspector, it's been eight hours; Inspector, it's been fourteen hours . . . But the Inspector just sat there and picked his teeth and nodded his head and then picked his nose. He asked us some random things. Like if the girls had a mobile phone. What a stupid question. But I knew why he had asked me that question, that Inspector, because he was from around here, around Murwani, he had some jack in Nagpur or something like that and he had managed to halt his transfer somehow. That's what I had heard. That he wanted to settle down in Murwani for some time, at least until he got transferred to a city. That's what I had heard. So he had been around Murwani for many years, and he asked us: Did they have mobile phones, your daughters; did you call them on the mobile phone? No, bhosadichya, I wanted to tell him, they don't have a mobile phone. They are girls! They are little girls! And they haven't returned from school! I wanted to scream. I wanted to cry. I wanted to hold his collar and shake his useless body and kick his flat butt, but I composed myself, just as I composed myself every day in front of Aaji. It's not difficult for me to stay calm in front of chutiyas like that Inspector, it comes with practise, it comes with experience. Then that Inspector simply looked at me—you won't believe this—that Inspector simply looked at me, in front of Ajoba, my father-in-law, and he rolled his tongue and closed his eyes and opened them again and said: What about you then? Do you have a mobile phone? How about you give me your contact number? If I find your daughters I can call you. How about we do that?'

PI Dighole

'Ajoba, asa kasa chalaycha? You have to look for them na, Ajoba? I asked you a hundred times in five minutes, who saw them last? Where did they see them last? You need to look around na, Ajoba, I am not saying we won't look around, we are the police, but this isn't a police case yet, Ajoba.'

PI Dighole adjusted his pants and realized that its size was almost the same as Patle's, which meant that the noose with which Patle had hanged himself—or someone had hanged him—could well have been *his* khaki pants. That sent a shiver down his spine, and he wished that Sangere was present and around and not on a long leave. That would have taken his mind off the pair in front of him, and off Patle as well.

'But, Inspector, it has never happened before—'

'But it happens. First times happen all the time. I went to Nagpur last month and had a medu vada sambar for the first time in my life, can you believe that? It happens.'

'Inspector . . . they usually return by this time, and they should have—'

'Mai, Mai, Mai, listen to me. I am telling you. I am not saying we won't search for them. I am not saying we won't help you. All I am saying is that you go back, ask their friends. If the friends don't have any clue, come back and we will see. Okay? Understood?'

Ajoba said: 'Tell him about the bag . . .'

Then, impatiently, to PI Dighole: 'A classmate returned Priyanka's bag. Because she did not come home.'

Inspector Dighole stretched back on his chair and scratched his cheeks.

'Did not come home. As in?'

'As in the classmate returned her bag because she went off to play.'

'Haan, see. They went off to play and they lost sense of time. It's simple, Ajoba, they must be—'

'It doesn't happen like that with my daughters,' the mother screamed. 'It doesn't. It doesn't. It doesn't. How many times should we say this, Inspector? Every second, every minute—'

'O Mai, keep the drama in the cinema hall, haan, this is a police station and I am an Inspector. I am not your personal bodyguard, kalla ka? I am a public servant, I have other work to do. Don't waste my time.'

'This is a waste of time for you? Inspector, this is—'

'O Mai, mind your language, haan. You are ladies so I am—'

'They are also ladies. My daughters. They are ladies. They have disappeared. We have come to you because—'

'You shouldn't have come to me, Ajoba, Mai. I am trying to explain this to you na, this is not a police matter—'

'Then what matter is this? What matter is this, Inspector Dighole?'

'O Mai, I am giving you last warning, haan. I am telling you, you are ladies and Ajoba here is an old man so I am not saying anything to you, but if you—'

'Inspector, please. Where did they go? Please find out.'

'Ajoba, listen to me: you said their bags, some friend came and gave you their bags—'

'Janhavi gave Priyanka's bag to me,' the mother said.

'Haan, to you. Whatever. Janhavi, na? You go and ask that Janhavi. Did you go and ask Janhavi?'

Silence.

Inspector Dighole knew he had scored.

'Did you ask Janhavi about your daughters? Where they went off to play?'

'They were . . . they were playing. That's all she said.'

'And did you ask her where they were playing?'

'No.'

'Why not?'

'I didn't think . . . I didn't think it was important.'

Sixer number two.

'You didn't think where your daughters were and what they were doing was important?'

The Mother

(Excerpts from an interview transcript. Interview conducted on 23 February 2019.)

'He started saying: What can a policeman do if the mother is so irresponsible about her daughters? If a mother can't keep tabs on where her daughters are, where they are playing, what can a policeman do? The madarchod said that policemen are helpless when it comes to such daughters and such parents. I asked what he meant by such daughters. He scratched his useless head and said: You know, daughters who have mobile phones, daughters with shiny new clothes and loads of money. I don't know where that money comes from, he said, but you know your daughters are famous because of that. Because of the money. Like I said, Anisha, Priyanka and Sanchita: what they did or didn't do was everybody's business, but . . . And he said: If that elder one, what is her name? He asked me her name, and poor Ajoba thought he was being genuine and said: Anisha. Haan, said that haramkhor Inspector, that Anisha, excuse me but you have to keep an eye on what she does, that girl is a firecracker. That's what he said: That girl is a fatakdi, you keep an eye on her because one day she is going to burst, *boom*, and then you won't be able to handle her blast. Then I couldn't handle it. Then I started calling him a bhadva. I started calling him a randibaaz. I started calling him a bhoknalya. I started telling him what I thought of him: I told him he should take a look at his malnourished son who looks as if he comes from a fucking beggar's family; I started telling him to focus on his son, because his son might become a bailya one day and a policeman such as himself won't be able to handle that. And that got his goat, because then he started abusing me in turn and he started telling me about how Anisha was always hopping into some bus and going off to the neighbouring towns to fuck older men; how she is a kept woman and a whore and how the money that comes into our home is all through our . . . I can't . . . it's just . . . eventually Ajoba had to pull me out of the police station, and you know what that Inspector said while we were going out? He said: Check in Futane Wadi, maybe your daughters are rolling on the mat with some mullah; maybe they have eloped with one of those men and are too ashamed to come and tell you . . .'

PI Dighole

Dighole sighed with exhaustion and relief as he saw the grandfather push the mother down the steps of the police station. She struggled for a bit and Dighole watched her as she glared at him and pointed at him and shouted a number of things about his mother and sister and daughter. He rolled his tongue around the walls of his cheek; let that bitch say what she wants, what the fuck is she going to do anyway? One punch and half her battishi will scatter down the station's floor, Dighole thought with a smile.

They finally disappeared behind the police station's crumbling outer wall, the old man and his daughter-in-law, and Dighole gave a long and satisfying burp.

Police this, police that. Can't keep their chuts in their panties and want to blame it all on the police.

Dighole's shift had just begun and he wasn't expecting anything or anyone to come up during the course of it, except Constable Karamble, who should have returned by now, that A-one kamchor. Long since he went out for his after-dinner paan, Dighole thought.

He called his wife because he wanted to calm himself down and he wanted to praise that marvellous potato bhaaji.

'I was waiting for your call,' his wife said, and Dighole slumped into his chair.

'You are in mood today or what?' Dighole asked hopefully, picking his teeth and smiling slyly.

His wife went silent for a few seconds. 'No. Bring six pavs on your way home,' she said.

Dighole grunted, and before he could add anything his wife had cut the call. 'A test of will, this woman,' Dighole murmured as he watched Karamble walk in.

'Kay Karamble, kuthe jaun rahila be? I thought you took VRS or something and went back to your village.'

'No, saheb, sorry, saheb.'

'You fixed that paan yourself?'

'No, saheb, sorry, saheb.'

'Did you bring a paan for me?'

'No, saheb, so—'

'You know what, Karamble, sometimes I think it should have been you hanging by that tree instead of our dear old Patle. Sometimes I tend to think that way, you know why, Karamble? Because at least Patle fetched water and ensured the pot was always kept filled.'

At the mention of the pot, Karamble hurried towards it and peeped inside.

Dighole picked up the glass paperweight on his desk and hurled it at Karamble.

'Aai zavli tujhi, Karamble, what are you checking that pot for? Don't you trust what I just said to you?'

Karamble picked up the pot and hurried outside through the back door towards the unkempt privies, which was where they got their drinking water through a municipal pipe that looked ancient and dangerous. Dighole sat back, waiting for Karamble to return.

He drew his cell phone from the upper pocket of his uniform and started the snake game he had come to like. Inevitably, his tongue sneaked out when he played that game, and he spent hours trying to fatten his virtual snake. Dighole's son liked that game too: it was the only time Dighole thought he was bonding with Jayesh, when they played the snake game together.

'Saheb . . .' Karamble held out the glass of water, and Dighole gestured at him to keep it on the table. 'Eh, Karamble, this snake game is solid,' Dighole said, not taking his eyes off the screen. Karamble didn't respond, and instead began gazing into his superior's mobile screen. Silence reigned in the police station as Constable Karamble and Inspector Dighole deployed the entirety of their detective brains to get a pixelated snake to eat pixelated food.

'Saheb,' Karamble said suddenly, making Dighole look up at him. 'Saheb, the three sisters are missing.'

Dighole paused for a bit before nodding his head and dropping his Nokia on the table.

'Hmm. I know. That mother came here asking me to look for them. For her daughters, those sisters.'

'Whose mother, saheb?'

'Your mother, chutiya.'

'Achha, the sisters' mother, saheb? She came here, saheb?'

'Haan na. Behenchod, what "missing"! You know how those girls are . . .'

'Saheb, Raju Bokle told me he saw the elder sister at the petrol pump at three o'clock. She was wearing a sexy green top. That's what Raju Bokle said, saheb, not me.'

'But even if you say it, what's the harm? Sexy is sexy, Karamble.'

'She is a . . . I mean, she is just a kid, saheb . . . she is . . .'

'How the fuck does that matter? A kid can be sexy too. And little surprise Raju Bokle observed it. Madarchod sits at his paan shop all day watching little girls dancing on that shit smartphone of his. It helps him get his bandook loaded, if you know what I mean.'

'Saheb . . .'

'And what was Raju Bokle doing at the petrol pump at three in the afternoon anyway? He should have been at his shop na, handing our Deshmukh Saheb his post-lunch paan.'

'Saheb, he went there to—I mean, it's that, he had been going there for, I mean, not that I would know much—'

'Tujha aai la, Karamble, start speaking in single sentences na, chodhichya. I went to bed. I fucked my wife. I wet my pants. I want to pee. Then full stop. Full sentences, full stop,' Dighole said and burst out laughing, patting Karamble on his back.

'Haan, so you were saying? Raju Bokle?'

'Raju had . . . Raju went to the petrol pump to meet one of the employees,' Karamble informed Dighole, his voice turning into a whisper with every word he spoke.

'Interesting,' Dighole said, scratching his cheek. 'And who is Raju Bokle's friend at the petrol pump, Karamble?'

'I don't know his name, but he . . . well, Raju is his supplier.'

'Supplier, meaning?' Dighole was getting a hang of where this conversation was going.

'You know . . .'

'Behenchod, Karamble.' Dighole kicked the stool from under Karamble, who was covering his face, expecting a slap. The wooden stool tumbled and Karamble lay sprawled on the floor, but Dighole nudged him with his foot. 'Stop the fucking drama and get up, chutiya.'

Then: 'How much have you been getting out of all this?'

'Nothing, saheb, nothing. Sorry, saheb,' Karamble said, recovering from the shock of the kick and sitting back on the stool.

'Nothing? What do you mean "nothing", Karamble? Why *nothing*? You think you can make a chutiya out of me just because I fuck around with you or what, Karamble? How much?'

'Just the free paan, saheb, sor—'

'A free paan? Aai zavli tujhi, Karamble. And what—wait a minute, how do you know all this about Raju Bokle?'

'Saheb, Raju Bokle asks me to look after the shop . . . sometimes when he goes . . .'

PI Dighole motioned as if to slap Karamble but did not. He merely stared at him.

'You are an A-one chutiya, Karamble, that's what you are,' Dighole said.

Anisha, Priyanka, Sanchita

What we now know for sure is that the three sisters were together. Well, that should be a relief. But hear Raju Bokle out: 'The grandfather and the mother came and asked me if I had seen the sisters. Now, I am not going about the village looking at girls, rao, but I didn't tell them that because they looked worried, and I don't mess with worried people. Worried people are crazy people, and as it is that family is weird. So I told them what I knew, which is that—yes, I had seen the eldest sister at the petrol pump at around three, rao. Wearing a nice green top. The mother tells me: Impossible, Anisha doesn't have a green top. Well, what do you know? Anisha did many things that the mother wouldn't have had any idea about. But entire Murwani knew, rao. She was alone and I was alone and I thought: why don't I go talk to her? But then dhanda is dhanda, bhau, you can't keep it waiting. By the time I had finished my deal, Anisha was nowhere to be seen. Of course I didn't tell all this to Ajoba and that mother, obviously not.'

So Anisha was alone, at around three in the afternoon, standing at the petrol pump. What was she doing there? And where were Priyanka and Sanchita? Baffling.

We know, however, that they were together later. Because Pranil, who was watching the cricket game, did see them at around four-thirty, sometime before it started to drizzle. Remember Pranil? Prateek's elder brother, Datta Mama's nephew, the one who was destined to be an engineer. He was sitting on one of the scooters, watching the game when he saw, or so he claims, the three sisters walking in the direction of the temple from the petrol pump side. That's quite a lot of walking in the course of a single day, from the temple side to the petrol pump side, but it can be done. Most would have walked along the highway, but that is fraught with risk for children of Anisha, Sanchita and Priyanka's age. Which is perhaps why they took the inner road, where Pranil, at least, saw them walking towards the temple side. One of the questions to confirm the authenticity of the sightings was to ask if they had been holding hands. Because most of those who remembered the sisters from that day said that they had been holding hands. But Pranil didn't remember whether they were holding hands or walking in a line or walking abreast or hopping: all he remembered was that he had seen Anisha, Sanchita and Priyanka, and while Sanchita and Priyanka were in their uniforms, Anisha was wearing something green. Pranil saw them walking off in the direction of the temple, and that was the last anyone saw of them. Apparently.

The Mother

(Excerpts from an interview transcript. Interview conducted on 23 February 2019.)

'Perhaps it was my fault. I should have asked that girl Janhavi where my daughters were and what they were doing. I should have looked for them in the afternoon. I should have asked around before going to that madarchod, because I know he must have started mocking us the moment we stepped out of that police station. That wouldn't have mattered had he been of any actual use . . . We went to Janhavi's place first. They were having their dinner, those poor people. I knew Janhavi's father because he worked in the factory and he was a decent person. He had helped me before at the factory and I asked him to call his daughter because my daughters had gone missing. What do you mean they have gone missing? he asked me. They haven't returned home yet, I said, and Janhavi . . . Janhavi was the last person to have spoken to Priyanka. So he called Janhavi and Janhavi told me about how Anisha had come into their classroom and taken Priyanka away because of some emergency. I started to sob. It meant that little brute was up to something, I thought. Why didn't you tell me about this earlier? I asked Janhavi, almost shouting at her. I said: I don't know about any emergency. There was no emergency! Everything was normal, everything had been normal, until that point—in that moment I realized that something had gone wrong. Horribly wrong.'

Chorus

A number of people saw the three sisters and a number of people saw Ajoba and the mother trying to search for them.

Said Vandana Armale: 'The poor grandfather could hardly walk. He was wearing a sweater and had covered his ears with a shawl. But the shawl was torn, I could see. He was dragging his feet when I saw him. When did I see him? Hmm, let me think. Around nine-fifteen, I think. At night. At night, imagine, that old man and that woman. Where did I see him? Hmm, let me think. I think it was near Maharaj Putala. Yes, they were heading somewhere fast. But he couldn't walk properly. He has always had trouble na, that Ajoba, with his leg . . .'

Said Abhiman Landole: 'It's not uncommon to see people out and about at that time of the night; of course, Murwani is a village and all, but it's not as if it's a dangerous village or anything like that, and I don't mean things don't happen in Murwani; of course, there are some occasional lafdas, but it isn't like Uttar Pradesh or Bihar or any of those BIMARU states; Murwani is safe, Maharashtra is safe; but it isn't common to see an old man and a woman walking on the road at ten in the night, mostly because the light situation here is a little problematic. Matlab, you will see streetlights everywhere, or not everywhere, in some places, but you will see the streetlights and you will think, oh good, if I need to walk out of the village at night, no problem: just follow that road down the petrol pump or towards the temple side and walk out on the highway and on the highway of course there are those car lights and truck lights and lights in general . . . but no, saheb, no. Only two or three streetlights work here; the rest are just for show. Just for people from outside to look and say: waah, Murwani has streetlights. No, saheb, no. The panchayat steals electricity here, it's a big problem . . . What was I saying? Haan, I saw Ajoba and that woman walking around, poor things, searching for the girls, asking if anybody had seen those three sisters. It's a wonder, rao, how three girls disappeared in such a small village, but if you actually look at it, Murwani is not that small, and when you actually think about it, you shouldn't just let your little daughters roam about anywhere they wish, rao, because the village is so close to the highway, what if a truck comes and crushes your daughters under the . . . but then again, that's not what happened na . . .'

Said Rajni Khotele: 'They asked me if I had seen the girls. I was with my husband at that time. We had gone to watch a movie and we were returning when they surprised us. That woman suddenly pounced on me, out of nowhere, and asked, have you seen three little girls? I got scared and looked at my husband and my husband told the mother that no, we hadn't. I was new to this village, we had just got married, and my husband told me later that the woman is considered to be mad in this area. No surprises there, I told him, she looked like a madwoman all right to me . . . well, it was around that PHC area, near the bus stop, that's where they asked us about their daughters.'

Said Gadya Rambhau: 'Vishnurao, the grandfather of the girls, knocked at my door at around ten-thirty or eleven. We have been close friends since we were very young, in our twenties. I grew up in Dhule, he grew up in Madhya Pradesh, but we came to this district because of work, rao. There were odd jobs available here. At first Vishnurao worked in the fields, then in some factory in Madhya Pradesh, then he came back and I got him a job as a mechanic, even though he had no experience as a mechanic. Then once this factory started, rao, everything was set, because it gave a lot of jobs to our people. There was an entire village where the factory now stands, called Pansala, which got a lot of money and new places somewhere else . . . our people protested, rao, Tatya and all, because we also wanted money and new places and flats. But the factory management said no, we will give every man and woman in this village a job, which I think was for the better. Tatya didn't agree, but he was the first one to take a manager-wala job when it was offered to him. It's another thing that he doesn't work there now . . . Anyway, Vishnurao found stable employment there, and then he came with me when my cow dung cake business got going. To be honest, Vishnurao was bad luck, rao, because the moment he joined me, my business began to dwindle. Complete loss. I had to tell Vishnurao, look, Vishnurao, friendship is friendship and business is business. You will have to go because you are bad luck. I was frank because I always like to be frank, especially with my friends. And Vishnurao was a practical man, he understood. He even apologized to me. I said no need to apologize, not at all, it's not your mistake that you are bad luck, it's just the way your planets are placed. Then Vishnurao went back to the factory and I continued with my business, which began to draw in profits from the next quarter, so you see . . . it's just a matter of how one's planets are placed when one is born, nothing else. Anyway, that did not affect our friendship at all, and he came to me that night and he told me—he was almost crying—that his granddaughters had disappeared. Well, what do you mean, Vishnurao, what do you mean they have disappeared? I asked him. They must be around somewhere, come inside, have a glass of water. The sisters' mother was with him, too, and I asked my wife to talk to her while I spoke to Vishnurao and tried to understand what the matter was, where the sisters could have gone and where to search for them.

'But let me tell you, the moment he told me that the girls had gone out in the morning and not returned since, I felt as if . . . I felt strange. I thought, this is not good. This is, in fact, terrible. The mother sounded calm, more or less. I don't know how, because I was panicking, and I could see that Vishnurao wasn't doing that well either. But that mother was very calm, which was strange, because which mother would be calm about her daughters disappearing? And disappearance is always worse than death because death, let me tell you, is knowledge while disappearance is void. Sant Barabanki has said that. I am a follower of Sant Barabanki, and Sant Barabanki, who disappeared long ago, had said that. Disappearance keeps the faith alive, but death is final. In this case, of course, death was—no, what I mean is . . . Anyway, the long and short of it is that Vishnurao told me about how the Inspector had treated them, how he had told them to come back tomorrow, how he had insulted his granddaughters and called Anisha a randi and how he had behaved with the mother, and I wasn't surprised. I know that Dighole, a very disgusting fellow. But our friend Tatya, who is a social worker here, he had a very good hold over Dighole, I knew that. So we decided that we must call Tatya and the others, although Vishnurao was a little hesitant about that, I could see that, and I wouldn't blame him: Tatya was our friend but he was not exactly the most . . . I mean, his methods were different. He had a lot of goondas who surrounded him and who were ready to do things for him—bad things, of course, but also good things—if Tatya so much as whistled. Tatya was very influential around here, rao, Tatya Bhau was everybody's friend . . . he really cared about Murwani and the surrounding villages. So I said: Don't worry, Tatya is our friend, he will straighten out that Dighole madarchod.'

The Mother

(Excerpts from an interview transcript. Interview conducted on 23 February 2019.)

'Gadya Rambhau was a sensible man, as far as I remember, and he had helped Ajoba before by taking some sensible decisions on his behalf. That day Gadya Rambhau said: Let's take Tatya's help and teach Dighole a lesson. Let's make a rat out of that tiger, or something such. I agreed with Ajoba's friend. Normally I would have stayed away from Tatya and all those people, but I knew Tatya had a hold over Dighole and I wanted Dighole to suffer. At that moment, I wanted nothing but for Dighole to suffer. The madarchod had called my daughters whores. He had called me a bitch and also a whore. You can't expect me to sit and swallow that insult. And of course I wanted the police to act, to start a search, to register a formal complaint. So I told Gadya Rambhau that I will come along and let's all go together to the police station again. But I remember Gadya Rambhau said that it wasn't safe with Tatya's men, because they were all rowdies and they might be drunk at this time of the night. Besides, they might be sleeping and Tatya would have to wake them up, which means that they won't exactly be in a good mood. That was a logical thing, and Gadya Rambhau was always logical, as I said. Even so, I kept insisting. I argued for a bit, but then it started to rain. At first it rained, then it became a drizzle. Gadya Rambhau and Ajoba both said that it isn't advisable for women to come out at night with such people while it was raining, since the saree gets stuck to the body . . . eventually I had to agree, and Gadya Rambhau's wife walked with me to my house and Gadya Rambhau and Ajoba went to the Gram Panchayat building to fetch Tatya.'

PI Dighole

'Karamble, you have an umbrella?'

'No, saheb, sorry, saheb.'

Police Inspector Dighole sighed as the rain crashed down on the tin roof of the police station, designed such that the water had to trickle down and form a puddle on the station floor that made it difficult to walk outside without getting the lower part of the khaki uniform wet. Patle would no longer have that trouble, Dighole thought, he had made creative use of his pants, that randichya.

'She will have to be content without the pavs, if this continues,' Dighole murmured, cracking his fingers and following it up with a loud burp.

'Saheb?'

Dighole's son loved those pavs. He ate so many pavs, but he was still a fragile lad. So much money I spend on those pavs, Dighole thought, so much hard-earned money, and yet the boy was hardly strong. He should look like khatya pitya gharatla, not some malnourished kid from the streets, yellow with fever and hunger. Jayesh definitely did not look like a policeman's son, that randi was right about that, and it was Dighole's personal project to make him look and act like one. But perhaps he had gone a tad too far in the implementation of this project and perhaps that had alienated Jayesh from him.

It was obvious his son loved his mother more than his father. He didn't love his father, he feared him; PI Dighole wanted it to be a balance of both, because it had never been that way when he was growing up: he feared his father and then he hated him and that was that. PI Dighole wanted something better from his son, a mix of respect, genuine respect, and love, real love. His actions, however, had put paid to all those plans: one day PI Dighole had pointed his revolver at Jayesh—hardly seven—and told him to study hard. 'Otherwise you will know the difference between your toy gun and this one here.' He found the comparison witty, but apparently it was crass and unnecessary.

In retrospect, though, it *did* help improve Jayesh's marks in school. And he *did* study seriously now, more than before the incident, Dighole liked to believe, though that belief was strictly opposed by his wife, who had grown even more distant ever since that incident. Dighole was of the opinion that they were overreacting, his wife and his son. It wasn't something that serious. Obviously, he wasn't going to shoot his own son; it would be ridiculous of his wife to think that way. But she had remained that way, adamant and screwed-assed, and Dighole was the last person who believed in talking to resolve issues. It is what it fucking is, Dighole thought, his finger cruising through his teeth in search of tartar. If anything, it had led him to someone and something better: an attractive alternative, Dighole's solution to all problems these days.

'I hope they have found the sisters by now,' Karamble said.

'Hmm,' Dighole groaned.

The sisters.

'Tell me, Karamble, what do you think about that family?'

'Which family, saheb?'

'Karamble, are you as stupid in front of everybody else as you act in front of me? Don't tell me this is special for me.'

'Saheb . . . they say a lot of things about them, but I don't know.'

'Started calling my Jayesh things, Karamble. She started saying Jayesh is a bailya, that Jayesh might actually be a . . .'

'Ignore na, saheb.'

'You have seen Jayesh. What do you think?'

'Saheb . . .'

'You think he is a chutiya, Karamble?'

'Saheb . . . of course . . . of course not, saheb . . .'

'Behenchod. Is that what they say about Jayesh outside, Karamble? That he is a pussy?'

'Of course not, saheb.'

'Madarchod doesn't even go and play cricket. Can't even pick up a fucking bat. Stays home all day and sits there like he has no purpose, chutiya saala.'

'Who, saheb?'

'Karamble bhadvya, sometimes I look at you and I am reminded of Jayesh. Fucking useless pricks, both of you.'

'Saheb . . .'

'Chutiyas, both of you. You could have made good money off that Raju Bokle, Karamble, and look what you did. All you did was mooch a fucking paan out of him as if nothing else matters in your shit life, Karamble. Be ashamed of yourself for a change.'

'Saheb . . .'

Chorus

Said Ganpat Lawane: 'Haan, bhau, they came, that Ajoba and that Gadya. Haan, bhau. Tatya Bhau was with me at that time. I don't remember what we were doing. Well, I remember what I was doing. I was drinking beer, bhau. Mast chilled beer. Why shy away? I like mast chilled beer, I was drinking mast chilled beer. Arey, behenchod, people in cities can go to posh, big restaurants with mast videshi music and drink mast videshi beer and come home mast drunk and pengat pengat but we poor people drinking mast chilled beer is a problem? Behenchod, I will drink chilled beer whenever I want and wherever I want, and I was drinking beer at that time. But I wasn't drunk, bhau, like I said the last time we met. I wasn't drunk. Na. It was only my second khamba, bhau, so I was happy, I was nicely sitting there with Tatya Bhau, who doesn't drink, like I said the last time we met, Tatya didn't drink and I was drinking and we were discussing something, this matter or that matter, there was always some matter, and these people came and Gadya Bhau was panting and when Tatya saw that old man crying, he became very disturbed and he got up—we were sitting on the stairs of the Gram Panchayat—and he touched Ajoba's shoulders and asked him very politely, ekdum politely, like this: What happened, rao? Any problem? And Gadya Bhau started to whisper: The old man's granddaughters have gone missing, and the old man has been looking for them everywhere and the old man went to the police station, but Inspector Dighole kicked them both out. Both? Tatya Bhau, sharp as a hawk, asked. Then Gadya Bhau told us about how the poor mother was called a whore and a slut and all sorts of things, when the poor Mai was only looking for her daughters. That got Tatya Bhau all riled up, bhau, let me tell you that. He respects women like anything, bhau, let me tell you that. Best respect for women he reserved. He never shouted at womenfolk, bhau, never saw such respect for women in anybody but Tatya Bhau . . . And then Tatya Bhau looked at me and said, Ganpat chal, behenchod, let's fry Dighole in Murwani masala today. Call the boys, we will take them along, and tell Fawdya to bring out the cricket bats from earlier today. We had a practice match because we had organized a cricket tournament. So we had many cricket bats and stumps stored up for the tournament, and Tatya Bhau said let's get everything out and let's penetrate the madarchod's ass with them. I had never seen Tatya Bhau that angry, but that night he was like a haivan, a rakshas. I was scared of him, but I called Fawdya, our man who handled the labourers in the area, and I could see that Fawdya had been drinking too, but I told him to get the boys here with stumps and cricket bats. Then Tatya Bhau said, no, not near the Gram Panchayat, call them near the playground, we will walk from there. So that's what I told them: Come near the playground with bats and stumps, let's give that Inspector some Murwani masala.'

Said Gadya Rambhau: 'I remember that we went to the playground and they were already there, all of those burly fellows, red-eyed and sweaty and smelling of tobacco and cigarettes and alcohol. I was scared, but I expected this, of course I expected this, that's what I meant when I said that Tatya's methods are . . . but this was required. Tatya was a good man, but all this is also required in his trade. Social work is not a joke. All this is necessary. And from the playground we started walking towards the police station, which was towards the petrol pump side. I think we were fifteen or twenty of us, and it took us fifteen minutes to reach the police station.'

PI Dighole

'Haan, exactly, behenchod. Listen to this message Sangere sent me the other day . . . what is common between floods and wives? Get caught in between any one of them and you can get choked to death. Slowly. Ha ha ha. Eh, Karamble?'

'I wouldn't know na, saheb, I am not married . . .'

'But in general, Karamble, in general, you have known women in your life na. Sister, mother . . .'

'Haan, saheb, in general I—'

'But tell me something, how do you manage without a woman in the house, Karamble? What shit life. Go home, make your lunch, make your dinner, eat, wash utensils, jerk off and go to sleep. It's a sad life. No wonder you are so sad all the time, Karamble.'

'I am not sad all the time.'

'Why don't you do one thing? Why don't you seduce some woman here in the village, Karamble? Or if that's too much effort for you, I can arrange for someone from Futane Wadi, those randis are always up for a—'

'No, saheb, I have told you na. I am not . . . I am happy the way I am.'

'Every single man who hasn't managed to get a woman to suck his dick has the same things to say: I am happy the way I am. Listen to me, sometimes I fear Jayesh is going to turn out like you, and I don't want Jayesh to turn out like you. I don't want anybody to turn out like you, Karamble.'

'Neither do I, saheb.'

'Well, that's good. But what is not good is that you don't have—you have some brother? Sister? Call your sister, na, to clean up your mess of a house? To cook for you some days. I am sure your sister wouldn't mind that.'

'Sister lives in Mumbai, saheb.'

'Aai zavli, Karamble, Mumbai? What is she doing in Mumbai?'

'They have a food stall there, my sister and her family.'

'Achha. See, she has made a life for herself there in the city. And look at you, Karamble. I feel disgusted about the way—what the fuck is that sound, Karamble?'

Police Inspector Dighole, who by that time was using both his hands to demonstrate a point for Karamble, paused. He strained his ears. His mouth was open in anticipation of the words he had been about to utter but did not get the chance to. They could hear collective muttering, some chants. A group, getting closer.

Constable Karamble stood up from the stool, picked up his baton and walked towards the door of the police station, where he stood for some time, looking around indifferently.

'Check the gate,' PI Dighole said, getting up and making sure that his revolver was in its holster. There had been some communal incidents recently, not for months now, but one never knows. Some bike crashes into someone's yard and it sparks a riot. One never knows in this country.

Communal procession or not, PI Dighole realized that a crowd was on its way—either for them, the police, or passing through, in which case Dighole would have to stop them and check them out. But of course, why the fuck was a crowd passing through the village at this time of the night?

As soon as Karamble reached the gate he beat a hasty retreat, running the short distance between the station gate and the station door. 'The sisters' Ajoba . . . saheb . . . with people, saheb, hockey sticks and . . .' Karamble gasped for breath and struggled to form sentences as Dighole tightened his hold over his holster.

Ajoba

(Excerpts from an interview transcript. Interview conducted on 2 March 2019.)

'Yes, I think you are right, because as soon as we reached the police station, I could see the Constable and the Inspector, and they were standing there as if they were ready to run for their lives or as if they were ready to shoot. The Inspector was ready to shoot. He had his hand over his . . . that thing where they keep their revolver. And I could see, I am telling you that I could see that I wasn't needed there. That Gadya wasn't needed there. I wanted to lodge a complaint. An FRI they call it na? An FRI, I wanted to file. But Tatya and his men were not interested in that. They were only interested in intimidating the Inspector, Inspector Dighole, his name was. They had some lafdas from before, and I could see that Tatya wanted to . . . even at that time my granddaughters were not really important. My granddaughters were already being used for something else. It's how the world works, haan? Yes. So when we reached the police station, Tatya and his men confronted the Inspector.

'Dighole Saheb said: What is all this, Tatya? What are you doing here? And Tatya said: Inspector Saheb demands to know what is all this, what am I doing here. Nothing much, Inspector Saheb, out for a stroll. And people started laughing. As if it was a joke. As if they were a part of some movie. Tatya continued: I will tell you what all this is, Inspector. It's your randigiri. Your randigiri has brought us here, as usual. We have had enough of that. Kay barobar na? This poor man's granddaughters haven't turned up yet. Bhosadichya, they have been gone for more than six hours and you told him to come tomorrow. *Tomorrow.* This isn't a sarkari bank, Inspector, have some shame. Tatya said something along those lines. I cannot be sure about the exact words, but I am sure those are the exact words. I am sure. And the Inspector tried to calm the situation. The Inspector said: Calm down, Tatya. But Tatya was in his own world that night: Look at the gall of this chodhichya. He thinks this is the time to relax. You think three young girls disappearing in the dead of the night is a matter to be calm about, Dighole? And Dighole Saheb, that bumbling idiot, he said: We can sort this out calmly. Tatya, now very angry, said: Arey, madarchod! Again the same thing. What did I just say? Is this the time to be calm? You are an Inspector, Dighole, you should be the one going around the town trying to search for those girls and getting your car . . . this is your car na? Kay re? This is the Jeep you take for rounds na, at night?' And Dighole Saheb did not respond, he simply clutched that part where he kept his revolver. What if those girls are kidnapped? someone shouted. I don't remember who. But I thought: It is possible. It might be possible. To be honest with you, my mind at that time was completely blank. There was nothing there. Empty. I remember that feeling. Feeling as if there is nothing going on in my mind. That there are no thoughts. That everything has ended. Kidnapped? I heard Dighole Saheb say. And then: Did you receive a call, Ajoba? Demanding money? What a stupid thing to say. Tatya said: This is not your chutiya movie, bhokichya. No one phones and demands money here. And Tatya said: You think just because you have a phone everyone here has one? Not everyone whores himself in this village, Dighole, what do you think? I remember I agreed with what Tatya had said, but my mind was completely blank. Completely dark.

'This was before Dighole said: Tatya have you started drinking again? Because these days the moment you open your mouth, all the shit of Murwani . . .'

PI Dighole

Dighole did not see where it had come from, but a stone the size of a fist crashed into one of the station's windows and shattered it in half. Then another, smaller this time, the size of a grenade. It did not shatter anything: it simply went through the hole in the chowki's window. Dighole considered pulling out his revolver and firing in the air, but it hadn't come to that yet.

'Bhadvya!' someone from the crowd shouted. It came from the group of youngish-looking men huddled in the corner, beside and behind each other, looking angrily at Dighole. One of them brought down the cricket stump he was carrying on the bonnet of the only police Jeep at the station, indeed, in the vicinity. But that didn't dent the white bonnet, so he brought the stump down again and again, until the hood over the engine looked sufficiently crumpled. Dighole pointed out the obvious by shouting that the man was damaging public property.

'Look who's talking about damaging public property,' Tatya said, and that somehow made the man with the cricket stump more purposeful. 'You use public property to go for your randi rounds and now you are accusing us of damaging public property? No, no, no longer! Police ki dadagiri nahi chalegi, nahi chalegi. Gaandit ghal, aai zavadya, Dighole,' a young man shouted and aimed the stump in his hand at Karamble, who managed to dodge it.

At that moment Dighole decided that he needed to pull his gun out. He had thought he could deal with Tatya by bantering and letting him vent his frustration, but the men seemed determined to create a scene. Well, if they wanted a scene, I will give them a fucking scene. Departmental inquiry, if it ever happened, can be handled. Things were escalating quickly: shooting in the air or, if circumstances forced him to, *at* them, in self-defence, was not a crime, and he could wriggle his way out of it if it came to that—he had plenty of jacks in the force for that.

Gadya Rambhau

(Excerpts from an interview transcript. Interview conducted on 27 February 2019.)

'Then I saw Vishnurao struggle his way through those thirty or forty men, which isn't as easy as it may sound, let me tell you that. He was tapping someone and trying to push aside someone else and trying to shout that he is the grandfather of the sisters and that he needed to speak to the Inspector, but he couldn't achieve much with that old and frail body of his. I was watching all this and I rushed to him and I asked him what the matter was. He told me that everything was falling apart. That this is all nonsense. We are not here to smash police Jeeps and start a fight, we are here to lodge a complaint. I said that is true, but let Tatya handle this in his own way. But Vishnurao was very sure that nothing was going to be handled, and he was right. Tatya . . . well, Tatya was a good man. A decent human being. He helped a lot of people around here, with all sorts of things, but at that time he was trying to do . . . something else.

'Then Vishnurao started waving his hand in the air, and fortunately that Constable saw him and I think he saw a way out of this, a peaceful way out of this mess, because he shouted, at the top of his voice: Let Ajoba come forward! He wants to say something! Let Ajoba come forward! That little Constable almost lost his voice shouting that. By then the Inspector had pulled out his revolver, so there was that too. He pointed his revolver at Tatya and said: Let Ajoba speak, let him come inside the police station.

'I started walking with Vishnurao and everyone gave way now. When we reached the stairs of the police station, the Inspector looked at me and shook his head: Only Ajoba inside. All of you wait. But Vishnurao, who by that time had gathered strength from Pandurang knows where, my friend Vishnurao said: No, Inspector, I want Gadya and Tatya to come with me. Otherwise forget it. It was a very brave thing to say, as you can imagine.

The Inspector thought about this for a while, and then with a defeated look he nodded his head and told that Constable to keep an eye on Tatya's people: Make sure they don't damage anything. The moment he said it, one of them smashed the windshield of the Jeep. The Inspector was stunned into silence, but Tatya being Tatya turned around, walked up to the man who had smashed the windshield and whispered something to him. Then he looked at everybody else—there were many in the mob who were not Tatya's men by that time—and he looked around at the mob and said: No lafda while we are inside, kay? Let's see where this goes. No lafda. I want *no behenchod lafda*. Then he looked at the Inspector: Haan, Dighole, they will do nothing now. Tatya looked at the Constable and smiled: Let's go inside and discuss now, kay? Chalo. I remember Tatya was the first one to enter the police station, even before the Inspector . . .'

PI Dighole

The first information report was filed at 11.25 p.m., almost exactly two hours after the mother and grandfather duo had come to the police station for the first time.

'Madarchod therda returned with a crowd to lynch us, Karamble,' Inspector Dighole said as he flicked a piece of glass off the Jeep's bonnet and thought about the report he would have to write about the damage and the hundred other bureaucratic hurdles he would have to deal with, all because Tatya Khandle had decided, as always, to turn this into a personal matter.

This was not exactly new: last time it was about Constable Patle, and since Patle belonged to the Powar caste, and since the all-important local body polls were in the offing that year, Tatya had resorted to making a tamasha about murder-not-suicide, no doubt on the orders of his masters. By those standards, this sisters' thing was a fucking gold mine for that gaandu, Dighole thought. Nobody in this village gave a shit about the sisters or that family, but look at those ghename sticking to each other like leeches all because Tatya liked to whore himself around.

'Karamble,' Inspector Dighole said, his hand still running over the damaged bonnet.

'Saheb?'

'Remind me to ask SP Madam if we can put a hundred holes into Tatya's body and toss it down some well.'

Karamble nodded his head.

'How many holes, Karamble?'

'A hundred, saheb.'

'Correct. A hundred fucking holes, and that's not counting the four he already has.'

'Four, saheb?'

Inspector Dighole looked up, pointed at his mouth, 'One,' his ear holes, 'Two, three,' and down at his groin, 'Four.'

'And, saheb, the gaand?'

Inspector Dighole sighed and nodded his head slowly. 'You are right. A hundred holes, not counting the five he already has.'

Janhavi

It was impossible to sleep. Priyanka was missing. Anisha was missing. Sanchita was missing. The sisters were missing, that's what her father told her when she heard the commotion outside. Her father had reassured her that they were searching for them, all of those who were outside. 'They will find your friend, don't worry. Go to sleep. You have to wake up na, tomorrow, you have to go to school . . .'

But Janhavi didn't want to go to school if Priyanka wasn't going to come. What was she going to do in those horrid classes without her best friend? No, she would go to school only when Priyanka returned. And she would return, of course, she would return. She would have to. Priyanka would never leave her alone and go off somewhere, she would never do that. They did all things together. Priyanka had her sisters, but she never left Janhavi alone, and she always ensured that she was a part of everything the sisters did together. Some people even called Janhavi the fourth sister, but Janhavi didn't like that because she didn't like being associated with the other two.

It wasn't as if Janhavi didn't like them. That wasn't it. And it wasn't as if Anisha and Sanchita excluded her or anything. There was always some whispering and some giggling between the three sisters, but they never treated Janhavi as if she were not one of them. At least Janhavi had never felt that way with them, but it was simply . . . it was simply that her mother had told her to stay away from them. And her mother had told her that Anisha and Sanchita were not the best-behaved girls in the village. And that aunty, their neighbour, had told her that she had seen Anisha going around with boys, that she, Janhavi, should be careful of such girls; that she, Janhavi, because she was always with Priyanka and her sisters, should be careful and not mingle much with the sisters; and that she, Janhavi, should especially refuse anything that Anisha gave her or asked her to do.

Now all that was making sense.

Many men and women had come to Janhavi's house that night asking questions. 'Where did you see Priyanka last?' 'What did she tell you before leaving?' 'She must have said something, you are her best friend. Try to remember.' 'What was Anisha wearing when you saw her?' 'Which way did they go when they left?' Questions that had reduced Janhavi to tears.

The rain had been a saviour. Because when it started to rain, most of those who were outside, searching, had returned to their homes. And no one had bothered to come to Janhavi's house and ask her questions then.

But Janhavi hated rain. She was thankful that people had stopped coming to ask her those stupid questions, but she hated hated hated the rain. The atmosphere outside, darkness everywhere, the *tap tap tap tap* noise of those large drops falling over the roof of her house, the pools of muddy water everywhere, those black clouds like black horses in the sky . . . and now her friend, out there somewhere in all this.

Her father pinched her cheeks and smiled at her. 'Janhavi beta, go to sleep. Tomorrow when you go to school, Priyanka will be right there at her . . .'

Prateek

Prateek was sleeping when his elder brother woke him up.

Pranil was pouring sweat and the expression on his face said: emergency. Prateek had been thinking about that word since the morning, so when Pranil woke him up, the first word Prateek uttered was: emergency.

'The sisters . . .' Pranil said, panting, 'the sisters . . .'

They were led to Datta Mama's house by their parents. On their way there, Prateek saw a number of men holding bats and stumps talking to each other, shouting across fields, running on the road, umbrella-less in the rain, some smiling, others anxious. Prateek couldn't understand what was happening, but he could gauge that this *was* an emergency. Had something happened? But he knew better than to ask questions while they were walking with their parents.

Datta Mama was talking to his son when Prateek, Pranil and their parents entered. The door was open, and Datta Mama looked tense. His face was grim, and the moment he saw them enter, he told his son to close the door behind them.

'What is happening, Datta Mama?'

'Those daughters-of-bitches have fled their homes. Not surprising, if you ask me.'

'Who?' Prateek asked.

'The sisters.'

'What has that got to do with us, Mama?' their father asked, suppressing a yawn.

'You were always dumb, Ghanashyam. My only concern is that you display your dumbness too much. Now listen, whatever it is to do with the sisters, the police will be involved. And you know the police here. They are going to round up every boy coming of age, and that means Pranil and Prateek, but Pranil especially. We need to prepare.'

'Prepare?'

'Where were you when they disappeared? What were you doing? Can anyone vouch for you? All those things.'

'Mama . . .' Pranil began, averting his eyes from Mama's gaze, 'that eldest sister, Anisha, she . . . I saw them, those sisters and Anisha . . . she had a . . . she had a lafda . . .'

Mama didn't put too much into that kick, but it hit Pranil right under his chin and he screamed. No one was shocked. This was simply Mama's way, that was how he had raised his sons and that was how he would bring up his sister's sons as well.

'When you lose a tooth or two you will understand when to speak what and where, Pranil. I hope you got the message. Lafdi, lagna, elopement this and that. I don't care. You stick to your story and you stay out of it. Forget everything else, do you understand?'

Prateek was planning to tell Mama about how he had seen the sisters walk out of the school gate and turn right instead of taking the left, how he thought that the sisters were actually bunking school and going off somewhere to have fun, but of course he kept mum. As the younger one, he would perhaps only receive a slap or two, but Prateek had always preferred the schoolteachers' ear-twisting to Mama's stinging slaps.

Mama was about to launch into another tirade when they heard shuffling and whispering and general commotion outside. 'You stay inside,' Mama instructed Prateek and Pranil and their mother. 'And you two, come with me.'

Mama gathered his lungi, picked up his walking stick and walked out of the house.

Gadya Rambhau

(Excerpts from an interview transcript. Interview conducted on 27 February 2019.)

'I remember a lot of things from that day, but I don't remember who called me to the well. Someone told me, or I heard someone say that they have found the sisters. I thanked Pandurang. I joined my hands and closed my eyes and began to say a prayer. Someone tapped me on my shoulder: Gadya Bhau, you will have to inform Ajoba. I said okay. Then someone else told me: Gadya Bhau, come to the well. The well, the well, the well, everyone was suddenly talking about the well. It had been raining, so we had . . . we had stopped the search for some time. By that time it had stopped raining, but the skies were still dark. By the time I walked to the well, I knew that something was wrong. I saw a tramp, that lukhya, he was standing near the well and that lukhya was the first one to say: I know who did this.

'Who did what?'

Ajoba

Ajoba had almost dozed off when someone knocked on the door, only to find it open. It was drizzling outside. The grandmother did not move while the mother continued to sleep.

Gadya Rambhau peered inside the room.

'Vishnurao?'

'Gadya?'

'They have found the girls.'

As Ajoba peeped inside the deep, dark cavern of the well, someone hurried to his side with a torch. The man's hands were shaking, but he managed to turn the torch on. Framed inside the torch's yellow circular beam were the grandfather's three small granddaughters, their bodies floating gently in the black water of the night.

Someone whispered, perhaps to assure Ajoba, that the girls looked unharmed. It didn't make any sense. To Ajoba nothing made any sense anyway. He saw the three bodies. Anisha's left leg over Priyanka's right, Priyanka's face on Sanchita's neck. He kept looking at them, his granddaughters. His lips quivering, his breath laboured. He felt panic and then he felt pain.

Ajoba looked away at the surroundings: a vast, empty wilderness, punctuated by shocked murmurs permeating through the foggy expanse. Someone sobbed, someone else stifled theirs. Ajoba couldn't breathe. For a couple of minutes he thought he was going to die. He slumped down, but then realized that his back was touching the well's parapet wall.

He jerked away. A shiver ran through his spine. He couldn't cry.

By this time a bunch of women had brought the mother and Aaji to the well. The yellow light of the many torches partially illuminated their faces. Ajoba got up and peeped inside the well again. Someone came along purposefully with a torch, but Ajoba pushed him away with his hand and stared into the darkness inside, unbothered by the noxious, chemical odour that emerged from the well's black, moss-infected walls.

'Don't let them look inside,' Ajoba managed to murmur. Someone heard him and understood. There were whispers among the women, and then more sobbing. Someone said, urgently, 'What is happening? Call the police.'

It was dawn already, and Ajoba knew that the day would allow everyone to peep inside and look at his granddaughters without the need of a torch: their dresses blown up like balloons, their eyes half-open, their lips slightly parted.

He broke down.

Chorus

Said Constable Karamble: 'We were preparing to leave. Our shift was about to end. Dighole Saheb's phone began to ring. He spoke to someone. It was his wife. I observed his face. I always observed his face when he spoke on the phone to determine who he was speaking to. He always started with "Haan, bol" when he was talking to his wife, so when he picked up the phone and said, "Haan, bol," I understood that it was his wife. But madam calling at that time? It must have been around five-thirty or maybe five. Maybe four-thirty. Sorry, I don't remember. I remember it was dawn, and Dighole Saheb's wife never called him at dawn . . . so I knew something was wrong. His face changed. You know that balloon going poof when the air exits? Like that, Dighole Saheb's face collapsed. He started shouting. "Where? Where? Which well?" I got up and picked up my baton. "Ae, don't tell me not to shout . . . Smita, don't tell me . . . don't tell me . . . ae, behenchod, where are they going, answer me!" He never swore at his wife. He might say bad things about her in the station, but he never swore at her. So I knew something was wrong. Something had happened.'

Said Fawdya: 'Haan na, ekdum suddenly it got serious. I was in charge of the cricket kits for the night cricket tournament. Everyone was excited. The workers were also excited. They also wanted to play. I was explaining to them that they can't play because only four teams were allowed: two from Murwani and two from outside. And the Murwani teams had already been formed. Besides, these workers were from outside states. They worked on a season-by-season basis. February–April here, April–July somewhere else, and then back to their native places. Things like that. They were outsiders, basically. But they wanted to play. They said we will form our own team, and I was trying to tell them, chup bhokichyano, that is not possible. They weren't ready to understand and I was about to tell them that Tatya himself will come and talk to them. The problem is that they had heard about the amount we were giving out to the winning team—one lakh rupees, a good sum—and they wanted to compete for their share. What "your share", I asked them. You have no share in this. So we were having this jhaka-jhaki when Ganpat called me. He said, "Fawdya, matter jhalay. Come to the playground with all the boys. With cricket bats and stumps." Now that was a problem because cricket bats and stumps would remind these drunk chutiyas again of the cricket tournament. But if Tatya asked us to assemble to revolve a matter, we had to. No questions asked. So I told them, okay, let's discuss all this later, let's go and see why Tatya has called us. They were all very loud until Tatya told us what had happened. Three sisters had gone missing. Three little girls. Then those workers became serious. Very quiet. I think they were thinking about their daughters or something. Or maybe they were just sad that the tournament would now be cancelled . . .'

Said Ganpat Lawane: 'The Inspector was shaking when he arrived on the scene. Naturally, bhau. What do you think? Three minor girls . . . and the moment they were found, everyone, *everyone*, haan, bhau, everyone started whispering to each other, because they looked . . . how to say this now, bhau, without sounding . . . they looked violated. Yes, they looked violated, and someone told Ajoba that the girls looked unharmed, but everybody knew that the girls had been violated and murdered. I won't use the term raped because I am not . . . but they had been violated, especially that girl in the green top na, bhau. But the Inspector was not ready to agree. He came and he peeped inside the well, and we stood and stared at him silently, which is what Tatya Bhau had instructed us to do. "That gaandu Dighole will come and start making useless statements, but don't do anything. Just stand silently and watch him go about his business. Observe his movements but do nothing and the chodhichya will get scared." Then Tatya told some of the workers to go and arrange for rasta roko on the highway because this needed media attention. Our Tatya Bhau was very smart and very sharp, bhau, you must have understood that by now. He knew in advance how everybody was going to behave. It was too good. It was fun watching Tatya Bhau go about instructing everyone to act, as if he was Shahrukh Khan or Salman Khan in a movie, haan, bhau. So Dighole chutiya arrived with his napoonsak constables and he asked Ajoba, of all people, about the bodies. Poor thing, that old man. He was sitting under a tree with his head held in his hands and this randichya goes to him and asks him where his granddaughters' bodies are. Imagine that, bhau. Then after Dighole had done all his bullshit, he came back to Ajoba and said: "Ajoba, I know this is a difficult . . . this is very . . . but this is not a murder or anything. This looks like an accident."

'"Unbelievable," Tatya Bhau whispered. It was clear the Inspector had lost it. So Tatya Bhau went to the Inspector at this point and told him clearly. "Enough of your gaandupana, everyone here knows the truth, which is that it's a murder. Everyone here knows it's murder and not just murder, but rape. *Rape*. Rape and murder, madarchod, and on your watch. Look how I fuck with you now, Dighole." All this our Tatya Bhau said, and Dighole was about to say something when Tatya Bhau pushed him and looked at his Jeep and pointed at it and said, "You decide, your life or this Jeep?" Before Dighole could respond, Tatya Bhau said, "Of course, the Jeep because namarad chutiyas like you won't have the daring to give up their lives, and you call yourself an Inspector, lavdya?" So then Tatya Bhau told us to ignite the police Jeep . . .'

PI Dighole

When the Taluka Magistrate arrived, he looked haggard, irritated and confused all at the same time. PI Dighole knew that the Magistrate was an asshole, and when he barged in he made everyone stand at attention in front of him like school students during PT period.

Then the first thing Rammadhav Sanjay did was examine the burning Jeep. He stood staring at the flames leaping out of the shattered windshield. Then he gave a slight nod and began walking towards PI Dighole.

'Dighole, that Jeep is burning.'

Dighole was about to launch into an explanation, but the Magistrate had already moved on.

'Three minors,' Sanjay said, sticking out three of his fingers. 'Three minor *girls*. They are telling me it could be rape. Rape *and* murder. PI Dighole, what were you thinking?'

'Sir . . .'

'You know SP Madam is going to be directly involved with this, na? *Directly*,' Sanjay said, his hands comically fixed on his waist. Like he was Vithoba Mauli, PI Dighole thought.

'Yes.'

'Good. Because you better be ready with your answers, not that it seems you have any. Where are the bodies?'

No one answered.

'Where the fuck are the bodies, Dighole?'

'Inside the well, sir.'

Rammadhav Sanjay scratched his arm and then rubbed his temple.

'Pull them out, yaar, quickly.'

A random local whispered into Sanjay's ear and Sanjay turned to PI Dighole again. 'Dighole, they are burning a truck right at this moment on the highway. Burning a truck *and* blocking the road. Deshmukh is handling that right now. We are all handling *your* headache, get that into your useless head.'

Dighole felt the bile reach up to the edge of his throat. He had had a spectacular dinner, but that, he realized, was going to be his last peaceful meal for a while. He sighed and glared at Karamble and Narvankar. 'Baghtay kay, bochyano? Pull the bodies out.'

Others

The Taluka Magistrate conducted the inquest panchnama but sent the bodies for post-mortem the next day. Two days later, the post-mortem report established that Anisha, Sanchita and Priyanka had been raped and murdered. It wasn't clear, however, whether all three sisters were dead by the time they were thrown into the well.

According to the traditions of Murwani, dead minors have to be buried, not cremated. Someone knew the logic and the legend behind it, but the family of the sisters didn't. They were told by Tatya that the sisters would have to be buried and they agreed to it. Then Tatya asked them about the heights of the sisters and proceeded to instruct two of his men to secure the required land and two others to dig the required graves.

Not many attended the burial. Those who did said that the sisters' grandmother did not come and that Ajoba, inconsolable, tried to lower his granddaughters' bodies but could not, so Tatya and his men eventually had to perform the ritual. They also said, those who attended, that the mother did not shed a single tear for her daughters. But then again, who knows?

When they discussed the incident—in Murwani, in Nagpur, in Mumbai, in Delhi, in party offices and official buildings, in Assembly corridors and Parliament halls (for a day or two)—they said, maybe this wouldn't have happened had she been wearing her uniform. That green top had invited attention. It was like a signal, and what does a green signal mean, gentlemen? But in Murwani several people pointed out the obvious: the two other sisters were in their uniforms, and yet . . . Then the discussions moved on to other topics.

Part Two

CRIMES

22 February–27 March 2013
Murwani, Maharashtra

Ganpat Lawane

(Excerpts from an interview transcript. Interview conducted on 28 February 2019.)

'The important question was: what to do with all the biryani now? We had ordered a lot of biryani for the opening match. For the entire village, bhau. Tatya Bhau sponsored it. He had told Rafik Bhai from Futane Wadi that the biryani should be Hyderabadi style, ekdum chatakdar. People should lick their fingers clean, he had told Rafik bhai, and I will be observing if people are licking their fingers clean. No piece of chicken and not a single grain of cooked rice should go to waste, Tatya Bhau warned. But then look what happened, behenchod. You never know how Pandurang works, bhau—not Pandurang Shishathe, haan, I am not talking about that chutiya car mechanic, I am talking about our God Pandurang. You never know how He works, He is always sending signals, because at that time, when Tatya Bhau told Rafik Bhai that nothing should go to waste, that the biryani should be tasty, I thought: Bhau, now the entire order is going to go to waste. I am not lying. Mother promise, I thought, bhau, there is going to be some jhamela, and look what happened. Jhamela.

'Right after the three little sisters were buried, Tatya Bhau whispered to me as if he were revealing some top-secret information: Go to Rafik and see what you can do about the biryani. What do you want me to do about the biryani, Tatya Bhau? I asked a stupid question.

I know I did because then Tatya Bhau said: Lavdya, thoos it in your gaand and sit on it until it gets digested. I said sorry, bhau, but I couldn't resist asking another question, which was also stupid: Is the tournament not happening then? And Tatya Bhau looked very disturbed because then he asked me: Ganya, what has happened to you? Are you drunk? Did you drink first thing in the morning? No, no, no, bhau, I said, I am not drunk and I haven't had a drop since this entire thing started. Good, said Tatya Bhau, now go.

'I went to Rafik Bhai's biryani corner and it was as if he was waiting for me because he said that I had come too late, the biryani masala and all were already made, and that he had prepared so-so many kilos of biryani. I tried to tell Rafik what Tatya Bhau had told me, which is that Rafik should shove the biryani inside his asshole and sit on it to see whether it gets digested, but Rafik Bhai didn't like the joke because he then called his chokras out and they were all topiwale with their black eyes and their machetes and they all stood there like they were ready to pounce on me and my boys. Now we are not afraid of anything, but we didn't want another lafda right then, especially after what had happened to the three sisters. I told Rafik Bhai I was joking, but that it was Tatya Bhau's instruction: Cancel the order. But Rafik Bhai shook his head and folded his hands over his chest. He said: No, tell Tatya it's not possible, and ask him to come and speak to me, man to man. That got my balls. What do you mean? I asked Rafik. Be within your limits, Rafik, you think I am not man enough to talk to you? But Rafik Bhai then said: No, chutiya, what I mean is ask Tatya to come and talk to me businessman to businessman. That confused me even more because neither Rafik Bhai nor Tatya Bhau were businessmen. Rafik Bhai sold biryani and chicken and Tatya Bhau was a social worker, so . . . but I let that go. I gave one look to all those mullehs and I said to Rafik Bhai: Rafik Bhai, I will ask Tatya Bhau to handle this. And Rafik Bhai said: Yes, you better. What the hell did that mean? I was very confused . . .'

State Home Minister

On 22 February, the State Home Minister arrived in the village with an entourage. Police cars, sirens blaring. The enterprising people of Murwani pitched up cold drink and snacks stalls, but there was hardly a person from the security detail who wanted to taste the local delicacies, which of course were hardly local. Except for the biryani. That, the State Home Minister had been told, was procured from Rafik Bhai's especially for his visit. Enticing as the pot of biryani was, though, he wanted to check out the scene of the murder first.

The State Home Minister, who was wearing a crisp white kurta and sporting pitch-black shades, walked slowly and spoke in whispers to the Director General of Police (DGP), who in turn instructed the police detail around him to take exhaustive notes of what the State Home Minister was saying. The State Home Minister then turned to the Chief of the State Women Commission, who was trying to listen to the State Home Minister's instructions to the DGP. If all this made their walk a little awkward, they did not notice it, busy as they were trying to look busy.

The State Home Minister *was*, in fact, talking about an important matter with the DGP, just that the important matter was unrelated to why they were in Murwani. Eventually, the State Home Minister reached the abandoned temple, where he tried to pay his respects to whichever God had been installed inside, only to be told that the God had, in fact, been shifted out of the temple and into the village. In fact, near a mosque. This prompted the State Home Minister to praise the village's secular values, and then bemoan the fact that such an ideal village should experience such a tragic tragedy.

The DGP and the Chief of the State Women Commission stopped a few steps away from the well while the State Home Minister trudged towards it daringly and looked inside with a grave face. It was perhaps true that the State Home Minister, at least momentarily, felt sad. He must have thought about his daughters, his sons, his sister's daughters, his brother's sons. He must have, but there is no way of knowing. He looked inside the well for a long time, that much is true, and then he looked at the DGP.

'Is this where the bodies were found?' he asked.

'Yes, sir,' the DGP said, touching the peak of his peak cap.

'This is unacceptable,' the State Home Minister whispered. 'I want this case cracked. This is unacceptable.'

The DGP looked at one of the Additional DGPs (Law and Order) and mumbled something. The Additional DGP (Law and Order) nodded and excused himself, apparently to call the other Additional DGP, the Additional DGP (Special Operations). They spoke. Then the Additional DGP (Law and Order) returned to the DGP's side and whispered something into his ears. The DGP nodded and in turn whispered something into the State Home Minister's ear, who then thought gravely about whatever had been whispered.

Snapping out of his grave thoughts, the State Home Minister then looked about, as if he were looking for something or someone. The DGP put a hand on his chest and bent forward and asked the State Home Minister what the matter was. Then the DGP nodded thrice and asked the Additional DGP (Law and Order) something. The Additional DGP (Law and Order) then called for the SP from the security detail and a tall woman with a stony face approached the State Home Minister and saluted him. Then she saluted the DGP. Then she saluted the Additional DGP (Law and Order). All three of them nodded in return.

The SP pointed somewhere and spoke for some time with the State Home Minister, who looked on gravely in the direction that she had pointed. Then he started walking and the entire police detail, villagers, reporters and other miscellaneous followers trailed along. For a brief moment in time, then, the shack—isolated, ignored and avoided for the longest time—became the subject of intense attention.

'Is this where they live?' the State Home Minister asked the SP and the SP nodded. 'Well, hardly surprising . . .' the State Home Minister started but then he stopped and folded his hands as the mother of the three sisters peeped out. She invited the State Home Minister in, and as he stepped into the shack, the DGP whispered, 'Careful, sir,' because the State Home Minister's kurta was about to get caught in the edge of the sheet metal door.

The State Home Minister spent fifteen minutes inside the shack and then stepped out teary-eyed.

The visit was now in its concluding stages, so the State Home Minister asked his assistant to gather all the reporters around. This took another half an hour, during which time packets of biryani were served to journalists and police officials. White plastic spoons and happy faces. Cups of tea, cold drinks in dirty glass bottles with straws.

The local MLA came and met the State Home Minister and they joked and laughed and high-fived and praised the biryani, which indeed was excellent. These people indeed know their biryani, said the MLA. Then he began whispering things, and everyone could see that there was a discussion of vital importance in progress. One of the local reporters told a national reporter who had flown in from Delhi that the MLA and the State Home Minister were probably discussing terms.

'What terms?' the national reporter asked.

'Arey, MLA Saheb wants to switch sides. They are giving him a Lok Sabha ticket.'

'Achha? Interesting.'

Meanwhile, the DGP, Additional DGP (Law and Order) and the State Women Commission Chief chatted about a new office for the latter in Nagpur.

When the mics and the cameras had been set up and the reporters had had their tea and cold drinks, the State Home Minister took his place on one of the plastic chairs that had been arranged for the press conference.

He smacked his lips and burped and said 'Ram Ram' and then joked with a local reporter about his drinking tea instead of his usual cold drink mixed with alcohol.

'Kay Shatabde, no Thums Up with little little today?' the State Home Minister laughed, displaying his corroded teeth. The DGP and the police officials smiled shyly.

'Okay,' the State Home Minister's tone changed to formal and distant. 'I have taken proper cognizance of the situation. This is not just a tragic incident, this is a national tragedy. I am going to take this issue up nationally. But first of all, an ex-gratia amount of ten lakh rupees shall be given to the bereaved family. Secondly, I have instructed DGP Akbar Khan here to form special teams to investigate this crime. I am confident this case will be cracked soon.'

'Any chance the case would be handed over to the CBI?'

'Arey, bhau, I have just handed over the case to the CID. Give them some time, na,' the State Home Minister said with a sarcastic smile that made everybody laugh. 'See, you have to give them some time. I have DGP Saheb with me, he will tell you how he plans to go about the investigation.'

The DGP, his hands folded over his chest and his back pressed against his chair, cleared his throat as the faces turned towards him. He made some remarks about how tragic the entire thing was, and he said that the police would form teams, but appealed to the villagers to help the said police teams with the investigation.

'I have no qualms about admitting that the local people know this landscape and how things work here much better than any special teams. So we will require your inputs on this case,' the DGP said and then nodded, indicating that he was done.

No tough questions were asked. The reporters and their cameramen were tired. They had been told that the State Home Minister would visit in the morning, but it was almost evening by the time the conference ended. They knew that they should probably reserve the challenging questions that required long-winded answers for next time.

They dispersed as the State Home Minister and the DGP strode towards a duplex bungalow belonging to the Aangles, the richest family in the village. The State Home Minister and the Aangle patriarch went back a long way, from when the Aangles had sought to invest in the State Home Minister (then a first-time MLA) and his 'development projects' in central Maharashtra. Now the State Home Minister was, well, the State Home Minister, and he wanted to pay his respects to the Aangles—long time no see.

Of course, the State Home Minister spent more time inside the Aangle bungalow than he spent inside the Gudadhe shack, but that was to be expected.

The Mother

(Excerpts from an interview transcript. Interview conducted on 24 February 2019.)

'In the end I decided that I cannot keep crying. A week after they . . . a week after they found the bodies, I decided that I should stop crying. But what they have published in the media is all wrong. The media, you people, you people said that the mother did not cry at all. That she did not shed a single tear. Who told you all this? The villagers told you all this, but it is not true. I cried. I cried so much that I had nothing left to shed after a week, I was weak and I was hungry. I did not eat and I did not sleep. I vomited everything that went into my belly. The factory was helpful. My manager was helpful. He said: Take as much time as you want. But not more than a month, otherwise we will have to replace you. And I don't blame him. Everyone is a parent, after all, he said, but everyone has to work too. He gave me twenty days, for which he had to fight with his boss, but the boss eventually understood, he said, because it was a special case.

'But at that time I didn't want sympathy, I wanted justice. I wanted the police to be held accountable. First and foremost. So I said to myself: I cannot just sit here and cry and wait for someone to do something for us, for my daughters. I will have to do it myself. I will have to stand up for myself. I am capable of that. It's not as if I haven't seen death. I have seen my mother die, I have seen my father die, I have seen my husband die and now I have seen my daughters die. Death was always there, taking away everyone from me one by one, as if it wanted to nudge me and show me that this is how it feels, to lose someone but not to lose yourself. That is my karma, because when I was a child and when my father used to beat my mother, I would pray to God: Deva, take this man away. Deva, take my mother away. Deva, take this misery away. Deva, take *me* away. God sat in judgement and God granted my wish, and here it is—death everywhere. What would these villagers understand about all this? If I tell them all this, they will still go and announce to everyone that I am mad, that I am a witch, that I did not cry for my daughters and that I did not love my husband. But I have seen so much death that it no longer does anything to me. Yet, when I saw them for the last time, my little dolls, my . . . when I saw them for the last time, I cried and cried and cried and I couldn't stop myself, I cried so much. My head started throbbing and Ajoba came to me and gave me a glass of water and I cried into that glass of water. I drank my tears . . .

'But when the State Home Minister came to meet me, he looked at me as if he were looking at a demon. He pointed at me and whispered something to his PA. The PA noted something down and the State Home Minister folded his hands and spoke to me for a bit. How I am, whether I needed anything, whether I was doing well. And when I said: I am fine, we just need a new home, because I wanted to escape from that shithole, from all those memories, he went silent and almost said: Is this the time to demand all these things? He didn't say it, but I could see it's what he wanted to say. And of course that *was* the time because I wanted to escape the memories of my daughters. I don't dwell on them now and I didn't want to dwell on them then. But the State Home Minister merely smiled and said: You will get justice, Mai. I promise you. Then he looked at Aaji and Ajoba and folded his hands and whispered condolences and repeated the same thing: You will get justice, Ajoba. I promise you. You will get justice, Aaji. I promise you.

'Then he was gone, and the next day the local newspaper said: Mother doesn't cry for daughters during State Home Minister's visit.'

Chitranshu Chitale

Chitranshu should have been writing his weekend feature piece about the fate of police colonies across Mumbai and the ways in which their living conditions could be improved, but he wasn't. Because it was a Friday afternoon and soon it would be a Friday evening, which meant that it was time to follow Hamid and Dinesh and Tejas from the digital team to Dadar West's Gopalkrishna Bar and Restaurant, order their usual Old Monk quarters, dip their chakli in green chutney and schezwan sauce, bend their backs on Gopalkrishna's rickety benches and bitch about their bosses.

Even as he ate his lunch—garlic-bread sandwich from Rupak's Kitchen—Chitranshu could think of nothing but the sweet taste of rum with coke and the extra spiciness of Gopalkrishna's chicken fried rice. He could think of nothing but getting wasted, catching the last Borivali-bound train, getting off at Bandra, peeing in one of the station's acidic-smelling toilets and sprinting back to catch the train again as it gathers pace. Who the fuck wants to read about where the police shit and sleep on a Saturday morning with their cup of tea anyway? But his editor, Shantadeep Das, a grave man with a deep voice, wanted the piece to be subbed and ready by 7 p.m. *today*.

The notebook in front of Chitranshu had all the ingredients that would make a 900-word story. A few lines scribbled here and there about a visit to the Dadar police colony and a few quotes by one or two officials who wanted to remain anonymous for no good reason; and what they had provided Chitranshu was shit. Everyone knew the Mumbai Police's finances were fucked; bring me the numbers, get me the proof. But of course Chitranshu had only spoken to mid-level babus, so there was hardly any possibility that they could have provided him with any biteable information. But if nothing else, their quotes could always act as good fillers.

Chitranshu dipped his sandwich into the ketchup-pumpkin squash, took a large bite and closed his eyes. Heaven. He moaned and then smiled.

'Ae Chaitrali,' he said, adjusting his swivel chair's height to look at the new girl. He could see Chaitrali's back and the nape of her neck. She turned around and danced her eyebrows.

'Yes, sir,' she said. 'What can I do for you?'

Chitranshu paused before answering because it always aroused him when she said that. It was as if he owned her, as if she was waiting for his command and she would do *whatever* he wanted her to do with him. It was the stuff of Chitranshu's fantasies: and she looked particularly ravishing today, Chaitrali, in her kurti and patterned palazzo with diamond-shaped earrings and those nicely bobbing curls . . . There wasn't much difference between their ages, she was twenty-one and he was twenty-five, and things could work out if he played his cards right.

'You want this garlic bread sandwich?'

'Garlic bread? No, thank you.'

'Arey, take one and taste, na. Take it in your mouth.'

'No. I know you are chepaoing it to me because you can't finish it alone.'

'Untrue. I can. But I just like sharing things with other people. Sandwiches, books, beds, mattresses, even sofas if they find those comfortable.'

Chaitrali winced, but that was for a second. Then she shook her head slightly and tried to find something to fiddle with.

'Arey, take one. Here—'

'I said I don't want it, Chitranshu.'

'Fine. Your choice. There's a lot of mayo in here. You would have enjoyed it, dripping down your lips and all.'

Chitranshu shrugged, as if to indicate that he didn't care either way and sat back. Chaitrali had been at their newspaper for a couple of months, and Chitranshu thought they had forged a good friendship. They went for smokes together and they rolled their eyes together during meetings, and sometimes, when there was yelling and screaming, they looked out for each other. But things, Chitranshu had begun to feel, have to move beyond all this now. His friends were waiting for the day when this friendship would convert into a courtship, and frankly so was Chitranshu. So he had started giving her hints, making sly comments that indicated what he wanted. His logic being: if she doesn't distance herself after those comments, it clearly meant that she, too, was interested.

But then why act so weird? Why act so precious? It's a simple thing, Chitranshu thought as he slowly bit into his sandwich, you want sex, I want sex. We both want the same thing. It's not some Bollywood cliché, it's the truth. Why not act on it? Why wait for the boy to act? Where is the feminism now?

Chitranshu got up and stared at Chaitrali's back for some time. He had been disappointed when she was assigned that desk: he wanted to see her face, that pretty face, with those ample lips and intelligent eyes and thick curls . . . but then eventually he had decided that this was better. This way he got to check her out without the risk of being caught. And anyway, this view was the best view, Chitranshu thought with a chuckle.

He felt a bulge in his jeans and he looked around. The digital team was in a meeting, something to do with the weekend shift, and there was no one else around. So he whipped his phone out, opened his camera and focused it on Chaitrali's back. *Click*. *Click*. Ah, Chitranshu thought, superb stuff; all set. Now to get that feature piece done, get drunk, relax, go home, jerk off to these photos and wake up hungover. It was a lonely life, but at this point it was the only life he knew . . .

Later, at Gopalkrishna, with Hamid and Tejas—Dinesh had to rush home because his two-year-old had been involved in some domestic accident—Chitranshu, drunk, disturbed by the state of his life, declared that he was directionless and the only consolation now would be to ask Chaitrali out and sleep with her.

'But tell me something,' said Hamid, 'do you want to date her or do you want to fuck her?'

'Who would want to date a twenty-one-year-old?' Tejas asked.

'Especially if you are a twenty-five-year-old,' Chitranshu added.

'What has that got to do with anything?'

‘Arey, chutiya, he is twenty-five, she is twenty-one. In another year or two she would expect proposals, behenchod.’

‘Exactly,’ Chitranshu whispered.

Then they sat in silence, drinking to their stagnant lives and pitiful careers. At some point Chitranshu said that he wanted to quit and start writing something that he would be ‘proud of’.

‘For example?’ Tejas asked. Tejas was in his early thirties; he was unmarried and he lived alone. Sometimes he said that he was lonely and miserable, but often he proclaimed that he was living the bachelor dream.

Chitranshu might have been confused about what he wanted from life, but he knew that he didn’t want to end up like Tejas. That he knew for sure.

‘A real story. A book, you know. A fucking book.’

‘A book. Did you write that feature piece?’

‘Of course I did. Chutiya Hamid, I am not some lukhya who keeps his work pending. I do my work. Work hard, party harder.’

‘Lavda. Das must be working overtime, editing that piece of shit.’

Chitranshu was about to respond, but then his phone flashed Das’s name.

‘Speak of the devil . . . Haan, sir?’

‘Chitranshu, where are you?’

‘Sir . . . on my way . . . I was just—’

‘Gopalkrishna?’

‘Yes . . . any problem, Das Sir?’

‘I am sure you are hammered, but that doesn’t matter. Do you think you can take a taxi and board the 12.18 Rani Laxmi Express from CST?’

'Sir . . .'

'I'll message you the details. And note down your expenses, you will be refunded. Do you have a message pack?'

'Message pack—yes. Yes, sir. But send me the details on WhatsApp, na.'

'I don't have that on my phone. I'll just message. You need to go to Nagpur, and then take a bus or something to a village called Murwani. M-U-R-W—'

'Text it, Das Sir.'

'—A-N—haan, better.'

'What has happened, Das Sir?'

'Murder. Three minor girls. Sisters, they are saying, but not triplets apparently. Raped and killed.'

'In the village?'

'In the village, yes. Feature piece, next weekend.'

'All expenses paid?'

'It's a fucking story, Chitranshu, not your college field trip. I want a good hook and some meaty quotes. Find out something that others haven't. Understood?'

'All expenses paid then. Understood, sir.'

Narayani Bawane

Narayani Bawane watched as the police and the press swooped down on the school. The police took Principal Ahire with them before the press could ask him any questions, but the little girls and boys were left to fend for themselves. The reporters had their cameras and their notepads out, and they were asking some of the children if they knew the three sisters.

Narayani shut the wooden windows of the kitchen hurriedly and sat down in an unlit corner. She didn't want anyone to see her, much less ask her any questions. She gathered the edge of her dupatta into a ball and pushed it inside her mouth, like she always did when she was anxious. And then she began to cry.

Narayani had nothing to do with what had happened. But in a way, she did. In a lot of ways, she did. For starters, she couldn't bear the thought that she was one of the last to have seen the three sisters before what had happened had happened.

She had called out after them. The eldest, Anisha, had stopped while nudging her sisters to continue walking. Narayani, a midday meal cook at the school, knew Anisha as one of the smartest girls she had ever met, which isn't saying much, since Narayani had never really been out of Murwani in the thirty-one years of her life. But she had been working in Murwani for the last decade, and she recognized a clever mind when she saw one.

Anisha and Narayani weren't friends, exactly, but Narayani thought of herself as a guide to all the girls in the village. She had wanted to be a children's nurse, but it hadn't been possible because she didn't have the kind of money to go to a good school and then a good college to obtain a degree. But she managed to become a cook at the school, and that was enough. She liked children, she liked being among them, talking to them and advising them when they felt listless. She particularly looked out for the girls of the town because she felt that they needed to be moulded and protected. The world outside was gruesome but the girls in Murwani preferred being part of that world instead of this. They looked beyond the village and the tehsil: they were ambitious, these girls, not like the boys, whose ambitions Narayani felt were half-baked and marred by numerous distractions. Anisha was one of the brightest among them.

That day Narayani had asked her where she was taking her sisters because it was the middle of a school day. All three of them should have been in school, and Priyanka and Sanchita were indeed in their white shirt and yellow pinafore uniforms, but Anisha was wearing jeans and a dark-green top, the top she was found dead in.

Where are you going, Narayani had asked, but not very seriously. Almost playfully, in fact, because Narayani was aware of Anisha's bunking habits. She would bunk, disappear and then return by one and trot home pretending she had attended school.

Narayani never asked Anisha where she went, but she had seen the girl near the temple once, on her own, when Narayani was returning from the Ahneri market. At that time—this was about a year before the murders—Narayani had been inside a share rickshaw, so she couldn't stop to ask Anisha what she was doing around the temple premises when children had been told to steer clear of the area. Anisha was curious, so she must have wandered around trying to see what exactly was wrong with the place and why they had been asked not to venture there. And she must have found nothing, Narayani thought, because there was nothing around the temple premises, except an abandoned field where sometimes a drunk or two could be found sloshed and sleeping. Perhaps even a snake or two. But someone had started a rumour about a gang of rapists and murderers prowling around the temple long ago, and it had stuck, to the extent that the God being worshipped had to be shifted to new premises inside the village.

'Mummy has called all of us,' Anisha had told Narayani on that fateful day.

'What for?' Narayani had asked.

'Something has happened.'

To Narayani it didn't seem as if anything serious had happened going by the look on Anisha's face: calm, composed, jovial even.

'Okay,' Narayani had said, smiling slightly and getting back to the kitchen. That's it. That was the last time Narayani saw Anisha and her two sisters. When her Baba informed her about the murders or the accident or whatever had led to the death of those poor souls, Narayani couldn't respond. The moment was a blank; she felt empty and hollow. She couldn't bring herself to look at the bodies, even though they had been pulled out of the well and kept in the open for an entire day, which Narayani understood was a grave mistake. Substantial evidence was lost, they said, and PI Dighole, that bumbling idiot, had been suspended as a consequence. They said that the new Inspector was better, but Narayani didn't know who the new Inspector was. There were so many policemen around now in so many police Jeeps; a couple of police vans and many important-looking men and women running out and about. It was impossible to know who was who and what they were doing here.

It was a jatra, that's how it felt. Many of the people in the village, tired of the monotony of their lives, had plunged into the investigation headfirst. Narayani's father was among them: he roamed around the village trying to find 'clues' and had come home one day with a tattered doll, claiming that it belonged to the youngest and that he was going to present it as evidence to the police the next day.

The police had shooed him away.

'Good-looking officers, Narayani, bodyguard types,' her Pappa had said after returning home. 'Why don't you try sleeping with one of them? They *will* have to marry you if they knock you up. Two birds with one stone, haan?'

'Have some shame, this is your daughter you are talking about,' Narayani's Mummy had scolded him, but Narayani knew her mother would not have been averse to such a scenario were it to happen. They had been looking for a husband for Narayani for seven years, but nothing had worked out. Narayani had rejected some and many had rejected Narayani. She was their only child, and her parents wanted the prospective son-in-law to look after them. Who would agree to something like that? One or two had, on the condition they be paid a substantial dowry, unaffordable for Narayani's parents. They belonged to the Mahar caste, so nobody but a Mahar would even touch her, Narayani knew that. She had come to accept her fate: she would have to deal with the molestation and the humiliation that came with being the single woman of the village. Eventually, Narayani knew, she would be ignored and forgotten. That's what happened to women who could not even attract a decent husband.

Narayani sobbed into her dupatta, but she was no longer sure whether she was crying because she was scared or because of her sorry situation. Perhaps both: it didn't require a lot to reduce you to tears around this village.

The Mother

(Excerpts from an interview transcript. Interview conducted on 24 February 2019.)

'I remember a week after my daughters went away, everybody in the village was out trying to find clues. I couldn't watch all that. I couldn't believe what was happening. These chutiyas. These jobless lukhyas were trying to search for clues so that they can bring justice to my daughters. My daughters, who had been isolated and mocked and told to go away from this village because of me, their mother, because of how I behaved, because of how my daughters behaved, because they couldn't understand how women of a Kunbi household could be like us. They said that me and my daughters had brought disrepute to the caste and that we should be shunned, and the women, the women told me that it was because of you, and your daughters, especially that Anisha, it is because of you that we have to listen to our fathers and husbands say: See, this is what happens when you stretch your legs out of your blanket too much, this is what happens when we start educating you, when we allow you to think. It turns into a tragedy.

'These husbands and brothers and fathers and sons of these women who were warning them about such tragedies, they were all outside searching for clues. They were all outside trying to *help* the police . . . All they wanted, our men and their men and Powars and Vanjaris and Telis and Brahmins and Mahars . . . everyone who lived in that cursed village, all they wanted was some fucking entertainment.

'And in the killing of my girls they found it. They started scouring the village for clues. For clues! I couldn't believe it. What clues were they going to find, these lukhyas? I really should have told them that time, that time when they were searching for something around our shack: You are looking for clues? Look for clues within your fucking hearts, you will find plenty of clues there for what happened with my daughters. Plenty of clues . . .'

Kavita Aangle

A little before dawn, Kavita Aangle opened the creaky door of the only duplex bungalow in Murwani and slipped back into the makeshift bed she and her husband shared in the ground-floor hall.

Everyone thought they were lucky, the Aangles. The richest family in the area, and the most influential by far, in possession of a growing family business and a duplex (named Prerna) that looked like a palace. There was the land, of course, parcels of it spread across the district, but there were also a number of businesses, a finger in every pie, spread out across the state. Kavita knew that the Aangles had multiple sources of revenue, some white, many black, like most business empires: but her husband had very limited access to them, because her husband was, well, he was an Aangle, but he was counted among the black-sheep variety.

Still, people believed that they, Kavita and Sadashiv, had everything going for them: rich members of a rich family with connections across the societal spectrum. Yet how was it they failed to notice, Kavita always wondered, that there were fourteen people crammed inside Prerna; fourteen people—aunts and uncles and sisters-in-law and brothers-in-law and cousins and even a distant Mama who came and went as he pleased—who gathered to eat, shit and sleep under a single roof.

As she tiptoed across the main hall and slipped into her bed, Kavita had hoped that her husband wasn't awake. But a couple of minutes later she heard his whisper in the dark: 'Kuthe geli hotis?'

'Where do you think?' Kavita shot back.

'For forty-five minutes?'

'It's rough terrain outside, you know that.'

Her husband moved and she felt his breath on her face. Stale, sweaty, but not pungent, fortunately. He tried to lead her hand into his pyjamas, but she was too sleepy to make the effort now, since it was *always* an effort with her husband, and most times without any result.

'I am sleepy. Don't. Not today.'

'When then? I want—'

'Not today.'

'Why don't you shit in our house?' he asked, suddenly grabbing her neck and forcing his tongue into her ear. He usually did this: it was either the ear or the earlobe or her thumb or her toe. He would suck some appendage of hers and force her to jerk him off, but sometimes it just didn't . . . it just didn't *work*. He was either sucking her toes or grabbing her neck or trying to choke her or pushing his tongue down her ear . . . He never touched her vagina, and by this time she had come to realize that her husband had some *very* different ideas about sex. All she had known about sex before her marriage was that it is painful, until it is not, but that is only if you are lucky. Otherwise sex is to be endured. But this man . . . initially she liked all that he did: tying her up and slapping her and forcing her to suck *his* toes. Then she began to feel weird. Is all this normal? Is this sex? And she was sure he boasted about what he did to her with his friends on their drunken nights behind the temple, of course he did, it showed in the way they looked at her.

She said: 'I have told you before. It's disgusting. Tell your Aai not to shit on the floor of the toilet.'

'You are the shit on the floor of the toilet.'

She pushed him away and turned on her side and crossed her hands against her chest. Kavita half expected him to make her jerk him off, like he usually did, but he slid back over to his side quietly and remained silent for some time.

'It's not safe outside. Shit inside if you really need to. You know . . . you know what happened here.'

Her husband never mentioned the sisters. Just that vague *what happened here*, as if he was too disgusted to say what had actually happened, to utter the words.

That made her think about what the Inspector had grunted into her ears a few minutes ago as he came inside her amid the cracking twigs and under the distant stars: 'It was an accident, I swear . . .'

Sanjay Dighole

As far back as he could remember (which wasn't saying much), former Police Inspector Sanjay Dighole did not recall being drunk. More precisely: being piss drunk. To the extent that he would find himself sprawled out on an unlit street on the outskirts of the village, a street where he once used to swagger on his midnight 'rounds', looking for people who looked and probably felt exactly like he did at that point: drunk, hungover, exhausted, covered in vomit, a senseless mess of muttered phrases and uncontrollable bowel movements.

He closed his eyes and then opened them again. Wait a minute, where the fuck was he? The sky looked pretty but it began to circle around him. The fit forced him to sit up and vomit the dinner he had consumed—Chinese pulao. Bloody Chinese pulao. 'Anisha . . . the Chinese pulao-wala, right beside the petrol pump . . .'

Someone had told him about the eldest sister walking to the food stall where they sold the atrocious pulao before going to the school to fetch her sisters. But that's not as if it established anything, much less a pattern, because Anisha was known to bunk school and go around the village and the adjoining towns. She had been doing it for years: if someone wanted to murder them, they could have murdered them long ago. Why now?

It was an accident, Dighole thought as he sat up and cleaned his mouth with his crumpled handkerchief. He realized that he had nowhere really to go and no one really to go to: he had been suspended, and his wife had taken Jayesh with her to his in-laws' for a couple of days, until the storm passed. But when they left, Dighole realized that he wasn't very enthusiastic about continuing his life with them: Jayesh he could accept, but his wife had turned into a wall. She had stopped responding to anything he said, she took him for granted, she bossed him around and she was never ready for any of the adventures that Dighole proposed. With her, life was bland, devoid of any pleasure. That was probably true for most of his colleagues and friends and their sexual lives, but he had something that they didn't: the other woman. The rakhel, as Dighole called her.

Kavita was anything but a rakhel though. Dighole often thought that he was falling in love with her, which was not so bad when he was a PI, because then he could simply pick up her husband in his Jeep with some help from Karamble and Sangere and throw him down one of the wells dotting the village's outskirts. Or he could tie him up and kick him inside one of the ditches they had dug for precisely such use. What was that lukhya going to do? He would probably do the Aangles a favour anyway. Kavita's husband was a faggot, and he did or tried to do things with Kavita that Dighole got a hard-on thinking about. But if Dighole started doing those things with her now, Kavita would probably leave him because she wanted simple, pure, regular sex; sex that did not involve pain but unadorned pleasure. That's what she had told him as they sucked on each other's lips for the first time, inside the police Jeep, parked along a thick line of vegetation that shielded them from the national highway. Dighole had offered a lift to Kavita and then things had led to Kavita caressing the bulge in Dighole's pants as Dighole tried to control his desperation.

'This is what I want . . .' Kavita had whispered, her eyes closed and her lips sucking on Dighole's hungrily.

'Call me saheb, Kavita. Say it. Call me Dighole Saheb. Dighole Saheb, fuck me.'

'Fuck me, Dighole Saheb . . .'

This had continued, unabated, for months, and once Dighole's night shift began he took the Jeep out on his patrol rounds and they fucked in the fields.

That night when he was suspended, after he had come inside her—that had been against her wishes since the beginning, but he never bothered to use a condom or pull out, that was for the chutiyas of the world, real men always, *always* come inside—he had fondled her breasts for some time and then bit her lips and tried to give her a bite on her neck, but she had pushed him away and adjusted her nightgown and sat up.

'Was it really an accident?'

'Hmm?'

'Was it an accident? The three sisters.'

'Fuck the sisters,' Dighole had said, sitting up and looking at Kavita in the dark. 'There's some of my amrut left on the tip, you want to slurp?'

'Shut up. Tell me something—if it was a murder, who do you think murdered them?'

Dighole felt like grabbing one of the rocks and cracking open her head with it. But he controlled himself. 'It wasn't a murder. It's that bastard Tatya. Tatya did all this, to fuck with me.'

'So Tatya killed the sisters? You think?'

'No. Listen, come with me to my house. No one home. We can—'

'No.'

Then she had left, and Dighole had gotten drunk on the desi narangi that he had bought from Raju in the morning. The narangi had a different taste, a better taste, but it got Dighole dizzyingly high. Maybe it was spiked. Maybe someone wanted to kill him. Maybe Raju wanted him to die. Maybe Tatya wanted him to die. Who knows?

Dighole got up and swayed and slithered his way back to the village. Anna Topiwale's cloth shop was the first concrete building of the village from the temple side, and, unable to walk any further, Dighole plopped down in front of the shop and let his back rest against its walls. The fucking sisters. He felt something in his pocket and he took it out: the plastic narangi bottle. High Punch. Well, at least it's true to its name, Dighole thought, taking another swig. He had never really been a drinker, and when he did drink, he drank decent alcohol. This was new for him, but it wasn't bad. Just make sure you don't eat anything now, Dighole Saheb, he muttered, taking another swig. Tatya behenchod. He fucked them and then he tossed them into the well. 'I know it, I know it,' Dighole muttered and then sighed deeply and felt his face grow heavy and flushed, and his pants hot and wet. But by then he was already halfway into a deep slumber.

Chitranshu Chitale

There was a reason why Chitranshu, at the age of twenty-five, was still called a cub reporter, even though in designation he was a senior sub-editor—not that that was saying much.

Ever since he had entered this profession a couple of years ago, Chitranshu had been told that he did not have it in him to become a reporter or a deskie or even a journalist. He simply didn't: he was too lazy and he was too stupid. An assessment with which he tended to agree. And it was true, he did not deserve to be a journalist, or a reporter, not even a deskie, not really, because all of those were dead-end professions, staring into a void, and he did not have it in him to stare into the void all his life and then sit up on his bed and cry one night because he ought to have done something else instead of following his passions. Following passions was all that was left of him, but journalism wasn't one of them. Strange thoughts to think on a reporting assignment.

Chitranshu sat pillion behind Arvind Godambe, a local reporter who worked for the Nagpur–Yavatmal News Service. They had met during the press conference with the SP. Throughout that question-and-answer session, Godambe had been whispering the 'between the lines' of the SP's comments. 'Suspended the PI. That's your first scapegoat,' Godambe had said when the SP informed them that the station in-charge had been suspended for his 'lack of response'. Then when she let slip that 'there hasn't been any conclusive arrest, no Rajasthani man or anything like that', Godambe frantically noted down that a man belonging to Rajasthan had in fact been taken into custody.

But these were details, not of much note. Chitranshu was looking for a feature piece, one that would take up an entire weekend page. Perhaps, he thought, they should start with the suspended Inspector.

'Do you know the Inspector?' he asked Godambe.

'Which Inspector?'

'The suspended one.'

'Dighole na? Of course I know him.'

'I think I should meet him.'

'Hmm. Good thinking. Dighole. Dighole is the clue. If we get him talking, half our work is done. Do you have a bike?'

'No.'

'Okay. I will arrange one. But we will have to search for Dighole.'

Godambe's friend Shailesh had agreed to lend them his bike while he joined a 'search party' that was going to look for clues around the petrol pump. 'If you find anything, you tell *me* first, kay,' Shailesh, who looked seventeen but was actually twenty-two, had said. Godambe laughed heartily and nodded. 'Chutiya,' he said once they were out of Shailesh's earshot.

The village was buzzing. There was a light fog and the weather was a little chilly, but Chitranshu had expected far worse. He had always lived in Mumbai, and he had been told that the weather at this time in eastern Maharashtra could be unbearable for people from the west coast, particularly the city-bred. It was always about the city and privilege. 'You have lived in Mumbai your entire life, no?' his editor had asked him on the phone while Chitranshu was on a bus to Murwani. 'It's going to be hard for you there. Be careful.'

'Dighole is the clue,' Godambe kept repeating throughout their bike ride on the macadamized road. But where was Dighole? Chitranshu and Godambe went to his house first, but it was locked. At the police station, they were told that he hadn't turned up for attendance for the past two days, though no one was bothered about that because everyone was too busy handling the press and the case and the random raasta rokos on the highway.

Godambe was of the opinion that they would find Dighole somewhere around in the village. He had put two and two together and had concluded that a suspended Dighole wouldn't be home but would be sprawled drunk, wallowing in his misery and complaining about the injustice doled out to him.

'Dighole had claimed that it was an accident,' Chitranshu said, quoting a villager who had been around when the bodies were found and who had heard Dighole try to convince the girls' grandfather that it wasn't a murder.

'Arey, this bhokichya Dighole is like that. Murder means he will have to sit and solve, na. There was a Constable from his police station, Patle, he was found hanging here, outside the village, and everyone said it was a murder because Patle had been repeating to everyone he met that he was going to be murdered. But no one paid any attention. Then he died. Dighole was the first one to say it was suicide, not murder—'

'What was it then?'

'Suicide. But Dighole kept repeating that it was not murder but suicide. Not murder, suicide. That made it worse because everyone here used to think that Dighole hated Patle because Patle was a Powar and Dighole belongs to the Vanjari caste. So Patle got more respect than Dighole around here, and people thought Dighole had him killed for that reason. An inquiry was launched because the police station was gheraoed and all during the SP's visit. Cursed, this place is, that way.'

The bike turned into a narrow lane lined with cement flowerpots, quite a few of which were cracked. Godambe stopped the bike and kicked one of the pots and it broke into halves, scattering soil, like vomit and bile sticking out of a drunk's mouth. 'They run a community police service here,' Godambe explained. 'That's why you see so many people going around trying to find clues. Community police, kay. The community police gifted these flowerpots to drunkards when the drunkards promised to quit. But as you can see . . .' Godambe listlessly waved a hand around. Then he started the bike and they went deeper into the confines of the narrow lane. 'This is where they live, all the scum of the village,' Godambe informed.

'But where there is gham, there is rum. Excellent desi daaru,' he added.

The narangi shop was a hole in the wall, and at first Chitranshu thought that it was deserted, since he couldn't see anyone inside, shrouded as it was in darkness. But Godambe parked the bike, kicked the stand and strode towards the hole. 'Dighole kuthey?'

'Ala hota. High Punch. Now find him,' a husky voice informed from inside. Chitranshu never saw who it was because Godambe turned around and started the bike again. 'You wanted a drink?' Godambe asked after they had already left the lane. Chitranshu could have done with a quarter, but he had a story to find and only half a day to do it. He was planning to get back to Mumbai that night, but he needed to have a story before he left. If he wanted to stay back for another day, he would have to bear his own expenses.

They tried searching for Dighole almost half-heartedly, and when they did eventually find him, inside his home, it was three-thirty in the afternoon and Dighole was covered in his own piss. The door to his modest house was ajar, and he was sleeping on his bed, in a spare bedroom that was a colourless cement grey. Drool dripped down his open mouth and formed a little pool on the bed, and he had covered his groin with both his hands for some reason.

Godambe stared at Dighole for some time and then called someone who knew the disgraced ex-Inspector. 'Haan, Sangere, what is up with your friend Dighole?'

From the other end, Chitranshu could hear Sangere laugh. 'My friend?' Sangere said, his voice a distant static. 'That madarchod fucked up big time. Let him sleep all he wants now.'

'Bhokichya Sangere, he baray saalya,' Godambe said, a slight smile wavering on his lips. 'He saved your ass a hundred times. And now you all have left him to suffer alone. How did *you*, Assistant PI, escape suspension, madarchod?'

'Arey, Godambe Saheb, you know me, saheb. I do a lot of favours and I remember them. And don't get emotional on me, saheb. I did whatever I could to save Dighole Saheb's ass. I even lied to madam, but you know how she is.'

'Madam doesn't know shit, Sangere.'

'Arey, madam knows everything. Achha, what happened to that Nagpur transfer? Did you have a word with Jambhol?'

'Haan, that is in process. But you will have to shell out a lot more than a fake caste certificate, Sangere.'

'Behenchod. How much is he asking?'

'I am not a fucking middleman, Sangere. How much is he asking! I am just saying it might require more than you think.'

'But you put in a word na, saheb. Your word works there.'

'My word works everywhere, Sangere. I'll see what I can do, let Jambhol get back to me.'

'Rawas.'

Godambe cut the call and looked at Dighole. What a pitiful piece of shit. Abandoned by wife, abandoned by friends. But for all his machismo, Dighole was actually a soft fellow. Godambe knew that because he had gotten drunk with the man quite a lot of times during the Patle case. And Dighole had loved Patle, it was evident: there *was* the caste bit, but Godambe bore the impression that

Dighole never took it seriously; as far as Godambe was concerned, it was banter, plain and simple.

Dighole had felt genuinely sorry for Constable Patle because his life was the usual shithole with nothing going right and no hope of it going right, perhaps ever. A crazy wife, a boy who couldn't handle his alcohol and another boy who couldn't handle his studies. And Patle, who couldn't handle any of it. It was suicide, and Dighole felt sorry for him, and that was that.

'Well, do you want to wake him up or come back later?' Godambe asked Chitranshu, who had settled himself on one of the plastic chairs by the bed. Chitranshu didn't respond and looked around, taking in the room if he needed to describe it in his report. But what to describe? There was nothing worth describing. A cupboard right beside the double bed, depressingly unadorned walls; not a single photo frame, not a single wall unit. The house looked like a ghost, its death an ancient fact.

Chitranshu pulled out his packet of Gold Flake and offered it to Godambe, who shook his head. 'No, not that.'

'I don't know,' Chitranshu shrugged, lighting his cigarette and taking a deep drag. 'Tell me a good angle to this story.'

'Which story?'

'This story. About the three sisters.'

'The angle is that there were once three sisters and they were killed.'

'Haan, but everyone knows that. Something different. Something hatke.'

'Hatke. Arey, this is different na? Where else would you find this kind of explosive story? It's a gold mine.'

‘No, Godambe Saheb, I want a hook. Something that is . . .’

‘Arey, what hook—’

‘Something that would . . . you know na, Godambe Saheb, something to wake the janta up to this horror.’

‘Achha, haan, wait. Listen to this. I know what you are after. In 2007 Murwani elected an all-women panchayat. The sarpanch is a woman, open category. The deputy sarpanch is a woman, OBC. The committee is all women, SC–ST, Muslim, Buddhist. All the parties came together and agreed that the panchayat should be all-women. They wrote about it in the papers. Now—’

‘Rape and murder of three minor girls when the panchayat is all-women. It is still all-women?’

‘You are in luck. Yes.’

‘Sorted.’

Dighole contorted his face, as if he was denying someone something in whatever dream he was in, and then sneezed. Chitranshu and Godambe watched him silently for some time, and then Chitranshu stubbed his cigarette and got up. ‘Let’s go get a drink,’ he said to Godambe’s smirking face.

Others

Several people around a well. Sniffer dogs in the paddy fields surrounding it. Laughter and talk. Some men in plainclothes with gloves on examine a couple of beer bottles found in the paddy fields. The dogs had been there a little while ago, sniffing at the bottles. One of the men wearing gloves shouts for a man standing on the makeshift road that connects the well and the paddy fields to the main village road. The man wearing gloves shows him the bottles—brown with plastic stickers—and seems to be asking him something. The man who is being asked nods for a long time, and then walks back to the makeshift road, from where he calls someone.

'Haan, Tatya Bhau. Haan, they are asking for your men, bhau . . . Haan? I told them na, bhau . . . Because? Because they found beer bottles, bhau . . . Where? Near the paddy fields, bhau . . . Haan . . . Haan . . . Okay, but who all were there, Tatya Bhau? They are asking . . . No, they are asking . . . They are asking . . . I am not . . . What? I am not taking any—Tatya Bhau, I don't doubt you or your men, they were . . . Haan, you send them.'

The man who had called Tatya Bhau goes back to the men wearing gloves and tells them something. All of them nod. They discuss something and the man then walks idly towards the well and lights a bidi. The men in gloves toss down the beer bottles and stare at the sniffer dogs for some time.

The sniffer dogs are accompanied by three young men, who occasionally point at something on the ground. The men nod their heads and shake their heads. The dogs run off into other adjoining fields. The man who called Tatya Bhau, who had been squatting and watching all this while, walks up to the men in gloves and tells them something, and the men in gloves look at each other and then look towards the highway. They nod. They say something to the man who had called Tatya Bhau, and the man nods and begins walking towards the highway. But just as he exits the paddy field, someone from the sniffer-dog team shouts something. No one can hear anything, and then everybody can: Here, here!

A cloth bag stuffed with ripe black mulberry. There is commotion and barking. The men handling the sniffer dogs are trying to restrain them. The men with the gloves push everyone aside, even though it's not strictly necessary. It's as if they have found a bomb. One of them picks up the cloth bag and says something. One of the young men points somewhere excitedly. The sniffer-dog team follows the man who had pointed. About 200 metres from the site of the murder is a berry tree. The dogs bark. The men in gloves, who had followed the sniffer-dog team, look excited, tense and happy. Evidence, crucial evidence.

Janhavi

Janhavi sat in the kitchen area, facing one of the concrete walls. Every now and then she extended her hand and pressed her finger on the concrete and started drawing imaginary patterns over it. Ever since that day when she was told that her friend Priyanka had left her for some better place, Janhavi had been at it for hours. Drawing patterns. Janhavi knew that something was wrong, that Priyanka certainly hadn't left for a better place because if she was going to a better place she would have taken Janhavi along. They were inseparable. How could she even think of leaving her best friend behind?

Janhavi trusted Priyanka more than all these others who were telling her that her friend had left the village. Her best friend was either hiding somewhere, or something very wrong had happened to her, and she was not going to talk to anyone unless she was given an answer. That's how it was going to be.

When she was not drawing patterns on the wall, she was picturing her friend on it, in the paddy fields, holding hands with her as they walked and ran and walked again in the fields, as they shared the chocolates that Priyanka got from her elder sister, as they went to the berry tree and plucked berries and showed each other their tongues and laughed their hearts out. Priyanka always shared everything with Janhavi, no matter what. And Priyanka never shared anything with anyone, so that made Janhavi feel special because she *was* special. She saw, on the wall, Priyanka trying to balance herself on the bicycle. Sometimes, Priyanka would push while Janhavi sat on the cycle, and the three sisters would come to pick her up every time she lost her balance. The sisters were tight-knit, and Priyanka loved Anisha and Sanchita, but Priyanka loved Janhavi the most.

'Janhavi,' her mother mussed her hair. 'Khaun ghenar na thoda?'

Janhavi didn't respond, but she looked at her mother. 'Did Priyanka eat?'

'She did. She was asking whether you ate. What should I tell her?'

'Tell her to come back here and eat with me.'

'That is not possible, Janhavi. How many times to tell you?'

'Then I am not eating.'

Janhavi's mother held her chin and made her daughter look at her. She looked into her eyes and then slapped her once. 'How many times should I tell you? They are searching for her. She will come back. Now eat.'

The lady police officers had told Janhavi the same thing: that her friend was somewhere, and they were looking for her. She had to cooperate with them so that they could find her quickly and bring her back.

'What did Priyanka say to you before leaving?' one of the officers had asked Janhavi.

Janhavi could do nothing but shake her head and start crying. She missed Priyanka, but she also didn't want to face the police. She was scared of them, and there were too many of them now. All this while she had been cooped up inside her home, but now she was supposed to go to school. How was she to go to school with all the policemen around? And how was she to go to school if Priyanka wasn't going to come? And she wasn't going to come back, for a long while, her father had told her as much.

All Janhavi did was stare at the wall and cry.

'Did she tell you anything before going? Did she say anything about where she was going?'

Janhavi shook her head. That day, Priyanka had told her nothing.

'Think properly,' one of the lady police officers said a little aggressively. 'Think harder.'

Hurda.

As Janhavi sat staring at the wall, she repeated the word to herself. Hurda, hurda, hurda. What does hurda mean? She had asked her father, and he had told her that it was jowar crop that was still tender. Hurda. She didn't tell the policewomen about hurda, about the last word that Priyanka had muttered before she disappeared forever. It was their secret, and it was going to remain their secret. No one had to know about it.

Sanjay Dighole

Dighole woke up with a start and found two strangers staring at him and smiling stupidly. When he went to sleep, his head had been throbbing, but now he felt refreshed. That was a good sleep. He had needed it. But who the fuck were these people?

'Kon be?' As he tried to get up, it hit him, the odour. He knew that odour. He knew that strong, pungent odour like he knew his right hand from his left. Because that's the way it stank when he hit those drunken, jobless assholes inside his police station just because he could; that's the way it stank when he pushed the worst of his suspects into the ditches they had dug on the outskirts and aimed empty revolvers at them; that's the way it stank when they beat up black and blue all those women-beaters and whore-molesters with their belts. They always pissed their pants because it was the most natural thing to do.

What was his excuse?

The two men gazing at him looked as hammered as he had been for the past couple of days, and Dighole couldn't decide whether they had been mooching off his High Punch or had had their own, but they were all drunk, or had been drunk, in Dighole's case, on the same thing.

It took Dighole some time to orient himself to his surroundings, and when he did, he realized that he was inside his house, inside his room, and he thought he knew one of the two bastards.

'Well, Police Inspector Sanjay Sudhakar Dighole,' one of them said, slurring his Cs and his Ss, 'One week of suspension did this to you? I thought you had a lund, turns out it's a nunu.'

'Ae bhadvya, Godambe,' Dighole said, running a hand through his hair and coming off with dirt. 'What are you doing here madarchod?'

'Take a guess.'

'What are you doing inside my house, I mean.'

'Let me introduce you first to our crime reporter from Mumbai . . .'

'Chitranshu Chitale.'

'Chitale? Aai zavli, Godambe,' Dighole said, managing to smile despite everything. 'Chitale, he says. Since when did you guys start getting into this murky business? Isn't it dirty work for Konkanastha Brahmins? Where's your engineering degree? Don't tell me you returned from the US to do this.'

Chitranshu laughed. There is genuine warmth in this room now, behenchod, Dighole thought.

'No. I didn't even want to be a journalist.'

'Oh. What did you want to be then? Was your passion engineering but Mummy-Pappa said no we need you to be a reporter?'

'No. I wanted to be a writer . . .' and he slurs, too, 'I still want to be a writer.'

'How old are you?' Godambe asked Chitranshu.

'Twenty-five turning twenty-six.'

'Arey, you are young,' Godambe said. 'Plenty of village gaands around, if you are willing to wait for a while.'

'Madarchod Godambe,' Dighole said, getting up from his bed and burping. 'I pissed myself.'

'Too many times.'

'And I don't feel too well. Cigarette de.'

Chitranshu tossed him the packet. Dighole sat back on the bed.

'Chutranshu,' Godambe said and repeated it. 'Chut-ranshu.'

'Chut,' Dighole said, gazing away as if into an abyss. 'That's where the problems began. They began with chut. All problems begin there.' He motioned for a lighter.

'All problems and the solution to all problems,' Chitranshu said, even though he was distinctly aware that his woke female friends would have found the whole discussion misogynistic. But his female friends were not in the middle of a frenzied but listless investigation into the rape and murder of three girls. They were sitting on their comfortable beds and sofas, with their comfortable, cushy jobs and their weekly presentations and pie charts. What did they know about what happens here, in this real India, in this Bharat of the lore?

'Give me a swig, Godambe,' Dighole said, exhaling a cloud of smoke. Godambe handed over the bottle to him and then scratched his neck.

'So Dighole Saheb—' Godambe began but Dighole's smile cut him off.

'Dighole *Saheb*. Chutiya Godambe, I have known you for the past five years. I know your tricks. Saheb, behenchod. No, I don't know anything about the case. I was hardly on the case. What I can tell you is that it's not murder, and it's not rape. Tatya did this to frame me. It's an accident.'

'If Tatya did this, then you are essentially saying he murdered them. Are you saying that?'

'No, Godambe. What I am saying is—and listen carefully because I am not going to repeat it—Tatya found the bodies, and he should have rushed to the police because he found the bodies, because that's what normal men do, but Tatya is not a normal man because Tatya wants to fuck every Inspector up his ass, because Tatya is a gaandu. So he went to the villagers and gathered them around and filled them with all his gaandu kachra, samjla kay? Because he wanted all of this to look like a case of murder. Murder and rape, because when it's a matter of ladies and girls how can it not be rape? But it's not a rape case and it's not a murder case, Dighole's experience chi shapath.'

'The post-mortem confirmed rape.'

'The post-mortem confirmed rape. Gaandu, who conducts the post-mortem?' Dighole asked.

'Who?'

'Local doctors.'

'Jai Bhim wale?'

'Jai Bhim wale.'

Godambe nodded knowingly.

'Actually,' Chitranshu said, 'remember, the SP said it's not clear yet whether the girls were raped or not? They have sent the reports for further investigation.'

'What else can you expect from people who get a doctor's degree in the reserved category?'

Dighole stubbed the cigarette on the leg of his bed and shook his head. 'It's not murder.'

'But, Dighole, even if those who did the post-mortem screwed up on the rape, even they can guess when it is a murder and when it isn't,' Godambe said, his face and the tone of his voice devoid of any hint of banter. 'Plus, you were so sure of that Patle matter, people started saying that you killed the poor man.'

'Poor man. That's what killed him. Poverty.'

'What is the girls' surname again?' Godambe asked Chitranshu.

'Gudadhe.'

'Gudadhe. Kunbi na, Dighole?'

Dighole took another swig from the plastic bottle and grunted. Sitting on the bed, his legs splayed apart, the bottle of High Punch between them, he looked like a child playing with his toys.

'Kunbi. Last week that Ghotya came and went. Said he is going to demand a CBI inquiry. CBI, behenchod. You people blow it out of proportion, people like you, Chutranshu, and then our asses are placed on the line. You toh will go and write a nice article. What about us? Former PI Dighole said what about us. When are the elections by the way?'

'Next year.'

'I heard Ghotya is going to the other side. These people are not making him an MP.'

Godambe nodded. 'Yes, the deal is almost done.'

'But this will hamper it.'

'Not really. Kunbi girls, Kunbi MLA. They are going to go all in with the "our girls and our people are threatened" theme.'

'Delhi would be the bigger story,' Chitranshu said, taking the bottle from Dighole. 'This . . . I don't know.'

'You know what Ghotya asked when he came here?' Godambe said, shaking his head. 'He asked, "What were the girls wearing?" Then he focused on the eldest one. He assured a CBI inquiry and then he started lecturing. Girls wear this and girls wear that and then they get raped.'

Dighole extracted something from the gaps between his teeth and burped again. 'Barobar tar ahe. Nothing wrong,' he said, examining whatever it was that he had managed to extract.

'No rapes in Bharat, only in India,' Chitranshu said, thinking that they were mocking the notion, but Dighole looked up and snapped his fingers and pointed at him. 'Exactly. Behenchod. Exactly. Good one, Chutranshu.'

'What has dress got to do with rape?' Godambe said. 'Dighole Saheb, don't tell me you wouldn't want to fuck a nice, taut woman in saree with hot figure. Eh, Dighole Saheb, don't lie. You get a hard-on na, looking at those women in sarees?'

'Only if I can get to look at what is *below* that saree,' Dighole said, smiling.

'I have heard stories, haan, Dighole Saheb,' Godambe said, taking a swig from the bottle and sighing loudly and with deep satisfaction. 'I know who you fuck around with and what you do at night.'

'Ae Godambe, mind your own fucking business, na,' Dighole said, his smile evaporating. He tried to get up. Then, halfway between the bed and the floor, his hand moved to cover his mouth and he started to vomit, splattering the undigested contents of his gut on the floor and on his pants and on the edge of his bed. He retched and gladly grabbed a bottle of water when Godambe handed it to him. He washed himself as he continued to vomit, and then gulped the water, poured some over his head and washed his face again. He was breathing loudly and with effort, his eyes popped wide open and staring at the ceiling. 'Behenchod,' Dighole muttered, again and again. Then he said: 'Aai zavli.'

'Done?' Godambe said, glancing at the vomit on the floor and on the bed. 'Congratulations on the distinction. Vomit and piss.'

'Let's go get another quarter,' Dighole said. 'I feel sober. I feel hungover. I need another drink.'

'Arey, Dighole Saheb, control. Control. You are fucking that poor liver over and over again. Let her rest.'

'We will have another quarter,' Dighole said, almost growling and purring at the same time, 'and then I have some work I need to finish.'

Narayani Bawane

Narayani Bawane observed Janhavi as she walked into the school grounds. Narayani was trying to see whether there was any grief noticeable on Janhavi's face. There wasn't, but the poor child must hardly understand what was happening. Maybe she hasn't even been told anything yet. What does one tell a nine-year-old when her friend dies, and in such tragic circumstances? Death is new to them. They are not familiar with it. *We* are not familiar with it yet, let alone these kids. They have to understand it first, though, and it's going to affect how they see *everything*, Narayani thought, a tear ready at the edge of her right eye.

A girl, perhaps a year or two older than Janhavi, asked her something. But Janhavi did not respond. She didn't even stop. She walked past her. Grief. It doesn't always have to be displayed, Narayani thought. It's just felt, somewhere deep within. Even if you are a child of nine.

It was the first day of the school's resumption. The new principal had announced 'advanced security measures' at a sabha in the village the day before yesterday, and the police had set up white boxes for 'anonymous tips' outside this and other schools in the area, although Narayani doubted they could gather much from any of those other schools. All that they could get was going to be from here, Murwani Vidya Sadan. But even here, who knows what anyone else knows and who knows how much of it they are willing to reveal? Narayani had not dared to go to the police yet, even though she was one of the last people to have spoken to the sisters. Or at least one of the sisters. She was going to miss Anisha peeping into the kitchen and asking what she was going to prepare for lunch that day. There were almost never any surprises, except on the birthdays of the teachers and the principal, and yet, Anisha never failed to ask.

Narayani could imagine the sisters' faces; she had been doing that for the past few days: lying on her back with her eyes open and picturing those three sisters, holding hands, going into the paddy fields and then . . . disappearing somewhere beyond.

What could have happened to them, those poor souls?

Narayani started crying. It didn't take much these days. Just the thought of going back to school and into the same kitchen had made her squirm. These days, more than anything else, she was just sad. Often, she thought: it should have been me. It could have been me. Why those girls? Why little children? Here I am, an almost middle-aged woman. You could have finished your job with me and got done with it. Why drag children into this?

It wasn't right to think this way, Narayani had told herself. And yet. Of course, she also questioned herself. If she really cared about the sisters so much, why not go to the police and tell them? But tell them what? What was there to tell? That she had seen Anisha and that Anisha had told her that Mummy had called them? So what?

Mummy.

Did she say Mummy or Aai? Mummy. It was Mummy. Or was it Aai and Narayani had merely been assuming all this while that it was Mummy because that's what she called her mother?

Narayani clapped for no reason, wiped her tears off and started the preparations. She chopped the onions and she cut the potatoes. She prepared the dal and she measured the rice. She made the chapatis, two for every primary school student, and, simultaneously, tempered the potatoes in the cauldron, not too spicy and not too sweet: a little bit better than bland, but not too tasty. And watery, always a little watery. It took her two hours, but she liked doing the work. There was satisfaction in knowing that the children were going to eat the food you prepared lovingly, as if she was the mother of two dozen children who smacked their lips and licked their palms when they ate her food. She could do with that little portion of happiness. It helped her sleep well at night and it helped her wake up in the morning and look forward to the day.

Of course, everything had changed after those three sisters . . . but Narayani tried not to think about it much. It was hard not to, with everything being as it was, but what else could she do?

Narayani stirred the dal and tasted the potato bhaaji. Good, as always. Not exactly delicious, because the ingredients they provided her were not suited for delicious food, but she did what she could and she thought she did it to the best of her abilities.

Noon came quietly and the bell rang twice for those who wanted to have their midday meal. The principal himself came out that day and directed Narayani to provide more food to three students, who were seated side by side. But they were instructed to leave the food on their plates. They had to wait before they could eat. A photographer arrived. He clicked their picture. Then they waited together, the children and the photographer and the principal and Narayani.

An hour passed.

Half an hour before school got over for the day, the local MLA arrived in a car. A police van led the way. Another police van followed in tow. Flanked by two private bodyguards, the MLA, Abhiman Ghotya, was wearing a crisp white kurta and equally crisp and perhaps equally white pyjamas. The principal went to receive him. The MLA joined his hands and spoke discreetly with the new principal. Then he came and smiled at the three children who were waiting to have their meal and sat next to them. He asked, 'What is your name?'

The photographer clicked.

The MLA did not wait for an answer. To the next kid: 'What is your name?'

'Ganesh.'

Ghotya smiled and the photographer clicked. Then Ghotya looked around, confused. He said: 'I don't see a girl student here. Where is the girl student? The whole point is to have a picture with a girl student. A little girl.'

The principal nodded and muttered, 'Yes, saheb,' and ran inside the school. Ghotya then whipped out his phone and started checking it. One of the kids peeped into it, but Ghotya didn't seem to mind. A little while later, the principal brought a girl and told Ganesh to scoot.

The girl sat with Ganesh's plate in front of her, and Ghotya repeated his routine: 'What is your name?'

The photographer clicked.

But the girl had to be seated right next to Ghotya. So the boy sitting beside Ghotya was told to exchange places with the girl. When they did that, Ghotya resumed his perfected smile. 'What is your name?'

The photographer clicked.

The MLA had two morsels of food and pretended to talk to the girl again for some time. Then he looked at the photographer. 'Done?'

'Last one, sir, with you feeding the girl.'

'No, no, that would be too dramatic.'

'Then your hand on her head, as if you are blessing her.'

'Haan, that sounds good.'

The photographer clicked.

After Ghotya left, the children were told to go back to their classes. But they have hardly eaten, Narayani protested.

'Jhala na ata, ajun kiti?' the principal said, but relented when Narayani insisted that they finish their food. Afterwards, on the loudspeaker, Narayani could hear the principal list out the new security measures that the school was implementing for the safety of the children.

'New fence . . . new checks for entry and exit . . . No need to worry at all now,' the principal announced triumphantly, but he did not mention the sisters nor anything about what had happened to them two weeks ago. No one paid any tribute, and no one remembered them and their lives. There was no ceremony—no garlanded photograph, no candles. No one officially mentioned the three sisters.

While Narayani was walking back home, she saw Janhavi heading in a direction opposite to the village: towards the abandoned temple. Narayani followed her. It wasn't so much about where Janhavi was going or what she wanted to do, Narayani rationalized to herself, but just to ensure that she was safe. Times are such.

Janhavi walked on, her little cloth bag in her hand. People were scattered here and there in groups. The jobless and the slackers trying to give their lives some purpose by looking for clues. It was a genuine workforce the police had built here, Narayani thought. People whose sole purpose was to not laze around idly, as they had been doing for the past many years, but to give their lives much-needed meaning, even if that meaning was hollow and temporary.

Everyone ignored Janhavi. It had only been two weeks since the three sisters, two of them in their school uniforms, had wandered on the road Janhavi was now walking, but no one bothered to ask her anything. The girl finally stopped a few metres away from the well, on the side road between the paddy fields and the national highway. She stared in the direction of the well while Narayani watched her, standing a couple of steps away. Janhavi didn't cry or even whimper, her expression was blank, as if she were in deep meditation, or as if she were having a conversation with someone in her head. Then suddenly she turned and looked at Narayani.

Narayani had no option but to smile awkwardly.

'Are you doing well, Janhavi?'

'Did she fall inside the well?' Janhavi asked, her tone sincere and devoid of any emotion. Perhaps she was just exhausted, Narayani thought.

'I am not sure, Janhavi,' Narayani said after a pause. 'The police . . .'

'Someone said in school today. That she fell into the well by the temple.'

'No one is sure of anything, Janhavi. Come, let us go. It will get dark soon, na.' Narayani extended her hand and Janhavi took it. 'Don't worry about these things, Janhavi. Concentrate on your studies and get out of here as soon as you can.'

'She said something about hurda,' Janhavi said, looking straight ahead.

'Who?'

'Priyanka. She said hurda. That's what she said to Anisha.'

'Did you . . . did you tell this to the police?'

'No.'

'Well,' Narayani said, sighing. 'That makes two of us.'

Tatya Khandle

Tatya Khandle sneaked out of the panchayat hall and dialled one of Abhiman Ghotya's three numbers. His PA picked up.

'Saheb is in a meeting. Kay ahe?'

'Arey, bhau, you won't understand.'

'Try me.'

'It's not something that can be discussed on the phone. They are tapping phones right now.'

'Then why the fuck did you call?'

'To—you ask too many questions, rao. Tell Ghotya Saheb I want to meet.'

'Saheb is too busy.'

'Tell him this is big. There is an opportunity.'

'Hmm. Opportunity. Last time your opportunity turned out to be a phuski bomb, Tatya.'

'Ae Rambade, you mind your own business—'

'*This* is my business, Tatya.'

'You are new to this place. Mind your own business, chal.'

Tatya cut the call, spat, scratched his head, sighed, spat again and then walked back inside the hall.

Chitranshu Chitale

A suspended police officer, a city-born crime reporter and the editor-in-chief of Nagpur–Yavatmal News Service sat triply on the latter's bike and tried to balance their way to the local narangi–mosambi shop. It wasn't as if they didn't want to drink good alcohol, it was just that none of them had enough money to buy it. A good-quality rum wouldn't have hurt in this weather and in this evening of possibilities and deepening mystery, but it was not to be.

They bought High Punch, and while Godambe paid, Dighole opened the bottle and started drinking from it. Chitranshu didn't try to stop him. He was too hammered to understand what was happening. He had a bus to catch, and his editor had called him twice. But Chitranshu had been too drunk to take the call, and he was probably going to be too drunk to remember catching the bus. That's how it is, he thought, deal with it, you suckers.

Godambe had offered him a job with his Nagpur–Yavatmal News Service, and while it was an attractive proposition, it turned out that what Godambe actually did was provide quotes, stories and photographs from

Maharashtra's rural heartland, sometimes to Delhi-based national newspapers and often to Nagpur- and Mumbai-based dailies. He got some money in return, but just enough to get by. At some point, Chitranshu promised to establish contact between Godambe and his J-school, which was considered to be one of the best state-of-the-art journalism colleges in India. In other words, it was for the elite and the wealthy, and it provided campus placements in return for the high fees.

'Why did you spend so much money if you didn't want to be a journalist in the first place?' Godambe, also hammered, asked.

'What else could I have done? No, you tell me. As a writer, what else?'

'Anything!' Godambe said, spreading his hands wide.

'Come join the police force,' Dighole said, swaying.

'Arey, first you join the police force, chutiya,' Godambe said. Then, turning to Chitranshu: 'As for you, you join me. We will fuck every living reporter here.'

But Chitranshu, of course, was hardly a reporter. Before they left Dighole's house, he had opened his notebook to glance at his notes, but there were just three pages, not copious by any measure. Enough for one day, though, Chitranshu had figured and then rushed outside to join the duo on their bike expedition for High Punch.

Dighole took another swig and smacked his lips. 'I have work to do,' he repeated for the hundredth time that evening. But this time he probably meant to do it, because he handed over the bottle to Chitranshu and, facing Godambe, said: 'I have work to do.'

'You can hardly stand up on your feet, Dighole Saheb, your work can wait. What work do you have anyway?'

'Work, work.'

'Yes, what work, saheb? What work?'

But no one was in any condition to provide a real answer, and Dighole bid goodbye and started walking out of the lane, while Chitranshu and Godambe stood where they were, in front of the desi theka, unable to come up with an answer to the question of what now. So they continued to take swigs, straight from the bottle, smack their lips, utter passionate and painful 'Aaaahs' and stand looking at nothing and no one in particular.

'How the fuck did we get so drunk?' Godambe asked.

'Now I know what Geoffrey Firmin must have been feeling,' Chitranshu said. 'Oh yeah!'

'What? Who?'

'There is this book called *Under the Volcano* in which the main character gets drunk and walks around the town and gets fucked.'

'Good book. Indian writer? Maharashtra side cha?'

'No. Mexican.'

'Mexican.'

'No, no. I think Canadian.'

'Canadian.'

Godambe looked at his watch and said, 'Chal, chal, let's go. It's getting hot.'

'Arey, bhau, go where? It's not hot, it's cold. Very, very cold.'

'Sit, sit.'

They drove through a more or less isolated village: there were people, gathered in groups, whispering and laughing out loud, a grunt coming from some corner, a scream from somewhere else in the dark. Godambe rode confidently, the yellow headlights of the Hero Honda CD 100 guiding him through unlit lanes. Chitranshu did not have any idea where they were going and he did not care. At some point he felt dizzy and he felt as if the world was spinning and he held on to Godambe's waist, who asked whether Chitranshu was in love with him. Or something.

Then they reached a spot a little removed from the village. Godambe parked and waddled towards a house a few metres away. The house looked pretty, thought Chitranshu. A nice little house on the outer edges of the village, pretty and comforting, abutting a farm. That is life. How comfortable and how simple. Should probably shift here or somewhere to some village for the rest of my life. Retire at thirty or something, Chitranshu thought.

Godambe was now talking to someone at the door. He was touching that someone at the door, and then the door shut and Godambe returned with a smile. 'Are you a virgin?' he asked Chitranshu.

'No, no, no, no, no, no, Godambe Saheb, don't play that—'

'Arey, bewdya,' Godambe said, grabbing Chitranshu's cheeks. 'What am I asking? Have you fucked before? Just answer.'

'Yes.'

'A village ass? Have you fucked a village ass?'

'No, no, no, no, Godambe Bhau—'

'Haan, sit now. Sit quickly.'

They rode onwards, towards the paddy fields near the petrol pump. This time they were far away from the fields on the other side of the town, the temple side. Godambe swerved from the side road adjoining the national highway and parked the bike on the edge of the paddy fields. He left the key in the bike with the headlights on and headed into the fields.

They came to an empty patch of land, a sort of a swale in between the fields of rice.

'Does your phone have light? One of those lights?'

Chitranshu switched on the flashlight. 'Arey, too strong. Okay. I am already *very* horny.'

'Godambe Saheb,' Chitranshu suddenly said, joining the dots between the mention of village ass and the questions about his virginity. 'I am not that sort—'

'What sort? And show the light properly. I need to spread . . . where is that . . .'

'Godambe Bhau, please . . .'

'What please? Okay, now, listen . . . haan, here it is.'

Godambe spread a blue sheet on the ground. But then he picked it up and started clearing the pebbles and the broken stones and the grit scattered on the ground.

'Godambe Saheb . . .' Chitranshu, his throat dry, didn't really know what to say, how to explain without sounding offensive.

'Okay, now listen,' Godambe said, spreading the sheet again and looking at Chitranshu, 'I have a massive hard-on, but I am going to be generous for you—'

'Godambe Saheb, no, please, I am going.'

'Arey, Chutranshu Bhau, you want village chut or no? Listen to me. Switch off the light. Okay, I have this woman here. Decent enough, body-wise. You can hold them nicely and suck them and she moans properly . . .'

Chitranshu sighed with relief. If this is what he meant—fine then. He had sobered down a little and could do with some warmth.

Chitranshu said: 'But Godambe Saheb, would she be . . . willing?'

'Willing? Willing for what?'

'Willing to, you know—'

'Arey, leave all that to me. You want village pussy, I am going to get my friend some village pussy. Now listen, go hide somewhere. When I say I need to go and pee, that's your cue. Then you come.'

Chitranshu hid in the fields, but it wasn't strictly necessary: the night was moonless, and tufts of clouds ambled along the starry sky. Romantic, sufficiently romantic, thought Chitranshu. He saw Godambe caress his dick, and then he heard steps. Godambe looked somewhere, where he thought Chitranshu was hiding, and said, 'Shh. Be ready.' He laughed.

A woman's voice: 'Arvind?'

'Darling,' Godambe purred.

In the darkness, Chitranshu could see Godambe and a woman's outline. The woman handed Godambe something that Chitranshu could not make out and Godambe pocketed it. Then in a quick, swift movement, Godambe pulled the woman towards him and started kissing her neck and running his hands all over her body. Or at least that's how drunk Chitranshu saw it. Then Godambe pushed the woman down on the sheet and started undressing. What the fuck is going on, thought Chitranshu. Who is this woman? He thought, is this how they do threesomes in villages? Chitranshu had a hard-on and he was trying not to jerk off.

Then Godambe grunted and stood up. 'I need to pee, darling. Coming.'

'Wash your mouth, too, while you are at it.'

'Shut the fuck up. You want me to spray myself with deodorant? Take what you are getting na, chup chaap.'

He tottered somewhere and whispered, in the hope that Chitranshu would hear him, 'Go after two minutes.' Chitranshu listened as Godambe's piss hit the ground as he whistled some tune that Chitranshu thought he recognized but could not remember. Then he walked towards the woman a minute after Godambe was done. He didn't wait for the woman to say anything. He didn't utter a single word. He was too aroused to care, or understand. There was also the matter of secrecy: the woman probably had no idea who was going to fuck her, and that, in a twisted way, excited Chitranshu more.

The woman went along for a little while, but as he breathed into her neck, she purred, 'Say something, darling. You are not saying anything today.' Chitranshu liked that voice. He nudged her to turn over. 'No, like this,' she said. Chitranshu didn't like that kind of attitude. Especially now. He spat beside her and was about to slap her when she turned over. 'Darling,' he moaned.

Tatya Khandle

'Haan, Tatya, what is it?'

'Saheb, I want to meet.'

'Let's discuss on the phone.'

'Saheb, it's too . . . sensitive.'

'No one is tapping our phones. Don't worry.'

'If you say so, saheb. There is—'

'But don't take any names.'

'Okay, saheb. Saheb, they have arrested a termite.'

'Haan, I know. In this three sisters case, na?'

'Haan, saheb. They are saying he could be a big fish.'

'Haan, I know.'

'A big termite, saheb. This is a very big opportunity.'

'What are you thinking?'

'Anyway those people will not vote for you. And the tides are turning in our favour, saheb.'

'What are you thinking?'

'Futane Wadi has a lot of garbage, saheb. Let's call the Nagpur municipality and get it cleaned. Our people will help.'

'Pest control?'

'Haan, saheb.'

'No, not right now. Last time I got into trouble for doing that. And this time the DGP is their person.'

'That Akb—'

'Na na, no names, Tatya.'

'Haan, saheb.'

'Actually, it's a problem. I have to—'

'Why problem, saheb?'

'They are not making me an MP this time around, Tatya. I am switching sides. I can't be seen doing all this now.'

'All this?'

'Pest control. I am turning secular now, Tatya.'

'Saheb? This is not the time to . . .'

'Arey, I don't care who sits in Delhi. I want to become an MP from *here*, otherwise I am fucked. And I won't become an MP by standing as an independent. I need a party to back me financially.'

'Saheb . . . Don't, saheb . . .'

'No trouble, Tatya, not right now. This case is nicely set up. Don't stretch it.'

'Saheb . . .'

'I am busy, Tatya.'

'Saheb . . . there's another thing. The biryani, saheb . . .'

'What about it?'

'We . . . well, I mean we had to pay for it. You had promised that . . . from the funds . . .'

'Arey, once I become an MP . . . biryani hi biryani you will get to thoos, Tatya. Wait until I become an MP.'

Then Ghotya cut the call and switched off his phone.

Sadashiv Aangle

Sadashiv Aangle looked at his wife with weary and tired eyes as she went about doing her chores. He was sitting in the hall, on the chintz sofa, facing the wall-mounted TV, but he wasn't bothered about the TV. He was staring into the kitchen, at his vahini and at his wife. His sister-in-law was wearing a flower-patterned saree and had her wet hair shored up in a bun. His wife was wearing a semi-transparent parrot-green saree and her hair was open, falling over her butt. He observed all this, he observed their movements, he stared at their asses as they went about doing things that required them to stretch their bodies, and he tried to get horny thinking about his brother's wife sucking on his cock or even his own wife sucking on his cock, but none of those possibilities aroused him. And that was the tragedy, that's what they said outside: two women the village men would have done anything to get to bed, and this Sadashiv, this impotent asshole, he couldn't do a thing with them.

Why couldn't he? Sadashiv didn't know. He scraped the surface of the sofa with his overlong nails and tried to control his tears. His wife looked at him and, after a pause, asked him whether he wanted tea. He didn't reply. Then his brother's wife looked at him. She asked him if he wanted anything to eat. He just needed to satisfy one of them. Just one of them. Two ladies of the house, unsatisfied. How did that look on the Aangles? At least his brother had a reason. He was always busy. And at least his brother had a son. That made everything fall in place for Ashok. But what about Sadashiv?

He managed to shake his head and stare at the TV. There was an ad about a soap and then an ad about a Hero Honda bike. He would have preferred to work at the bike factory any day than sit at home and do nothing. He wanted to do something, but he couldn't do anything that had to do with the family business. That business required brains, and Sadashiv had been told enough times since his childhood that he had none. That he was more suited to work at home and in the kitchen, performing all the duties of a wife.

It had begun in his childhood. First the school in Bhandara, then the boarding school in Nagpur:

common toilets and teenage boys, the groping and the kicking. The silence of the night as Sadashiv lay on his bed, dreading and waiting for that first hand to grab his cock, for those fingers to squeeze his balls. He never knew who did it. At first he resisted, then he realized he liked it. The boys realized he liked it, too, and that's when it started to get worse. One day in his final year, as he was bathing, four boys—three of them his roommates—had descended on the bathroom, locked it from inside, pushed him against the wall and kicked him on his butt. Then, one by one, they had taken turns.

All these years later, Sadashiv still couldn't make sense of those days. Of what he was. He had left that hellhole to return to this hellhole, his house. He had a degree, he should start working. And he had worked. He went to sites and he travelled to business meetings and he stayed in expensive hotels, drinking away into the night and trying to masturbate over and over again, imagining everyone and everything. But to no effect. All he got at the end of it were tears of frustration.

One day his father, without any explanation, told him that he shouldn't travel and shouldn't attend meetings. He told him to stay at home. And do what, Baba? Do nothing, that's what your life is all about, his father had said. Ashok is willing to take care of the business. You are getting married.

Kavita was admittedly attractive, but Sadashiv never really had any urge to fuck her. He was happy, though, because he thought everything would be settled after the marriage. A warm body by his side: he would be able to try different things. He would be able to get it up. He would be able to fuck. That was good news. He was happy. His father was happy.

The wedding was a week long affair. His father wanted everyone to know that his youngest, Sadashiv, was getting married. To a girl from a prominent political and business family. His son was going to be normal, and he would have a normal family—his father wanted everyone to know that. The wedding day was a jatra for Murwani and the surrounding villages. People had come from as far away as Mumbai. That was the night Sadashiv understood how effective rum was in squeezing out the pain of not belonging to a place and a time and an event. Sadashiv didn't remember the wedding ceremony, but he remembered his first night, when he thought that he would feel lust for Kavita and it would make him free, happy. But that night he simply couldn't do it. Perhaps he was tired, she insisted. And he insisted back: suck me. Get it up with your mouth. It's what works, I know. But she would never do that. She thought that was impure.

Things unravelled soon enough. The rumours began again: Sadashiv Aangle, the youngest Aangle, can't get it up for his wife. Sadashiv Aangle, the youngest of the Aangles, is a namard. A bailya. A man interested in other men.

Eventually, his father told Kavita and Sadashiv to shift their bedding to the hall while Ashok and his family's room was expanded to include another toilet, only for their use.

That's how it was. And as much as Sadashiv tried to ignore it as just another fact of his failed life, he could never get over the everyday torment. The torment of not being considered worthy. The torment of being discarded, ignored, looked down upon. He preferred to drink and forget. Fuck everything. He had the money, and he was going to spend it on whatever he liked and whatever he wanted. As for sex, some of Tatya's pottis from other states, they were willing to suck him for a fee. The fee Sadashiv did not mind, but it came at a different cost: the rumours strengthened, and this time they were more mocking and more obvious.

It made a hermit of Sadashiv, a thirty-five-year-old man who sat in his house, sipped tea and watched soap ads and Hero Honda ads on TV while trying, for the umpteenth time, to get aroused by the display of abundant flesh inside Prerna.

He dug his fingernails inside the skin of his knees. He *could* do anything he wanted. But he couldn't do it to Kavita. The urge to hold her by her arms and take her to his brother's room and force her to take him in her mouth—that urge had passed, and it had passed because as he looked at Kavita he felt as if she was the only person who understood him. The only person who had chosen not to judge him and be with him instead; sleep beside him night after night, aware, surely, of the turmoil that was bubbling within him. The most important thing for Sadashiv was that he could talk to her. He could tell her how torturous all this was for him. Was she his friend? No, that would be going too far. But he couldn't hurt her. He would never hurt her. That much was true.

Sanjay Dighole

Dighole wasn't sure what he was going to do, but now that he had started walking, he thought he might as well finish the work that he had been thinking about for the past many weeks. Especially after his suspension and after his wife left him. That whore Kavita had to come and live with him, that's what he wanted. That's how tonight was going to end. She was going to come to his lonely house and she was going to spread her legs wide apart on his bed and he was going to fuck her through the night. And every subsequent night. That was her future, Dighole had decided it for her.

Like his counterparts for the day, Chitranshu and Godambe, he tottered much of his way, taking the support of a tree and falling down twice. But he managed to reach his destination, on the other side, a little away from the scene of the crime. Panting, sweating, unable to understand much of what was going on, but reaching there all right. There were some people on the side road, perhaps police, perhaps those local gaandus having the time of their lives. Who cares? Dighole certainly didn't. He stumbled up to the duplex bungalow. The Aangles. Living like rats in a burrow. Fourteen of them together, how was that for privacy?

But he didn't exactly know what to do now that he was there. He stood in front of the bungalow, thinking. What he was about to do could turn dangerous for both Kavita and him, and he desperately needed sex before any other tamasha. But his lust for Kavita, he had started to believe, was actually borne out of love. He loved her, that's how it was. He loved her because she let him do whatever he wanted with her, and he loved her because her skin had that sweet aroma of rich people. Washed, scented, cared for, Kavita was a catch, Dighole had always believed that. That bastard of her husband, what the fuck did he know about his wife? Dighole knew he could satisfy her needs and her desires better. That's what he was about to do. Free her from her master.

Someone tapped him on his shoulder. In the darkness of the evening turning slowly into night, he couldn't really grasp who it was.

'Arey, Dighole Saheb,' said Ashok Aangle, Kavita's brother-in-law and Sadashiv Aangle's elder brother. He was carrying something in his hand: a cloth bag.

'You are . . . Dighole Saheb, any problem?'

'No, sir,' Dighole stuttered. 'No problem.'

'I heard about your suspension,' Ashok said. 'I was disappointed. I think you could have handled the case better.'

'Yes.' Dighole was still trying to come up with something appropriate to say.

'So?' Ashok said. 'What are you doing here, saheb?'

'Arey, behenchod,' Dighole said, deciding to disregard any attempt to be decent. He was here for a reason, and his gut was telling him to go for it. 'Call your asshole brother outside, Aangle.'

'Dighole Saheb, any problem?'

'Yes, I have a problem. Now go call him outside.'

Dighole reached for his revolver, but there was nothing save empty belt loops on his soiled trousers. When Ashok moved a little closer, Dighole saw his face squirm and his hand move up to cover his nose.

'Dighole Saheb . . . what has . . . what is happening?'

Dighole searched for something to grab. As a defensive mechanism. He spotted a medium-sized rock and picked it up and looked at Ashok in a stance that he hoped was sufficiently threatening. But Ashok looked far from threatened. He was muttering something under his breath, which Dighole knew Ashok did when he was nervous.

'This has nothing to do with you, Ashok,' Dighole said. 'Just call Sadashiv.'

'Dighole Saheb, you have had far too much to drink,' Ashok said. 'Maybe come back tomorrow when you are in your senses.'

The rock hit where Dighole wanted it to hit. His aim had always been good. Often, as a kid, the other children of his village and the elders used to ask him to knock down unripe mangoes from branches because his was always a guaranteed hit. That's how he decided to join the police force: so that he could practise his aim, fight crime on the side and pick up some medals, climb up the police hierarchy and retire somewhere in some city. Perhaps Pune. What dreams!

Dighole had hoped that there wouldn't be any blood, but there was blood, trickling down in three distinct lines from Ashok's cracked forehead.

The eldest of the Aangle sons dropped down on his knees, and the fruits from the cloth bag wrapped around his wrist rolled out. Then Ashok, who had never really had to see blood drawn in all the thirty-six years of his life, began to scream and shout.

The screams brought a couple of people out of the bungalow. One of them was Kavita's husband, Sadashiv.

The other was his father; the patriarch looking frail and old and exhausted. But even then the father was probably faster than the useless son, thought Dighole, who by this time had walked towards the gate, ignoring Ashok and his pleas for a doctor or an ambulance, whichever was faster.

'Ae Sadashiv,' Dighole said. 'Call your wife outside.'

'Dighole, what do you think you are doing?' the father said with a voice that, despite his age, was stern and deep.

'This has got nothing to do with Ashok or with you. This man Sadashiv,' Dighole pointed at him, 'this man has trapped a woman and I have come here to free her.'

'What woman?' the father turned towards his son, who looked clueless. 'What have you done now, Sadashiv?' the father asked, again.

'Nothing, Baba. Dighole, bhadvya, what are you blabbering about? You can't even stand properly, have some shame. Decent people live here.'

'Decent people!' Dighole laughed. 'Decent people. Baba.' He turned towards the father. 'You think it's a mystery outside why this chutiya hasn't begot you a grandson yet?'

'Ae Dighole.' Sadashiv loped ahead, towards Dighole, but stopped when Dighole lifted his hand and the rock that he held in it. 'Takkal phodin haan, Aangle. Yours and this therda of yours, his too. I don't want any trouble. Call Kavita.'

'Kavita?' the father repeated.

Sadashiv gritted his teeth and he held the edge of his trousers and pulled at it. 'I knew that bitch . . .' he muttered. 'I knew—fucking bitch. Fucking bitch.'

'What is happening?' the father said. 'Dighole, what is it? Why are you asking for my daughter-in-law?'

'Because I want to fuck her,' Dighole said, tossing the rock from hand to hand.

'What nonsense, Dighole, why would you—'

Dighole slapped the old man. Or perhaps it was a punch. At any rate, the Aangle patriarch almost lost his balance. He stood, stunned, his hand on his left cheek, unable to grasp why he had been subjected to this.

Sadashiv, meanwhile, remained fixed to the ground like a pole, gritting his teeth and muttering something to himself.

'Now you understand why she has been coming to feel my dick inside her, old man? Because your son is a faggot. Not a real man, a faggot, that's what he is, and Kavita needs a real man to satisfy her.'

'What is he saying?' the father asked Sadashiv, disbelief and shock replacing the sternness and confidence in his voice. Powerful people, these, Dighole thought, but suddenly not so powerful when confronted with the loss of honour of their family and the impotence of a male family member. Not to mention the infidelity of one of their women. The harshness of raw life makes them piss their pants. All of these Aangle company boys are like that. Swaggering in their dream world, chutiyas in reality, thought Dighole. Eventually, of course, they will act, have him beaten up, kicked into a ditch, something of that sort, because officially they can do nothing: officially he was already persona non grata.

Ashok ran past all of them into the house, still screaming.

'He is saying,' Sadashiv said, 'that Kavita, my wife, has been fucking him. Kavita! Kavita!' This last bit Sadashiv screamed.

Dighole chuckled. The man screams like a woman moans.

'Arey, just try to sound like a man for once na, Sadashiv,' Dighole said, burping loudly. 'She will come running out quickly. She wouldn't dare disobey a man's orders. I know Kavita, she is very submissive like that.'

'Dighole madar—'

'Arey, yaar, Sadashiv Bhau. You should watch Salman Khan movies, rao. I thought you would have come to punch me like Salman Khan or Sanjay Dutt or Ajay Devgn, rao. But you are still standing there. What are you waiting for? Want someone to suck your dick before you can gather some strength? Is that it?'

Sadashiv didn't move. Instead, Kavita walked out of the main door and, ignoring Sadashiv standing at the gate, flitted outside and lunged at Dighole. She was carrying a sharp object that Dighole realized far too late was a kitchen knife, nine inches long and two wide, which she thrust, at first, into Dighole's torso and then into the side of his neck. Blood splattered on the ground and formed a pool, and Dighole pulled Kavita down with him. This time she bore the knife into his round, pudgy belly. 'Randi saali,' Dighole managed to mumble as he struggled to breathe. Kavita stood up as Dighole groaned and continued to whisper something reedily. She spat on Dighole's convulsing body. 'Another word about my husband and I will cut you up and feed you to the dogs, you asshole,' Kavita said, still holding the knife firmly.

But it is doubtful Dighole was alive to hear that. He had stopped struggling and his eyes gradually became lifeless. For some time, the Aangles waited to see whether he could blink. When he didn't, the patriarch, the father who had been slapped and who had now recovered from his shock, sighed. 'Where is Mama? Hand over this knife to him. He will take the blame. We will bail him out. Dighole was suspended, na? Nobody will care about him.'

Kavita looked at her husband and then at her father-in-law.

'He had been trying to molest me for a long time. Nothing happened between us. But if you don't believe me, you can send me away and I won't protest.'

'Send you away?' her father-in-law asked, disgusted but his tone inching towards politeness. 'This is a matter of honour, Sunbai. These things get out. You should have told us about this before. Now go inside and wash up. We will think about how to proceed.'

Sadashiv stormed inside the house, but it would be all right, Kavita thought, almost smiling. She had some news they would like.

Dighole. He would live on.

Narayani Bawane

When Narayani Bawane met Arvind Godambe again, about a month after their last encounter, Godambe was in a particularly talkative mood. Narayani had decided to ask Godambe whether he was willing to marry her. It had only been two months, and it had only been five or six encounters, but Narayani liked Godambe, his innocence, his passion and his empathy.

'Arvind,' she said. 'Call me darling.'

'Daarling,' Godambe purred, sending flying kisses at her.

'Listen,' she said, breathing faster than she would have liked, 'do you think . . . I mean . . . I think—I have been thinking . . . should we get married?'

Godambe was silent for a while and then he backed away as if Narayani were a dead cockroach. He was disgusted by her presence.

'I am pregnant with your child,' Narayani said, although this was not entirely true. Or at least Narayani wasn't sure yet: she had been vomiting, and she had been having dreams. She had missed her period, but it had only been two days. It could be food poisoning. But . . . but she liked Godambe and he would understand. But Godambe only sniggered.

'How do you know it's mine, Narayani?'

'I haven't . . . I haven't . . . nobody else has called me darling.'

Godambe laughed. A cruel laugh, the kind that scared Narayani and made her skin crawl.

'You don't know then? That kid *was* good,' Godambe said, patting Narayani's left cheek.

'What?'

Godambe heaved with laughter. He was in Murwani to check how the case was progressing, and he had contacted her the way he usually did, by knocking on the backside window. But they hadn't gone into the fields, which Narayani saw as a sign that Godambe didn't just lust after her but was also interested in having a conversation, maybe even loving her as she hoped someone someday would.

'What are you saying, Arvind?'

Godambe's stare turned cold.

'Listen, Narayani, you are a slut and a whore besides. You are good at sex, that's what the kid said too. I suggest you start whoring yourself out, you will earn decent money. Besides, you won't lust after people like me. People who have more important things to do. Marriage. We give you people a little sympathy, a little bhaav and there you are, thinking you are like us. Behenchod, look at your face sometime, get a fucking mirror, all of your kind are haivans. Rakshas. You want *me* to marry *you*? Have some sense, Narayani.'

Godambe started his bike and looked at her pitifully: 'And about that baby inside your belly. I don't have anything to do with it. Last time some kid from Bombay fucked you instead of me. It's his. So go after him, not me.'

'Anisha said she was going to see "Mummy" when I met her. It was around 12.30 p.m. She also said something about a hurda party.'

Narayani folded the piece of paper and walked out of the school kitchen. At the gate, she looked around. Nobody was paying her any attention.

She dropped the chit inside the white box placed at the gate to receive anonymous tips.

Part Three

CRIMINALS

22 February–13 April 2013
Murwani, Maharashtra

Datta Mama

Datta Mama glanced at the Gudadhe shack every now and then and shook his head. That family is a curse on this village. God knows what sins the people of Murwani had committed to deserve them, but the sins must have been grave. This family has never got it right, and it never will.

Murder. Mama didn't believe that for a moment. Someone had told him that the police didn't either. The sisters used to loiter around too much, and that had got them killed. Mama didn't know *how*, exactly, but it was an accident. Either that or the girls had killed themselves, it was as simple as that. And even if it was something else, our Pranil had nothing to do with it.

'What are you crying about?' Mama asked his sister, who was sobbing into her handkerchief. He looked at her husband and clicked his tongue. 'Who has died? Has anyone died?'

'Don't say such things!' his sister snapped. 'At least not right now.'

'I simply don't understand why your wife is crying, Ghanashyam. Care to explain to her that she doesn't need to cry?'

'Malati,' Ghanashyam started but then Mama screwed his face, shook his head again and let out a series of 'chya chya chya chya'.

'Listen to that voice. Weak and ladylike. Don't you have a proper lunch, Ghanashyam? A proper dinner?

A man should have proper lunch and a man should focus on building his body, his personality. And a wife should ensure that her man is well-fed and tandurust. Don't you feed your husband properly, Malati? There is no strength inside that belly. Can't scold, can't shout and wants to raise two boys. Malati, shut the fuck up. Pranil will be back soon, fit and fine. This is a simple procedure. Shut the fuck up or I *will* have your mouth swollen shut.'

Pranil had been picked up for interrogation, like all the teenage boys in the village, and he had been gone since the morning. Now it was afternoon, and while Mama had had his hearty lunch, Pranil's parents and Prateek had decided to eat after Pranil came back.

'Why are you being so emotional? Every boy in the locality has been picked up,' Mama said, wiping the sweat off the nape of his neck with his blue towel. It was February, and chilly. But for some reason Mama had been sweating since the morning.

Malati continued to sob while her husband continued to look around listlessly. They were all outside, on the veranda, and Prateek was ripping up the dried brown leaves scattered on the floor and then shredding them carefully. Mama tapped his walking stick on the floor and was about to ask Prateek to get some water for him when he spotted Shabbir, one of Pranil's friends, walking towards Mama's wadi.

Shabbir had been picked up along with Pranil, and Mama knew Shabbir was a good boy, very bright, honest and straightforward in the way those people are. He lived in Futane Wadi, and things with those lot had been tense recently, but Mama did not believe in pinning blame on individual people for the faults of a community. A community is a community and a person is a person.

'Ae Shabbir,' Mama called out, getting up from his chair and grabbing his walking stick. 'Come here. Where is Pranil?'

'He is still at the police station.'

'Then how come they left you?'

'They are done with me.'

'But they aren't done with Pranil yet? What kind of interrogation is this?'

'Yes, how come they left you and not Pranil?' Ghanashyam asked.

'I don't understand that either,' Shabbir said, scratching his head. 'We all were together at that time. That's what I told them.'

'At what time?'

'Between three and six.'

'What do you mean you were together?'

'We were watching the . . . the cricket game.'

'That haramkhor wasn't studying then?'

'I don't know, Mama . . . I mean, I don't—'

'But if you were together, how come they let you off and not Pranil?'

'Mama . . . I am not sure. But they think—I know this is a lie, this is not true. But they think something was going on . . . between Anisha and Pranil.'

Mama tightened his grip on the walking stick. He glared at Shabbir and gritted his teeth. '*What*?'

'Mama . . . it was Valentine's Day na . . .'

'What has that got to do with my Pranil? Kay bolun rahila be tu, Shabbir?'

'It's not me who is . . . That's what . . . someone ratted Pranil out.'

'What do you mean ratted Pranil out?' Ghanashyam asked, but Mama raised his hand and glared at his brother-in-law.

'Ghanashyam, let me handle this and you do me a favour and shut up. I think we need to go to the—'

'No, Mama, stay here. Too many policemen. It will only complicate matters because they are pulling in anyone who is minutely related to the girls.' Shabbir frowned. 'I think that's what got them suspicious about Pranil.'

'What?' Mama asked, suddenly dizzy.

'That . . . your house is here, and people used to talk about—I mean, Pranil was . . .'

'*What?*'

'People said he was in love with Anisha.'

'*What?*'

Mama had to sit down. He signalled with his stick to Prateek, and Prateek helped him to his chair. Then Mama hit Prateek on his leg with the walking stick. 'What is this? What is this? What is this boy saying?'

Prateek didn't know what to say. This was the first time he had heard anything like this. Pranil? His brother in *love* with one of those sisters?

'Mama,' Shabbir said, calmly and with confidence. 'It's nothing. These are all rumours. Pranil is innocent. It's probably because of your house—'

'Watch your mouth. Are you blaming me for this?'

'No, Mama, it's just that the area—'

'If *area* is the problem, your entire lot should be rotting inside that fucking jail. Not us.'

Shabbir had been about to say something assuring, but he stopped.

'Mama, I will go back after namaz and check what is happening. You don't worry.'

Mama said nothing. He looked toward the shack and spat at the floor.

'You three,' he said, glaring at his sister and Prateek, 'go home. I will call you when you are needed.'

Pranil

'Haan, you.' Inspector Gungale, a waning star from the Crime Investigation Department, pointed at fourteen-year-old Pranil and smiled. 'Come here, beta. Don't be scared.'

Pranil stepped forward and Inspector Gungale stared at him for a minute. He was chewing something and spitting something out occasionally. Just like Dighole, but Dighole looked far less menacing than this person. Gungale was sitting on a metal chair, his khaki shirt undone and his belt out of its loops. He was holding the belt by its buckle and cracking it on the floor, like a whip.

Pranil, trembling, started to sob. His ears had turned pinkish red and his lips had a small, deep cut. Something had happened to one of his front teeth but he wasn't sure what. He wanted to look into a mirror, look at his face, ascertain that it hadn't been changed during the course of these three hours—the worst of his life.

'Hmm. Tar ha na? This person was one of the sisters' boyfriend, na?'

'Sir.'

'Hmm. Bhunk re. What did you do to her?'

It took Pranil every ounce of whatever remained of his strength to answer.

'Sir, nothing . . . sir, please . . . sir, I wasn't . . . sir, I am not her boyfriend.'

'You are not her boyfriend. Ka? Break up kela?'

But Gungale didn't wait for an answer and turned instead to the Constable. 'See, this is the problem with today's people. Use and throw. Use and throw. What love, baba. What prem kathas. Imagine, Shri Ram went all the way to Sri Lanka from UP for Sita Mai. To rescue her. To bring her back. That is the kind of dedication we had. And they say *this* is Ram Rajya.'

The Constable shook his head and scoffed. They stared at the five young boys in front of them. They were standing inside one of the police station's three square-shaped cells. This one was furthest inside, hardly illuminated, damp and reeking of sweat, shit and piss. The best place to intimidate impressionable young minds.

'Hmm. So? Not your girlfriend. Then whose girlfriend? Yours? Yours? No? Then maybe yours? No? They are all saying no—what is your name again?'

'Pranil.'

'Yes, well, Pranil, they are all saying no. And we received a tip. What did the tip say? Pranil and Anisha went up the hill to fetch a pail of water, God knows what they did, but they came back with a daughter. What does that tip mean? What do you think it means?'

The constables sniggered. The one standing beside Gungale acted as if he was going to slam his baton on Pranil's legs but stopped mid-air.

'Next time,' Gungale said, pointing a finger at Pranil, 'next time, it will hit. And not just once, haan. Enough of this bullshit. Your uncle's farm is right next to the sisters' home. Your friends tell me that you used to like that girl, that elder sister. It was 14 February. You know what 14 February means?'

When Pranil didn't answer, Gungale slapped him, once on his right cheek and then on his left.

'What does 14 February mean?'

'I don't—'

'It means Valentine's Day. Valentine. It means Love Day. Lavde. What does Valentine's Day mean?'

'Love . . . love—'

'Ah?'

'Love . . . Love Day.'

'That is correct. The day when you tell your chakuli you love her. You want to marry her. You give her flowers. Did you give her flowers? That elder sister?'

'No, sir.'

'Did you tell her you love her? That elder sister?'

'No . . . no, sir.'

The slaps stung. Pranil thought he was used to this; that he had been brought up this way. But this was worse than what Mama did to him. This was humiliation.

'Sir . . .' Pranil whimpered, 'sir, Akbar . . .'

'Hain?'

'Sir, Akbar liked her.'

'Akbar? Who is Akbar? That king? Chutiya samajun rahila ka be amhala?'

'Akbar Futane.'

Gungale looked at the four boys standing in a line behind Pranil, stuck to the wall like lizards. 'Akbar Futane ahe ka koni? Who is this Akbar?'

A sick-looking boy with thin arms and thinner legs stepped forward and croaked, 'Me, sir.'

Gungale pushed Pranil gently and told him to stand in Akbar's place. 'And you, Akbar Futane sakhar futane, you come here. Madarchod that Akbar Khan is one headache, now this one, behenchod. Come here. Let me see how you live up to that name of yours.'

The Mother

(Excerpts from an interview transcript. Interview conducted on 24 February 2019.)

'But then no, I remember they began saying: Actually, this has got nothing to do with Murwani. This has got nothing to do with the people of Murwani. Because it has everything to do with the people who came from outside Murwani. I, the mother of the girls who were killed, did not agree. I did not agree that people from outside Murwani could have done this. Who are these people? I asked. But nobody gave me any answers, because by that time everybody had started ignoring me; by that time I was, once again, a madwoman, and not just a madwoman, but also a suspect. Because there were people who said that I was a witch and that I practised black magic, and the police, instead of saying, no, this is nonsense, the police said: Let us check every angle, let us check what people are saying, and then they took me away and asked me all sorts of questions. They asked me about my black magic practices, and when I told them that I don't know anything about that, that I don't practise any black magic, they began asking me about the Kalandariya tribe. What Kalandariya? What Sufi? What Taj Baba? I didn't know anything about this, but they said that they had arrested some Mullah Chacha and that Mullah Chacha could be a part of the Kalandariya tribe and that they had been given a tip that I, too, was a part of the Kalandariya tribe. I had to laugh at that. But when I laughed they looked at each other, as if to say, see, she *is* mad. But I laughed because it was ridiculous. All this. I had never heard about all this before, and anyway, I said, if people are saying that a Murwani resident cannot do such things, how come they are accusing me of doing these things? And the Constable, that thin lady with black teeth, that thin lady with almost-closed eyes, she stared at me for a minute and then smiled: Because you were never a part of Murwani, madam.'

Cacophony

'We haven't done anything, saheb. We came here to do business, saheb, nothing else—'

'The business is good but we are poor people—'

'We have very limited means—'

'Routinely. And almost everyone here knows me personally, you can ask anyone—'

'Ask that boy about us, he will tell you—'

'We will never do such a thing, my God—'

'We came here to collect what we were owed, nothing else—'

'I have two daughters of my own, how will I even think of—'

'And we left that very evening for Rajasthan, only Kader was here—'

'See, we have spent extra money to come here—'

'Even thinking of such a thing makes my skin crawl—'

'Horrific, truly horrific, but we really had nothing to do with it, I am telling you—'

'We are willing to cooperate fully, no problems at all—'

'Around evening, I think, but it could have been late night, I am not *very* sure—'

'Those who did this should be hung publicly, that is for sure, sir—'

'It gives me the creeps, really, to be here at this point, but what can one do—'

'Almost three to four days, I think, before the—'

'We have lost our daily wages because we were called here, at least pay us for the travel if you can, sir—'

'These things happen regularly where we live, to be honest with you, but—'

'We know each other, none of us would even think of such a thing, really these are—'

'Horrors unknown.'

Kader Muhammad

When they left, they told Kader to be careful. Rajasthan, Maharashtra, Haryana, Tamil Nadu—it doesn't matter, the police everywhere are all the same. Everywhere they are looking for someone on whom they can pin the blame and close the case once and for all. They will try to trap you, they warned the old man, don't fall for their trickery. The more experienced and the more travelled among them told him what would probably happen if he wasn't smart: they would pin the blame on Kader, since Kader is a conveniently criminal name. The fact that he was from Rajasthan also helped. An outsider, twice over.

Kader knew that, but he was also convinced that nothing would happen to him. He was Mullah Chacha for the children, he always had been. He had been coming to the area since he was in his thirties, for thirty long years. Everyone knew him here.

Someone had told the police that they had heard an 'old man from Rajasthan' ask the eldest sister to accompany him. Ah, the morning shift Inspector thought, here we go, case closed. The blanket-sellers from Rajasthan had arrived in Murwani last week and had left—take this—on the day of the murder, so the police had called them back from Rajasthan. Kader and six others sold blankets in the village and the surrounding areas on credit, and they had been in this business for years. The villagers didn't exactly doubt them, but who can say anything with any certainty these days?

Everyone was questioned one by one by serious-looking men, but only Kader was told to stay back while the others were told to return home immediately. It was probably because Kader looked the eldest of the lot. But maybe it was also because he was the only Muslim man among them, although the rest did not think of themselves as Hindus as much as they thought of themselves as belonging to different castes, because their castes differed and their egos were inflated accordingly.

No one from the village came and spoke to Mullah Chacha as he sat alone outside the police station while the PI sipped his tea and read some magazines. Then he called Kader inside and asked him to sit on the chair. PI Deshmukh asked him all the usual questions: where, what, why, when. Then he leaned back in his chair and said, 'Did you offer one of the girls a chocolate, Chacha?'

Kader shifted in his chair uncomfortably. As a matter of fact he had, but there was nothing unusual about that. He did it every time he was on a visit to these areas: he bought a bunch of toffees and chocolates to distribute to the children when they swarmed around him like stray dogs. He liked children, he had a few of his own, but they were all scattered across the country and the globe. Kader lived alone, and he loved children, and this is how he had spent his life: going around selling things and distributing chocolates to children everywhere.

'Yes. I gave a chocolate to a girl, but I give many chocolates to many girls and boys, saheb. Is that a crime?'

'No, it's not. At least until it's proven otherwise,' Deshmukh said, eyeing him and clicking his tongue. 'Let me be frank. I have worked on many cases in my life, Chacha, and I know your sort of people. Acting innocent and thinking nobody would doubt your tharak because of your age. But it's you people who are the worst. I have dealt with enough people of your landya lot. You come here thinking you will lure little teenage girls and enjoy your jannat on earth, barobar na? Enjoyed then, young, fresh, virgin girls, mast ekdum? Chocolate. I will open one case against you here and the complaints will start pouring in, behenchod.'

Kader kept quiet. What could he say? It was always like this. His sons used to get very agitated but Kader knew this is how it is and this is how it is always going to be. It doesn't matter who says what or who you have known for how many years: at the end of the day, it always comes down to the name and the clothes.

'Now,' Deshmukh said, 'tell me. How did you do it?'

'Do what?'

The PI made a circle with the fingers of his left hand and put the middle finger of his right hand through it. 'This. How old are you?'

'I am not sure . . . but sixty-four, I think.'

'You *think*. Changlay behenchod. Don't you have a birth certificate?'

'No.'

'Then how will you prove you are not Pakistani or Bangladeshi?'

Deshmukh didn't wait for an answer. He shifted in his chair and looked at India's map behind him. 'Haan,' he said, loudly. 'Rajasthan na. Barobar behenchod. Border state. You are Pakistani, no?'

'No, saheb, I was born here, in Rajasthan, saheb, and—'

'How will you prove it?'

'I have a ration card somewhere . . .'

'Ration card. I can get a ration card for my dead father right now, that's how easy it is to get a fake ration card. I will tell you what, you come clean about the girls and I won't open a case against you for spying.'

This was not something Kader had expected. Spying? He had spent all his life in Lalwadi. And Lalwadi was in Tonk, which was very far away from Pakistan, as far as he knew. He had never even given a thought to this before, but now he needed to think fast. He couldn't. He sat there silently, tears welling up, his hands enjoined automatically.

'I am innocent, saheb. I am . . . please believe me. I came here for the—I had to collect my money. That's all I did, I swear.'

'Swear on what? Allah? No, you swear on . . . Mahakal. Say Jai Mahakal.'

'Saheb—'

'Swear on Mahakal and Hanumanji. Say Jai Mahakal and Bajrang Bali ki jai. Say it.'

The constables gathered around, some of them mulling tobacco paste in their palms, enjoying the bullying.

'Saheb . . .'

Kader was crying now, sobbing into his shirt and heaving. PI Deshmukh got up from his chair and slapped Kader across his face. 'Stop crying and say it and we will let you go.'

Kader nodded, composed himself and said: 'Jai Mahakal.'

'Is this how you chant Allahu Akbar? No na? Say it with passion. Chant it, behenchod.'

'Jai Mahakal,' Kader whimpered, his face stoic now. 'Jai Bajrang Bali!'

The Inspector delivered another sharp slap. 'Bajrang Bali ki jai. Say it.'

'Bajrang Bali ki jai!'

'Good. Ae Karamble.' The Inspector snapped his fingers. 'Lock this gaandu up.'

SP Anjali Shukla

'We have formed ten teams, and we already have a suspect apprehended. And . . . yes, the family is going to be provided with special protection. Home Guards have already been placed outside their house. We are doing everything we can,' SP Anjali Shukla told a bunch of reporters who were scribbling on their notepads frantically.

At this point, right now, this was the biggest story in Maharashtra. But maybe next week, Shukla thought, the storm would have passed. No reporter was going to stick around for more than a week. At the most two. But beyond that, the press was too broke and indifferent to follow up on such stories, Shukla thought with relief.

But right now it was important to show conviction.

'We have suspended the concerned PI and the teams are—'

'What is the name of the suspended PI?'

'Sanjay Dighole,' a local reporter prompted.

'Do you know the Inspector?'

'Which Inspector?'

'The suspended one.'

'Dighole na? Of course I know him.'

'I think we should meet him.'

'You have a bike?'

'No.'

'Okay, I will arrange. We will have to find him, though.'

Someone asked the SP: 'What about the cases of arson?'

Someone else said: 'Who is the suspect? Can we get info on him?'

'I cannot divulge too many details, since the investigation is in process, but we are making progress and we are heading in the right direction.'

'Ma'am, off the record. What is the progress?'

'Look, Shalini . . . Shalini, no? Yes, well, Shalini, it's a sensitive case and we have to proceed cautiously. It's not about who the suspect is or who isn't, or whether the suspect is from around here or Rajasthan—it's about facts. We are after facts.' Shukla cleared her throat and adjusted her police cap.

'Were the girls raped?' one of the reporters asked.

'This is off the record?'

'If you want it to be.'

'Then this is off the record. Report it, but say sources. Look, initial evidence pointed towards rape, but we have consulted some experts and they don't support that theory, so we are in the process of gathering more evidence. We have sent the samples for forensics, so once that report comes in, things should be clearer. That's all I can divulge.'

You have to give them things sometimes, these media people, carrots and sticks. Of course, the information was true. Some medical experts and some senior police officials had ruled out rape, and Shukla had her own theory about that. After the inquest panchnama, the bodies were kept in the open for twelve hours, which would have damaged the skin, and that could have led the medical officers to conclude that the sisters had been assaulted. But SP Shukla also recognized, privately, that this was a botched investigation to begin with: from the delay in registering the FIR to the autopsies conducted by a bunch of inexperienced doctors who were no forensic experts (an MBBS, a physician, a gynaecologist, an ortho and an ENT specialist) and who had failed to preserve any samples for the diatom test. It was a disaster handed to her on a platter. Besides, the rains had complicated matters, as had bloody Valentine's Day. Too many young couples calling each other. That had made checking call records nearly impossible.

But all this would be revealed much later, and that was only if anyone bothered to keep tabs on this investigation. Right now, harmless information in bits and pieces.

Shukla dismissed the press conference, entered the police station and called for PI Deshmukh. She needed 'fresh inputs' for her meeting with the DGP and the Inspector General, also attended by the District Magistrate, the Deputy Superintendent of Police (SDPO) and the Police Surgeon. Too many things would be alleged, too many people would be baying for her blood. The State Home Ministry was involved, the

Centre was surely asking questions. The suspension of PI Dighole was not going to satisfy them. She knew her transfer would be the next logical move. She needed something to salvage the situation.

PI Deshmukh entered her cabin, saluted purposefully and stomped his foot.

'Jai Hind, madam.'

'Haan, what is it about that man from Rajasthan you were saying?'

'Madam, he will talk. We will get him to talk.'

'What do you mean he will talk? What are the grounds on which we are holding him anyway?'

'Madam, he was here on 14 February. And he left the very next day. And he had offered the eldest sister a chocolate, madam.'

'Does he have an alibi?'

'He says he came here to collect some money.'

'What kind of money?'

'Some debt, madam. He sells blankets along with others of his group in the area.'

'Did you confirm the alibi then?'

'Yes, madam. His collection was done by afternoon, madam. His group left that evening, but this man left the next day, madam.'

'And why is that?'

'Something about the timings of their train, madam.'

'Where are the others from his group?'

'We let them go, madam.'

'On whose orders?'

'Madam . . . they . . . Santosh Sir . . .'

'I'll talk to him. You call this man.'

Karamble and Sangere brought Kader before the SP.

'What is your name?'

'Kader Muhammad.'

'Where are you from?'

'Rajasthan.'

'Where in Rajasthan?'

'Lalwadi, Tonk.'

'I was posted in Rajasthan once,' Shukla said, smiling slightly. 'Sit down.'

Kader sat down but then he got up. It hurt too much. Shukla realized this and glanced at Deshmukh and the two constables. 'Kader, what were you doing on the afternoon of 14 February? It's a simple question.'

'I was . . . I was collecting my money.'

'Till what time?'

'Around . . . around three, madam, I think. After lunch, madam.'

Shukla looked at Deshmukh and arched her eyebrows.

Deshmukh said: 'His friends said he went alone to collect, at around two. The man he collected the debt from confirmed this.'

'Confirmed the timing?'

'Yes, two in the afternoon.'

'So, Kader, what did you do after collecting the debt? Where did you go?'

Kader began to sob. Shukla offered him her glass of water, and he gulped it down. 'You want more?' Kader nodded, and one of the constables picked up the glass and rushed outside to fill it.

'Haan, Kader. Where did you go after collecting the debt?'

'I . . . I went with my friends, madam, for some tea.'

Shukla looked at Deshmukh.

'We did not—I am not sure this was confirmed by others in his group, madam,' Deshmukh said.

Shukla shook her head.

'So you have been coming here for . . . ten years? Fifteen?'

'Thirty years, madam. In this area. The people here know me. They know me as Mullah Chacha. Ask anyone, they know me. I will never do such a thing.'

'Why did you stay back? Why didn't you travel back to Rajasthan with your group?'

Kader took a deep, long breath.

'I went to Kovdi, madam. A friend lives there.'

'What is the name of this friend?'

'Nazir.'

'Nazir what?'

'Nazir Ansari.'

Shukla looked at Deshmukh.

'We have sent a team to investigate, madam.'

'When?'

'Today morning, madam.'

The Constable brought the glass of water. Shukla took the glass and placed it on the table but did not offer it to Kader.

'When did your friends leave for Rajasthan?'

'At seven, madam. In the evening.'

'Kader, did you offer one of the girls a chocolate?'

'Yes, madam, but I always do that. I swear. Ask anyone. I like children, I always do that. I swear.'

'Did anyone see you offer chocolate to the girl?'

'My friends . . . from Rajasthan, they did. They saw me. They . . . it was nothing. They all know I offer chocolates. That's why they call me Chacha.'

Shukla pushed three passport-sized photographs, cut out from a single photograph, towards Kader. 'Which one did you offer the chocolate to?'

Kader squinted at the images. Then he shook his head and cleared his throat. 'Sorry . . . None of them, madam.'

The SP darted a glance at Deshmukh, who gripped Kader's nape and pushed him closer to the photographs. 'Look closely, asshole.' But Kader stood by his word: he had offered a chocolate, but he hadn't offered it to one of the sisters.

'Madam, another night in the cell and he will start talking. I guarantee you. He will start talking,' Deshmukh insisted.

Kader Muhammad sat silently, but his hands were shaking, and he was trying to control his sobs. The man did not look like he was capable of handling three healthy girls. And one of them was fourteen, so it must have taken considerable effort: it didn't seem like a one-man job. But then again, he claimed that the children knew him, he had been around for the past thirty years, so who knows, he might have seduced the eldest one and then—

'Okay,' Shukla said. 'Deshmukh, I want every little detail accounted for. And no noise. And no marks anywhere. Get him to talk. Quickly.'

Datta Mama

Pranil had been told to come straight to Datta Mama's house once he was done with the interrogation, and that is what he did. Although, of course, his interrogation was hardly done. He had been told to come again the next day. Akbar was still inside the police station.

The house was silent and locked from the inside. Pranil knocked on the door and waited. When Datta Mama opened the door, he did not step out. Instead, without looking at Pranil, he simply stepped aside to let Pranil in. After he entered, Datta Mama closed the door behind him but stayed silent.

'Mama . . .'

'Is it true?'

'Mama . . .'

'Is it true?'

'Of course not, Mama.'

'Did they hit you?'

'A little bit.'

'Sit down.'

Pranil sat down and gulped. Datta Mama refused to look at him.

'Is it done now?'

'I have to . . . I have to go back tomorrow, Mama.'

'What for?'

Datta Mama was unusually calm, and Pranil knew that that was not a good sign.

'They have some questions.'

'Which means it is true. You had an affair with that filthy whore.'

'No, Mama. No. I didn't.'

'Despite my warnings.'

'There was nothing, Mama. Nothing. I didn't even look at her—'

'A thousand times. A thousand times I told you, those girls were a bad omen.'

'Datta Mama, really—'

'They are going to take your name and that girl's name in the same breath, Pranil. Do you know what that means for us?'

'Mama, I—I wasn't at fault.'

Datta Mama stared into Pranil's eyes. Then he examined his nephew's face.

'You call this being hit?'

Pranil didn't know how to respond. He simply shook his head, without knowing why.

'Tell your mother this is what the police did.'

'Mama?'

Datta Mama picked up his walking stick and gestured with it to Pranil: stand up.

Kader Muhammad

They asked Kader Muhammad who was waiting for him back home in Rajasthan.

The Inspector and the two constables. The Inspector asked Kader whether he knew someone called Afrima. Afrima Sayed. No, Kader told him. 'Because Afrima Sayed also lived in Lakhani and Afrima Sayed was also raped and killed and thrown into a well. And you were around then.'

'I don't know, saheb.'

'What don't you know?'

It was four in the morning and it had been eighteen straight hours since Kader had been forced to sit on the wooden stool. He wasn't allowed to get up and he couldn't stretch his legs. At first they limited themselves to a couple of slaps, but then the Inspector repeatedly pointed his revolver at Kader's temple and started asking questions which did not seem connected to the investigation.

'Afrima was converted. Married and converted. Why? Why do you do these things? She was married for seven years, and then her bloody katwa started fucking other girls. You can do that, na? Multiple wives you can enjoy. So he started fucking other girls. And she protested because after all she came from a decent culture. But the fucker beat her up. Then he killed her, because she threatened to reveal his conversion and terrorism business. The jihad business of you fuckers. That's why she was killed. And that's why there are so many of these people in our area.'

The last bit of Deshmukh's monologue was addressed to the constables, who stood behind Kader in their white baniyans and with expressions of intense concentration. It had been hot inside the cell, and the two constables had pulled off their uniforms dramatically, announcing that they were no longer part of the police but civilians angry at Kader and his ilk. Now, at dawn, the cold bit into their skins and forced their teeth into a steady chatter, but of course they couldn't put on their shirts *now*.

Sangere slapped Kader on the back of his head.

'You smell, you fuckers, you smell so much. Everything is muck and disgusting with you people. Never do a good thing for your country, you fuckers.'

For a long time during the night, the Inspector and the constables tried procuring tea. At first they asked Kader if he would like some, and when he said no, they pretended to be insulted and asked him if drinking tea was considered haram. If accepting tea from the idol-worshippers was considered a sin. Kader kept quiet. Truth be told, Kader didn't actually know a lot about what was halal and what was haram. He read his namaz but he had always been more interested in the economics of living than the economics of faith. So when they asked him questions about Islam, he maintained what he thought was an embarrassing silence.

But the tea never materialized because no one was selling tea at that time of the night. So Karamble was asked to go home, prepare tea in a thermos and come back. Meanwhile, Kader was allowed to sleep while sitting. When Kader did not sleep, Deshmukh stood in front of him and asked Kader whether he had a family.

'Yes, saheb, four boys and one daughter.'

'What pigs. Where are they?'

'The boys . . . saheb, one of them is in Kolkata. The others are in the Gulf.'

'Haan,' Deshmukh said, as if he had just proved a point. 'Gulf. Aiklat ka, Sangere? Gulf, he says his sons live in.'

'What he actually means is Pakistan,' Sangere contributed.

'Not really. It doesn't have to be Pakistan. These fuckers have too many countries to fund their jihad as it is. Where are they, Kader Miyan? Your terrorist sons?'

'Saudi and Dubai.'

'See. I am telling you,' Deshmukh turned to Sangere, 'we had a tip-off about a terrorist module here. I'm telling you, if we investigate this guy more, we'll get a lot of dirt. A lot of it. Thirty years he has been coming here. For what? To sell blankets? My gaand, behenchod. It's a racket. From the Pakistan border to Dubai to Saudi and Kolkata, which means Bangladesh, and now here, in Maharashtra. They are surrounding us, Sangere.'

'Ae bhadvya,' Sangere said, angered by his superior's claims, 'what are you guys planning?'

'What do you think? Another 26/11 type thing. What else would they plan?'

Karamble came back with the thermos and four plastic cups. They poured the tea and Deshmukh offered a cup to Kader. But Kader did not drink tea. He didn't drink milk at all, because he had always been allergic to it. 'Milk, saheb, milk is . . .'

'Milk is what?' Sangere asked, sipping his tea with one hand and waving his baton with the other.

'I am allergic to milk.'

'Oho. Allergic to milk. Why? Because it comes out of gau mata? Is that haram too? You can kill the cows, but you can't drink their milk?'

'It's a health issue, saheb, nothing else.'

'No, it's a cultural issue. Your Mughal blood cannot tolerate cow milk because your Mughal blood cannot tolerate cows because your Mughal blood thinks cows are a pure symbol of the pure Hindu blood. That's what it is. That is why your lot doesn't drink tea.'

There was hardly any relevant question to ask Kader. They tied Kader's hands to the cell's window bars and made him sit on the stool so that he was somewhere between hanging and suspended. They tried to see if they could get some chilli powder to throw into his eyes. Deshmukh and company were pitifully unimaginative when it came to actual torture, so the Inspector finally pulled out his revolver and pointed it at Kader and threatened to shoot if Kader didn't confess promptly. Once, Deshmukh almost pulled the trigger, but he stopped when he saw that Kader had pissed himself. At which point Sangere and Karamble pushed him down and began landing kicks into his balls. His hands were already stretched out and tied to the bars, so he could do nothing but scream. Once or twice he said, 'Ya Allah', which was enough provocation for Karamble and Sangere to induce more passion into their kicking.

But there was still no confession forthcoming, so at around 5 a.m., Deshmukh, sleep-deprived, hungry and exhausted, asked Karamble and Sangere to untie Kader and put him into the Jeep. But as they pushed him outside the station, they were stopped by two CID inspectors, who asked Deshmukh where he thought he was taking a suspect at five in the morning.

'For a stroll,' Deshmukh said. 'A morning walk.'

The two officers looked at Kader's face, which, to the annoyance of Deshmukh and the constables, looked bruised. Deshmukh wanted to slap Kader, but he had better things planned for him. Just get him out and put him in a Jeep and roll that pig into a fucking ditch, that's what will teach him a lesson. But he needed to deal with these CID assholes first.

'Don't act smart, Deshmukh,' one of the inspectors said. 'This man is going to screw you and your madam's behind like they screwed Dighole's gaand, because that is the only thing you people deserve.'

'Come back to me when they go to the CBI.'

'Another week at the most and we will catch the chutiyas who did this, Deshmukh. There's a difference between your lund and the CID's lund.'

'In size, maybe. But matter is the same, Gungale. We fuck as well as the CID does, I must say even better.'

'Now you will say it is because you fuck raw.'

'And that's the truth.'

Deshmukh pulled Kader by his collar and shouted into his ear: 'Naav bol re, madarchod.'

'Kader.'

'Kader kay? Didn't your mother fuck a man?'

'Kader Muhammad.'

One of the officers looked at the thermos in Sangere's hand and pointed at it. 'Some tea would be good.'

'Haan, haan, give them some tea, give them biscuits, sure, why not,' Deshmukh said and pulled Kader towards the Jeep. But Gungale, the second CID Inspector, stopped him again. 'Don't be a chutiya, Deshmukh. This is a suspect. Madam will come tomorrow and ask you about him. What are you going to tell her?'

'That he tried to run away and I shot him.'

Kader began to shake his head, his lips and his eyes widening with horror. 'No, saheb, no, no, no . . .'

'Don't be stupid,' Gungale said, his voice mellowing down. 'You will get suspended anyway. Think, Deshmukh, chutiya, it's for your own good. This is not your usual case. Think. What have you got on him?'

'He offered chocolate to one of the girls.'

'Saheb, I didn't, saheb—'

The CID Inspector slapped Kader. 'Chup. Ekdum chup.'

'And he has been coming here for the past thirty years. We can get his custody in that terror cell case.'

'I am not sure about that.'

'Some of their money came from the Gulf and Dubai. This guy's sons live there.'

'Haan, but there is no trail, na. It's not easy. But you see if you can find a connection between him and the other suspects. That would be good. And then it would be good publicity also. Some attention diverted from this hellhole here.'

'And you take the credit? Not possible, Gungale.'

'Arey, take the credit, Deshmukh, don't be a pain in the ass. Credit, credit, credit. Behenchod, solve a case for once.'

Deshmukh looked at Kader, paused for a minute, and then pushed him back inside the police station.

Constable Karamble

It was a tiring thing, working for a person like Inspector Deshmukh. He was right for the job, no doubt about that, but Karamble didn't quite feel as if he was working for the sake of justice, or even towards some conclusion, when he worked with PI Deshmukh. No, not quite. It was hard to believe, considering how PI Dighole treated him, but it was true: Karamble had started missing him.

His banter, his barbs, his harmless insults, his tendency to forgive and to forget; whatever one may think of PI Dighole, he had been a considerate boss, at times even going to the extent of taking the blame when the constables erred, as they quite often did. No other Inspector did that, and Karamble knew this for a fact because he had spent a considerable amount of time in Murwani, in the company of three 'distinguished' inspectors.

All of them were flawed in some measure, the inspectors, but this Deshmukh Saheb was a little over the top with his conclusions and his assumptions. And he had no real interrogation skills. The CID people were way better: they knew exactly how a criminal reacted, exactly how a man who had committed a crime behaved. And they knew the techniques to tease that out. But Deshmukh Saheb . . . for example, he had asked Karamble to bring kitchen tongs when the Constable was on his way home to bring another flask of tea.

'Bring tongs on your way back, Karamble,' Deshmukh had said. 'Let me introduce this bastard to a world of pain.'

Ridiculous.

As expected, the kitchen tongs had done nothing to Kader Muhammad's fingers. Deshmukh had tried to crush his fingers, but the tongs weren't made for those sort of things, and at any rate Kader Muhammad was too strong to have his bones—or his morale—cracked under the negligible weight of kitchen tongs made of stainless steel.

'Nail cutter, bring me a nail cutter.'

Of course, no one had a nail cutter inside the police station, so Karamble had to make another trip home to fetch his personal one. But that was useless because as it turned out Kader Muhammad had recently cut his nails.

'Surprising,' Sangere had said, eyeing Kader's bruised fingers. 'Considering how dirty you people are supposed to be.'

Later, when they were given a break to grab some shut-eye, Karamble had tried to speak to Sangere about what was happening.

'He seems innocent,' Karamble had ventured, spreading a mat on the cold flooring outside the cell and lying down on it with relief, groaning and sighing as he did so.

'How does it matter, Karamble? They all are guilty of something. Not rape, not murder. Okay. Then maybe theft. Maybe terrorism. Maybe something else. Better inside the jail than outside, these people.'

Karamble thought about all that Kader had said: all the pieces really did fit together. He collected his debt at two, went back to his friends at around two-fifteen. Then they went around Murwani selling blankets, until around six, which is when Kader left for Kovdi and the others in his group left for Nagpur. Kader claimed that he went to Kovdi on a truck and reached the town at seven-thirty. Murwani to Kovdi was forty-five minutes, but Kader claimed the truckers stopped for some tea and snacks, which delayed Kader's arrival at Kovdi. All this was confirmed by Kader's friend Nazir Ansari. Now the hunt was on for the truck driver who had given Kader a lift.

Dighole Saheb wouldn't have stretched it this way, Karamble thought. Whatever he was, Dighole Saheb wasn't a monster. Maybe ignorant, perhaps lazy, maybe too disinterested in his job, but he wasn't cruel. Though perhaps cruelty has its benefits, because the torture had certainly revealed other troubling things about this Kader fellow. His sons *did* live in all those problematic places, Dubai and Bangladesh and the Gulf, didn't they? And Karamble had read and heard and known enough in his life to understand that those places were jhamela places, places where they trained and harboured enemies of our nation. But then again, Karamble had read somewhere that all sorts of people live there, in the Gulf: especially from Kerala. Hindus, Christians, Muslims. So who knows?

That and the subsequent night Karamble had continued to interrogate Kader, until PI Deshmukh had come up with some sort of 'proof' linking Kader to some person in the neighbouring taluka who had given Kader a loan. As it happened, that person had also provided loans to those belonging to the terror module.

Karamble had never seen a happier Inspector. PI Deshmukh had announced a tea party for everyone on him, and then he had promised everyone a 'jangi party' later. But then came the news of Dighole Saheb's murder, and everyone had forgotten about that party. Karamble had cried that day. But of course not inside the police station. He had walked to the outskirts of the village in the falling light of the evening and he had stood at the spot where they, Constable Karamble and Inspector Dighole, used to pee while out on their nocturnal rounds. At first he had smiled, thinking about all the drunks they had scared shitless and all the suspects they had brought here to 'bury' and all the quarters they had sometimes downed here, at this spot.

And then he had sobbed. By the time he started bawling and crying into his handkerchief, he was no longer sure why he was crying. Or rather: there were several reasons why he was crying.

Karamble felt alone, and lost, because he knew that no one would be waiting for him at home, readying his dinner, handing him a cup of tea, laughing with him, arguing with him about the lack of money, teasing him about his age . . . When he went home, with all his memories and his scars and his burdens, there would be just that one room with a single bed and an unclean bathroom.

That, Karamble realized, was all there was to his life. And that, Karamble realized, was going to be all there was to it.

The Mother

(Excerpts from an interview transcript. Interview conducted on 24 February 2019.)

'I was told that I would be interrogated by the SP Madam, the Police Superintendent. I even remember the date, because it was exactly two months after my daughters were killed—13 April 2013. But SP Madam never came. I was let off after two days and told to remain within the boundaries of the village, because I could be called back anytime. But I was never called back. PI Dighole was killed, SP Madam got transferred, PI Deshmukh got transferred, API

Sangere got transferred and Constable Karamble got sacked. Everybody was scattered, everyone who was investigating the rape and murder of my daughters, and no one had any clue about who did that to them . . .

'Actually, that's not true. Everybody else apart from the SP Madam and the inspectors and the constables had an idea about who did this to my daughters, and for days and months after that February they would come to our house and stand outside awkwardly, trying to peep inside, trying to decide whether they should knock on our door or let it be. I installed a proper curtain on our window a month or so later, so from the gap in that curtain I would spot those people who traipsed to our house confidently but then couldn't muster the courage to come and talk to me. But some did, and they told me their theories about who was responsible for the death of my daughters. I heard them out and I nodded and I even smiled sadly. Yes, I would sometimes say, yes, I believe you. Yes, I would sometimes say, yes, this is possible. And I could see their faces lighting up, I could see the smile form on the edge of their lips, because the real reason why they were sitting in front of me, explaining what they thought had happened to my daughters, the real reason they were investigating and trying to find clues and going around the town gathering information, the real reason why they were doing all this was because they wanted to find a purpose, something to make them feel needed and important and worthy. I understood and I smiled and I said: Yes, this is possible, this is certainly what happened. As the mother of the murdered daughters, I approve of your investigation. Good job. Keep going.'

Part Four

CACOPHONY

February–March–April 2019
Murwani, Maharashtra

Chitranshu Chitale

The Marathi that the Chitales—that's Chitranshu Chitale, our crime reporter, and his family—spoke at home and outside, in their little social circles in Mumbai, was a Marathi they considered pure and chaste, a Marathi drawn from the Pune lineage, which is to say *proper* Marathi. Proper Marathi that was sprinkled these days with English words and sometimes, though rarely, a mix of Hindi and Urdu.

Not that they were language chauvinists, the Chitales, because they couldn't afford to be. After all, their son wrote most of what he wrote in English, which was a good thing. Better to be writing and reading in English than in Marathi these days, they argued. But when it came to debates in the wider world about language and its apparent purity, they believed that they traced their lineage to those exemplars who had been speaking *original* Marathi—whatever that was—for generations.

All this is to say that when Chitranshu landed in Murwani six years after he had spent a night in the village, he was aware of the difficulties he was going to face in his task of interviewing the people of the village and compiling their testimonies. The last time he was there, he had had limited interaction: Godambe, the local journalist, and Dighole, the disgraced Police Inspector who . . . well, who had met with an unfortunate end. The people of Murwani spoke a Marathi that

Chitranshu could more or less understand, but they spoke it rapidly. Chitranshu knew it would be hard for him to immediately grasp what they were saying, which is why he was going to record it and then write it all down.

Yes, he would have to listen to the language carefully and transcribe those interviews. And then he would start cutting off the bits that didn't fit or seemed out of context or rambling and digressive. In any case, he needed to transcribe everything, every word, before he started giving it shape and form, and before he started writing in earnest. But writing what? About that, Chitranshu had very little idea.

He told himself that he was writing a book. A book about murder. Three sisters, possibly raped, possibly killed, found at the bottom of a well, years ago. He had covered the case and then he had forgotten all about it. But to those who bothered asking, he explained that this particular case was an obsession. He had been thinking about it, consciously and unconsciously, for years. Right from the day he had returned from Murwani. The case of the three sisters, unsolved, tossed aside once its importance in the news cycle had faded—this case had 'haunted' him 'forever', Chitranshu said.

'I got a call one night,' he could be found reciting. 'Three sisters killed, four days earlier. Raped and murdered and found floating at the bottom of a well. Fuck man, what a story. I took the first train out and reached there the next afternoon. But this was almost a week after the incident, right? Since news travels slow. So I had to see the bodies in pictures: three little girls, like discarded dolls. I can't erase that image. What happened to those sisters? Who killed them?'

Chitranshu told himself that he was trying to get to the bottom of those questions, but the fact of the matter was that he was listless, lost and jobless. At one point he had decided to change his profession and dive into the world of publishing, but no one was ready to hire him. Then he thought perhaps he could try and take a stab at teaching journalism in one of the colleges in the city: he had six years' worth of reporting experience, and he could confidently tell off those starry-eyed idiots that you shouldn't enter journalism to change the world, because you can't change the world, you shitheads, all you can do in this profession is try and stay afloat, survive.

But no one was willing to hire him to teach the Bachelor of Mass Media courses. An ex-colleague, taking pity, decided to try him out as a guest lecturer. 'Teach them about ethics,' she said. 'Teach them about the basics of journalism.' Well, Chitranshu tried. He tried to tell the kids that journalism was all about that: ethics and morals, truth and integrity. He even added a little bit about how the fourth pillar of democracy, despite everything, stood tall and proud. It was going well, until it wasn't: Chitranshu couldn't lie for forty-five minutes straight. After all, this was 2019, who was he kidding? After he had told them about cross-checking facts and information that came from sources, he paused and sighed a long and hard sigh.

'Nope. All nonsense. Fuck it. It's a shitty field. Get into advertising. Same kind of people, but better pay.

If you are going to be yelled at, you better be yelled at while getting paid, no?'

Of course, he was never called back.

Now he had anchored his hopes on 'the book', as a sort of redemption. But those who had known him during his last couple of years in the world of journalism knew that the former crime and civic reporter, who sometimes doubled up as a legal reporter, was incapable of writing even a decent feature-length piece. So the fact that Chitranshu was writing a book was rather hard to believe. Even so, his friends from journalism college from all those years ago believed that he had struck on to something. At least he was trying to break away and do something different, something big, something that they thought they weren't capable of: writing a proper book on an interesting case, forgotten and buried in the recesses of recent history.

Yeah, well, let's see how that goes, thought Chitranshu. As it stands, everything else is fucked anyway.

Ajoba

(Excerpts from an interview transcript. Interview conducted on 2 March 2019.)

'The tape recorder is on?'

'Yes.'

'Switch it off.'

'Why?'

'I can't tell all this to a machine.'

'But you are talking to me, the tape recorder is just a—'

'I am not telling this to a machine. When you reporter types turn that machine on you don't listen. You don't *need* to listen. I know you reporter types. My granddaughters . . . they shouldn't have been newspaper clippings. That part I can't change. But I won't allow them to languish in machines now. If their story is to be told, it has to be heard first.'

'I am listening, Ajoba.'

'How could they not find the man who did this? I can't sleep at night. I keep thinking, how could they not find the person who did this? But I don't find it surprising now. Of course, they couldn't find anybody. How could they, with all these many people that we have in our country? You just have to accept these things. Not forget. Because the moment you start thinking of forgetting, it all comes back, piece by piece. I should know. I tried to forget, but as you can see, I failed. My granddaughters . . . No, I don't miss them. They come back to me in my dreams, but they never tell me what happened to them, which is probably all the same since I never ask. That explains all the talking I do at night, my wife used to tell me I blabber but I remember making meaningful conversations . . .'

'Do you remember what—'

'No, I don't. I can make up something and tell you, but I don't want to because I have decided to tell this story as honestly as I can, without any . . . without missing out anything, and certainly nothing made up. I think at least that much . . . Careful with that stool, it's very old and quite a lot of people have fallen off it, but we don't change it because it's been in the family for a long time. No, I don't have any memories attached to the stool, neither did the girls, and I told you to stop searching for headlines. A straight story is the least my granddaughters deserve. Anyway, the point is that it's been six years, more than that actually, the people here have changed, nobody really remembers anything about that incident anymore, it's just one of those things that happened a long time ago in this village, and even the village has changed. More trucks have started plying and more dhabas have come up on the eastern side . . . Do you remember when they blocked the trucks a day after my granddaughters' bodies were found? The people here were very angry, or so they would have us believe. But a learned person, like you, this learned person told me that it's all a tamasha, that the village felt that they needed something exciting, which is why the whole village was up and about in those days . . . And that might be true, who knows? He wasn't wrong in saying that nothing had ever happened in this village. And he wasn't wrong in saying that people were fed up, which is probably why I believe him when he says everyone here used our tragedy as their entertainment. A part of me does. I wasn't born in this village, I arrived here with my wife, and at that time this whole village used to be right beside the road you came from. It expanded. There are three or four apartment complexes now, though the residents say they are not part of Murwani. But sometimes they also say that *we* are not a part of Murwani, and that this village could be a great colony of apartment complexes if only we parted with our lands. That even the politicians and the builders say. It's funny. The other day a politician, who was around when the murders happened, he came to the village and he couldn't recognize me. Six years ago the chodhichya had fallen at my feet asking for forgiveness and promising every sort of inquiry into the matter—'

'Who was this?'

'What?'

'The politician. What was his name?'

'I don't remember his name.'

'We can keep it off the record, if you are worried about that.'

'What? Off the record? What's that? No, I don't want to record anything, not off, not on. The politician was trying to convince everybody that a new project, some tourism project I think, would fetch us a lot of jobs. That he has been saying for the past seven months all around the district . . . I heard his party has promised him something, a ticket maybe, that's what they show in films . . . Anyway, his party has promised him something big if the project goes through. Or some such. That's not the point, the point is that they are building tourism projects on a land where my granddaughters were raped and killed and their murderer or murderers never found. Imagine this, that's what you should tell people. On this land, where the girls were raped and killed, on this land the children and the grandchildren of others will come to entertain themselves. Makes sense, doesn't it? Because this village has always craved entertainment . . .'

A Shopkeeper

(Excerpts from an interview transcript. Interview conducted on 23 March 2019.)

'I remember them, yes, especially that girl Anisha. Very bright. Very, very bright. And she was very short-tempered too. Quick to insult you if you start saying anything against her or her sisters. She didn't really care much about her mother or grandparents, I don't think so, but she really loved her sisters. Two little girls with pigtails. They were harmless, let me tell you that. I mean, of course, there were rumours, and people said things about them, like how Anisha had so much money on her—which is something even I've wondered about sometimes, because she would buy a bunch of Gems packets, sometimes five or six at a time, and she would distribute it among her friends, and she had many friends too. How did she get all that money? As far as I know, their mother worked at the factory as a cook. That couldn't have brought much money. Not as much as the girls carried around, not at all.

'But otherwise they were harmless. They didn't have any wrong intentions, they never bothered anyone, they never made fun of anybody or bullied anyone. Anisha, especially. That day, I remember, she had come here, Anisha, in the afternoon, with her sisters. Sanchita and Priyanka. Around twelve-thirty she came in, and the sisters used to either walk behind her or stand behind her, and that day they stood behind her. They were in their school uniforms, but Anisha was wearing a green T-shirt—'

'Top.'

'What?'

'Not a T-shirt, a top.'

'Whatever. It wasn't her school uniform, that's what I remember. She came in and said: Kaka, Gems packet dya na teen. Three Gems packets. I can't forget that sentence. I should have asked her what she was doing wearing that T-shirt and jeans, I should have asked her if she was going somewhere, but I didn't. I don't remember why. Maybe I was busy at that time, or maybe I thought, what's it to me? The truth is that the sisters were always out and about the town, particularly Anisha. So I don't think I found it unusual or anything . . .'

'Do you regret not asking them anything?'

'Yes, I do regret it, of course I regret it . . .'

'Do you think it has something to do with the rumours? That's why you didn't ask them perhaps?'

'No, it had nothing to do with the rumours . . . Wait, what do you mean by rumours? I don't know what you mean by rumours. Look, it's a small village—'

'That they were witches. Their grandmother said that . . . That there was some black magic . . .'

'Black magic? Witch? What witch? No, sir, you should not believe in all these things. I know you city people think these things happen in villages and rural areas because we are anpad and gawar and we don't know anything. But these things don't happen, sirji. That is your imagination . . .'

'Do you think the grandmother poisoned the sisters?'

'What? What are you saying? How can an Aaji poison her own granddaughters? Some people like spreading all this, Patrakar Saheb, don't believe in all these things.'

'But that's what the mother claims.'

'Achha, the mother said that? Maybe, I mean, I don't know. See, six years ago, when this happened, the family was not known to be particularly social. They didn't interact with others in the village or the town much. That is because of that disease. I don't know what disease, don't ask me the details, because I won't be able to help you there. But they were . . . outcasts, that's what they were. Imagine, this is the only stationery store in the area and I have never spoken to the mother or to the grandmother. Once or twice I spoke to Ajoba. He is a decent fellow, I think, but I mean, I don't sit here and judge people. All I know is that Anisha came to the shop with her sisters that day and it was afternoon and she bought three packets of Gems and then they went towards the petrol pump . . .'

'Someone saw them there, at the petrol pump.'

'Yes, yes, I know, someone saw them at the petrol pump. But I can't be sure about that. I can only tell you what I saw, and what I saw was pretty simple: the sisters came here, they bought what they had to buy, and then they walked towards the petrol pump. The next thing I hear is about the . . . it was unimaginable. Unimaginable. Even the way they were . . . for days I couldn't erase that image. I was awakened by the commotion, and I rushed out to the well when I heard someone say that the sisters had been found. I thought they must have found the kidnapper or something. I knew the sisters were missing. I knew that, and I told everyone who would care to listen to me that I am willing to help. That I may be one of the last people to have seen them, so I am willing to help the police. No problem. But the police never came to me. The police never asked me anything. Nobody from the authorities bothered about me, even though I was one of the last to have seen them alive. Imagine that, Patrakar Saheb.'

Janhavi

Every once in a while Janhavi drew a sketch that resembled her long-lost and perhaps even long-forgotten friend Priyanka. It had only been six years, but people had moved on. For a while, not unlike the rest of them, Janhavi, too, had forgotten the three sisters. It had been difficult to forget Priyanka, but it is a fact that almost no one is irreplaceable in life, and Janhavi, after all, was only nine at that time: eventually, like everyone else and everything else, she had moved on.

But, of course, moving on is never that easy either.

What she remembered from those horrid days of February 2013 was the weather. It had been cold, but it was always cold in February. It was the sudden change in the weather that had bothered her. The cold getting colder because of the rains, and the greyish-black clouds dampening the mood. It seemed as if the monsoon had set in unnaturally early. The day after the bodies were found, a pool of muddy water had formed outside Janhavi's house. She had seen her face reflected in that pool, that is what she remembered, although sometimes she tended to think that it was Priyanka's face and not hers. It was that reflected face or what she remembered of that reflection in the water that Janhavi repeatedly sketched, one after the other, until she thought she had the image right.

Not always, though. It wasn't as if she was obsessed. She sketched other things too: crows perched on branches, squirrels scurrying on windowsills, cute little puppies on the street . . . But more often than not—eight times out of ten—when she tried to draw something, secretly, inside her classroom, she ended up drawing a face that made her think, always, of Priyanka. Sometimes it was just the face: a sad smile with a touch of mischief, the eyes lowered and hair tied up in pigtails. But sometimes it was Priyanka standing or sitting, at some distance, against the background of paddy fields, trees and a well. Often, it was just two little girls with pigtails, holding hands, happy.

Janhavi had never shown those pictures to anyone. Until now.

She had seen this person around their village two days ago. He had been asking a tea seller: 'What can you tell me about them? Those sisters?'

'Which sisters?' someone sipping tea had asked him. Then this person glanced into his notebook and said their names: Anisha, Sanchita, Priyanka. 'What can you tell me about them?'

Apparently, he was a journalist. Janhavi, fifteen now, knew what a journalist did: he appeared on TV or wrote in the newspapers. This one had no camera with him, so maybe he was writing for the newspapers. That was good: maybe he could tell her what had happened to her friend?

It was a Sunday, and she had been sitting in front of the tea shop, waiting for her friend Bhushan. This is what they did, usually: they met in front of the tea stall, which was somewhere between Murwani's outer limits and the national highway, and then they roamed the outskirts of the town, looking for birds, animals and insects in the bushes. Bhushan loved these creatures, particularly the rarities. Once, he had rescued a bat pup from the forest and walked all the way to Janhavi's place to show it to her. He expected her to sketch the pup as it sat with its wings folded on the edge of his palm. 'I know I won't get to keep it,' he had said, 'but I want to remember its face. Make a sketch.'

Bhushan was late, which was rare because it was usually Bhushan who was the first to arrive. While waiting for him on a bench laid down in front of the tea stall, she had heard this man with a rucksack on his back and goggles on his face ask the tea-stall owner about the three sisters. It had been a while since she had heard those words: 'the three sisters'. Tya teen bahini.

'You are from the CBI?' the tea-stall owner had asked the man as he handed him a cup.

'CBI? No,' the man said, screwing his face and adjusting his goggles. 'Did they hand over the case to the CBI?'

'I think so.'

'Is there anyone—I am a journalist. I am writing a book about the three sisters. Is there anyone I can talk to? It's not about the crime per se. It's about the three sisters. I want to write about the three sisters.'

Three sisters, three sisters, three sisters.

'I don't know,' the tea-stall owner said and offered a jar of biscuits to the journalist. The journalist ignored the tea seller's offer and sipped on his tea in silence.

'Go inside the town, you will find someone there,' one of the tea-sipping customers advised, pulling out a ten-rupee note from the upper pocket of his shirt and handing it to the tea seller.

'This isn't the town?'

'No, this is the highway. Only factory workers and truck drivers here. Go inside.'

Janhavi watched as the journalist nodded and thanked the man. Then he pulled on his rucksack, paid for his tea and started walking towards the town.

Ganpule Sir

(Excerpts from an interview transcript. Interview conducted on 14 March 2019.)

'I will try and recall that day as well as I can. My memory doesn't serve me as well as it used to once, which is why I sought retirement from the school in the first place—'

'But weren't you suspended?'

'Yes, but they never found a replacement with my kind of experience, a replacement who can teach three or four subjects. It's not easy to replace Ganpule Sir. Besides, my salary was a pittance, the others asked for huge sums. They were professors and all, laid off from their college jobs. So they were used to big salaries and aaram and all. But Ganpule Sir is hardworking, the school knew that, so once the matter went silent, about six months or so later, they just hired me back quietly. And no one even questioned it. Why should they? It's not as if *I* killed the girls, no? I mean I was treated with a bit of scorn for a little while because I don't know, maybe because they felt I was careless, but it passed and everyone forgot about it in another year. Now toh no one even associates me with that incident. Because most of those who are here don't remember it as well as they used to, and the other thing is that a lot of those who were here then have moved on . . .'

'Where?'

'Sorry?'

'Moved on where?'

'To cities and towns . . . Mumbai, Pune, Nagpur, Raipur, Bhopal. I don't know. They are not here. Even the mother, na . . . she also left. Only that Ajoba is here, and he keeps muttering things. I never met him, Murwani is not a village anymore, it is a fairly big town now, with the trucks and all. So . . . I didn't even know Janhavi that well, one of the sisters—'

'Priyanka.'

'Sorry?'

'Priyanka, you mean, the sister.'

'Oh yes, oh yes. Janhavi was her friend. Right. But I didn't know them well. They were quiet children, and the girls here have always been quiet. Doing their homework and their schoolwork diligently. They get decent jobs outside. They make money. What else do you need these days? But yes, Priyanka I didn't know well. And I am not sure how this will help you, but you know I have always wanted to say this: I am not guilty. No one thinks I am, of course, not now, but this has been on my mind ever since, you know, it just comes back to me sometimes, how people treated Ganpule Sir.

'So, I was teaching them English. They were very eager to learn English, I remember that. These girls. Very curious. I am not talking about Janhavi or Priyanka particularly. I am just saying all the girls. Curious and enthusiastic. So I was teaching them English and the elder sister comes in and says: Ganpule Sir, I need to take Priyanka along. And I said: What for? And she said: Someone has called her. Now people say that the elder sister said Mummy, Mummy has called them, but she didn't say that to me. She didn't say Mummy or anything. At least I don't remember it that way. She did say someone, someone has called them, but I don't remember who. And these things happen. There's some problem with something at home, someone is sick, some old person is going to die, some old person needs to be taken to the hospital . . . Yes, she said, there's an emergency. Not someone has called them, an emergency. Now I remember. Hundred per cent that's what she said. So how could I say no? They had two elderly people at home, their Aaji and Ajoba, so I thought okay maybe something might have happened to one of them. They didn't have a father, and they were close to their grandfather, so I didn't ask that elder sister about the emergency. An emergency is an emergency, it's better to ask questions after it has passed. So I said okay, take that girl—Priyanka? Priyanka along. Okay. How would I have known about what was to happen? It's impossible to look into the future. No one even thought about this. All of them just blamed me. Ganpule Sir's carelessness. You tell me, your Ajoba is fighting for his life and I keep asking you questions about your emergency, would that be the right thing to do? No, of course not. But no, Ganpule Sir is to be blamed. Ganpule Sir this, Ganpule Sir that. Ganpule Sir for annual function, Ganpule Sir to manage the accounts, Ganpule Sir to watch over the children, Ganpule Sir to distribute the meals and then Ganpule Sir to be blamed for carelessness.

'Anyway, that's all that happened that day, as far as I am concerned.'

Godambe

(Excerpts from an interview transcript. Interview conducted on 21 February 2019.)

'What happened to Dighole. That's a good question, but I don't know the answer to it, and I don't quite understand why you, Chutranshu, are concerned with it.'

'I am writing a book on the incident.'

'What kind of book?'

'A true crime story.'

'What are you going to get out of it?'

'I don't know. Satisfaction. It's a story that I have been obsessed about, Godambe Saheb, come on.'

'You got piss drunk, you fucked a woman and then you went and wrote a front-page article. What else do you need? Why do you want to write a book about this? That case was hot then. No one has spoken about it for six years. No one spoke about it two months after it happened. Nobody . . . Do you know they are saying it could have been an accident? Did you know that? Turns out, Dighole was right all along, that gaandu.'

'Well, what happened to him?'

'He was killed by one of the Aangles. Some Mama-Tama. Then this Mama got bail and that case was never heard of again either.'

'So nobody knows who killed Dighole? And what happened that night?'

'Someone does, but I don't. And I don't know who that someone could be. Maybe go and ask the Aangles.'

'You told me you used to track the case's progress.'

'For a little while I did. But then the heat wave started and there was some problem with the orange festival, and someone else came for a feature story on tiger attacks . . . People move on, Chutranshu, I thought you would be somewhere in Delhi by this time, some top editor-veditor with a national newspaper, something like that.'

'Well.'

'Are you married?'

'No.'

'How old are you?'

'Thirty-one.'

'Then get married. Focus on those things. These things are in the past, no one cares about them anymore. Least of all the people here.'

'But they never solved the case. There were three sisters and they died, and no one was bothered.'

'You are one to speak. Were *you* bothered? You were supposed to ask tough questions and all. But who are we kidding, Chutranshu? You know it's one of those cases, one of those things. It's all in the past, let's move on. Let's look ahead.'

'I can't. I need to get to the bottom of this.'

'Aai chi gaand tujhya. You are watching too much Bollywood these days, chutiya. Bottom of this. There is no bottom to this. The lip of the well was small, the girls screwed around and then screwed up and fell into it and got themselves killed. They were reckless, and their recklessness killed them. That's what happened. Now go write your book.'

'They were raped, too, na Godambe. Come on, you are being recorded, let's be a little serious here.'

'Ae shanya, you don't teach me serious-verious, haan. Be within your limits, ek tar you are not from around here. One call and you will be thrown out, kalla ka? And the sisters weren't raped. Get your basics right, aai zavli. It's been years, chutiya, why are you after this?'

'I told you. I am writing a book. I want—'

'I will tell you a story for your book. See if you want to pursue it. I met a crime reporter once who was sent by his Mumbai-based editor to cover an important story about a crime in these rural heartlands but the crime reporter got drunk with a suspended Police Inspector and a local lukhya and then fucked a local randi and knocked her up and went back and wrote a fake story and is now doing the same thing all over again, which makes him what? Which makes him a loser, but the madarchod doesn't realize it. Go write that story.'

Janhavi

'Do you still go to that school? The same school?'

'No, she goes to a convent school now. I was promoted at the factory a year or so after that incident, so I decided to pull her out of that school and enrol her in a good school. It costs us a little bit more money, but Janhavi doesn't mind. Do you mind, Janhavi? No, she says.'

'How do you feel now, Janhavi?'

'She lost her speech for a little while, you know. Priyanka was . . . they always used to play together. They always used to be together. It was really hard on her. Only last year we told her about what actually happened to Priyanka.'

'Can she speak now?'

'Can you, Janhavi? Tell our Patrakar Dada. Say something. Only Baba is speaking he will say.'

'I can.'

'Can you tell me something about Priyanka? Whatever you can remember.'

'Tell dada. Your name will appear in the newspaper. Her photo also, na?'

'Actually I am writing a book. About the sisters. So . . . but her name will appear, yes.'

'Photograph also, Janhavi. Say something.'

'Only if you are comfortable.'

'Priyanka was my best friend . . . I don't really remember all that much about her. She . . . we used to play together. She was my best friend. I loved her. We were always together. Ever since we were children . . . but I don't remember her much now.'

'Do you miss her?'

'Sometimes.'

'When?'

'When I see children playing. I see them and I remember how we used to play. All of us. But more than anybody else, I remember Priyanka the most. We used to play in the fields, and out there . . . behind the temple, too, sometimes. She used to rush off with her sisters after school, but I wasn't allowed, so she always used to tell me to drop off her bag home. But never the other sisters' bags. She used to say I belong to her, that I was her best friend, so I should only drop her bag and no one else's. Then in the afternoon we would finish our homework and meet and we would go and play in the fields. Langdi dhawki and pakda pakdi . . . and we used to eat berries. I think about Priyanka when I see the berry tree. She loved those berries. I can't eat berries now because I keep thinking about her when I eat them. So I just quit eating berries . . .'

'This is good. Continue.'

'She always used to complain to her Mummy—'

'Mummy meaning the grandmother?'

'No, she used to call her mother Mummy. She always used to complain to her mother about the eldest sister stealing money to buy chocolates. Sometimes they even used to give me chocolates. They had a lot of money, because the eldest one stole money. And Priyanka never used to like it.'

'What else do you remember?'

'Priyanka was my best friend. She was never afraid of anything. She scolded her sisters, and she used to tell me when they did something wrong.'

'Something wrong as in?'

'They used to steal money. They would go and buy chocolates and other costly things for themselves. They weren't bothered about time and what others would say. But Priyanka was not like that. Priyanka was scared of her mother, and she was very particular about homework. She always encouraged me to study hard.'

'Priyanka was an intelligent child, Patrakar Saheb, very intelligent. You know how that family's reputation is, but we didn't mind Janhavi going around with that girl because she was very sharp and she was good in studies, so we thought Janhavi might learn a thing or two . . . Bichari got caught up with her sisters, otherwise she might have had a bright future.'

Janhavi didn't really know why she chose to show the journalist her sketches, but she did. Her father was as surprised as the journalist, but her mother showed no emotion. She simply glanced at the sketches and grunted, far too loudly.

'So this is what you do instead of homework?' her father asked her playfully. 'Look, Patrakar Saheb, isn't she talented?'

'Very,' the journalist uncle said and asked them if he could click a picture of the sketches on his mobile phone.

'Yes, yes, of course,' Janhavi's father said, adjusting the notebook such that the journalist uncle could click his pictures comfortably.

That is when her Aai chose to speak. 'What is the meaning of all this?' she said, looking not at the journalist but at Janhavi's father. 'The girls died six years ago. They lived their lives and they died. What is the point of living in their memories and living in the past, you tell me?' This time she looked at the journalist, who stopped clicking the pictures.

'I am . . . madam, it's not about—I mean, they were girls. And don't you want to know who killed them?'

'What's it to us?'

'One of the sisters . . . Priyanka was your daughter's friend.'

'I don't need you to tell me that. My daughter has suffered enough. All we want for her is to grow up and marry into a good family and get out of this life. That's all we want. She keeps sketching these things.' Now Janhavi's mother looked at her father. 'What should we make of them? It took her four years to make new friends, did you know that? She didn't have friends. She couldn't do well in that school, which is why we had to admit her into a convent school. We don't like the convent school, but she failed twice in that Murwani Vidya Sadan. All because of those sisters. All because those sisters chose to die. Priyanka, Priyanka, Priyanka. Don't we have our own lives to live? It's done. They died. Now let us live in peace.'

The journalist uncle left soon after Janhavi's mother's outburst but not before he clicked some more pictures, smiled at Janhavi and told her not to worry. But why would she worry? She was, in fact, happy. Here was someone who was willing to solve the mystery of her friend's death. Here was someone who could find answers to all those questions Janhavi had been asking herself for six years. Perhaps she would finally be able to stop sketching all those images of berry trees and wells and lonely girls in paddy fields.

Anjali Shukla, IPS

(Excerpts from an interview transcript. Interview conducted on 23 February 2019.)

'I am not sure what you want from me. I can't give you a lot of details, because I wasn't on that case for very long, as you would know. I was transferred soon after. Maybe about four or five months after I started investigating the case, since it took so much time to gather the details. Then they handed over the case to the SDPO, and I think now it's with the CBI.

'See, what I know is this: it had rained that night, and the rains made it impossible to establish anything clearly in terms of the sexual assault and in terms of the murder. What exactly happened? See, the girls disappeared on the afternoon of 14 February. Sometime between twelve and three. The family did not notice their disappearance until about eight-thirty or nine. Then they started searching for the girls, and finally reached the police station at around nine-thirty. This I remember. I think it was someone called Gunde, Inspector Ghole—'

'Dighole.'

'I am sorry. Yes. PI Dighole. He sent the family back saying the girls would eventually turn up. But they didn't, and the locals launched a manhunt. Some people went to the police station and there was some violence. Public property was destroyed. PI Dighole should have alerted us then, but he didn't. He waited. The bodies were found at around dawn, between five and six, I think. This is what I remember about that day. It's been a long time, and I—Can I say something off the record?'

'Sure, madam.'

'Well, I don't think about the cases that I have failed to solve, quite honestly. I could have solved this case, but they transferred me. Have they reached any conclusion about it?'

'No, madam, which is why I am writing the book.'

'Okay. Listen, you can contact Deshmukh. Inspector Deshmukh. He was on that case. I can find out his contact if you want me to.'

'That would be very helpful, madam, thank you very much.'

'I will WhatsApp his number. What happened to Dighole by the way? I never heard from him again.'

'He was killed by someone in the village, madam.'

'Oh. Related to the case?'

'I don't think so.'

'Oh. Unfortunate. Unfortunate. Anyway, I'll send you Deshmukh's number, haan, you contact him.'

'Thank you, madam.'

Reportage

The village of Murwani stands somewhere along the Mumbai–Kolkata Highway. Blink and you will miss it. Or at least that's how many would have described it before 2013, and that's how many would describe it today. But for a brief period of time in 2013, specifically between February and perhaps May of that year, everyone knew Murwani, everyone knew its location, everyone knew how to get there and everyone was aware of why people were going there. And by the end of February 2013, a lot of people were going there: police vans, police jeeps, politicians flanked by private security guards and ministers surrounded by the NSG; cameramen and reporters, local news channels and newspapers and magazines and dailies and international publications—everyone wanted a grip on the case.

But what was the case? On the afternoon of 14 February, as the world celebrated Valentine's Day, three young sisters, living, playing and growing up in Murwani, which is about 90 kilometres from Maharashtra's winter capital, Nagpur, and around 850 kilometres north-east of state capital Mumbai, disappeared. A search was launched, and by the dawn of 15 February, with all hopes fading, came the tragic news that would shake the village, the state and—some would say this only cautiously, however—the nation: the bodies of the three sisters were found floating inside a well on the outskirts of the village, a couple of metres away from the highway.

But six years later, this is still pretty much all that we know about the incident. Were the sisters murdered? Were they sexually assaulted? Did they fall into the well together? Was this a suicide pact, imposed upon innocent minds by someone they knew? What exactly happened to the three sisters?

As outrageous as it may seem, no one knows. And the only truth we have is that the sisters disappeared on the afternoon of 14 February and their bodies were found at around 5.30 a.m. on the morning of 15 February. Beyond that, it was open season.

I decided that the sisters deserved better than that.

At that time I was a twenty-five-year-old rookie reporter from Mumbai on his first assignment outside the city. I wasn't very young, but I was young enough to think of it as a thrilling assignment. The story was my first front page, and I was proud of it, and so, I remember, was my editor. Overall, the *story* itself was a success, but it was just an editorial success. I wrote it, I filed it and then I moved on to other things. Life went on, and I must admit that for a couple of years I wasn't really following up on the story of the three sisters, until one day I came across my notebook from that day, filled up with details and observations which I would eventually cut out of the printed story. But when I read those notes, I asked myself two questions: what happened to those sisters and their case? And can this be turned into a book, one that would try and understand the story of the village and its people and then juxtapose it with the story of the crime?

By the time I found my notebook, my career as a journalist was stuck. Or at least that's how I had begun to feel, as if I was doing nothing worthwhile, as good journalists should. And when I found out that the case had languished all these years without any solution, it deepened my career crisis, plunging me into a vortex of questions. Why is journalism vital if all we do is write a 'mood piece' and a 'spot copy' about a heinous crime that ought to make us question our very existence? What use is journalism if it's a pillar that doesn't shake and doesn't challenge the democracy that it claims to support? If journalism is merely running after the latest story and the latest trend, as it is today, while falling at the feet of power because the power controls your salaries, I decided that I didn't want to be a part of this rut.

So I quit my job and left for Murwani. As one could imagine, it wasn't an easy decision, but I felt that it was a decision I had to make. To save myself, but also to pay attention to the obsession that had been gnawing at me for years, perhaps ever since I left Murwani that night in the February of 2013.

Sugandha Miss

(Excerpts from an interview transcript. Interview conducted on 14 March 2019.)

'Can you introduce yourself?'

'My name is Sugandha Ramkrishna Junghare. Actually I teach Marathi and Hindi at Murwani Vidya Sadan.'

'And you used to teach the three sisters?'

'Actually I taught Sanchita and Priyanka. But I knew Anisha. I never taught her.'

'What can you tell me about that day?'

'Actually I don't remember much about that day. Except that there was a meeting that day. A teacher's meeting.'

'What was the meeting about?'

'Actually I don't know. Because I didn't attend that meeting.'

'Why didn't you?'

'The women teachers were told to manage the classes. All the sirs attended that meeting.'

'But you must have heard about what happened inside the meeting later.'

'Yes, someone said it was about salary cuts. Udasse Sir told us the management had asked for the salaries of teachers to be cut.'

'So you were inside the class at that time.'

'Yes, I was with my class. Actually I was that class's class teacher. Actually I still am.'

'Which class?'

'Fifth standard.'

'Priyanka's class?'

'Yes.'

'Didn't you notice Priyanka's absence then?'

'There were so many children at that time. And I remember I thought Priyanka was absent. I didn't check the attendance book. My mistake . . . actually I was unwell at that time.'

'You teachers were really careless.'

'Actually I was unwell at that time, that's why.'

'So then—'

'And there are many children inside the fifth-standard class. In sixth standard they get divided into sections A and B, but in fifth standard everyone is together.'

'Okay. So but then . . . okay, what can you tell me about Priyanka?'

'Priyanka was studious and Sanchita was quiet. Actually she was average in her studies.'

'Who? Sanchita?'

'Yes. She was average, just like Anisha.'

'Go on.'

'That's what I remember about them.'

'How were they otherwise? Priyanka and Sanchita?'

'Priyanka was intelligent. Very studious.'

'Yes, you already said that.'

'She used to complete her homework always. She also had a friend. Janhavi her name was.'

'Yes. But Priyanka . . . I mean, can you remember anything else? Any memory that particularly struck you when you heard about her death?'

'Actually she was very studious . . . and Sanchita was very average as a student . . .'

Pranil–Prateek

(Excerpts from an interview transcript. Interview conducted on 19 March 2019.)

'I don't want to talk about it.'

'What did they—'

'I don't want to talk about it. I want to forget all that.'

'Dada was beaten by the police. Black and blue.'

'You are his brother na? What is your name?'

'Prateek.'

'And age?'

'Eighteen.'

'Tell me.'

'The police hit Dada. When he came home—'

'Prateek, I don't want to talk about it.'

'No, Dada. They have to know what the police did to you.'

'No one has to know anything. It's all in the past.'

'The police hit Dada, and when he came home he was bleeding.'

'What did they pick you up for?'

'There . . . It was all fraud. I was—no one was . . . let's not talk about this.'

'They said that my brother was having an affair with Anisha. But he wasn't. They just wanted to beat up everybody.'

'Did you complain about it?'

'No.'

'Why not?'

'Our uncle wanted to put the matter to rest. After they cleared Pranil and said that he wasn't involved with the murder, everyone just wanted to move on.'

'But did you have an affair with Anisha?'

'No, of course not!'

'Why *of course* not? You were of the same age, right?'

'I did not have *any* affair with anyone.'

'Can I talk to your uncle? Where is he?'

'He has left the village.'

'So does he live nearby? Around here?'

'No.'

Narayani Bawane

(Excerpts from an interview transcript. Interview conducted on 15 March 2019.)

'Is that your daughter?'

'Yes.'

'How old is she?'

'Six.'

'What is your name?'

'Sheetal Arvind Bawane.'

'Hello Sheetal. Nice to meet you. She is six years old . . . it has almost been the same amount of time as the—'

'Yes. Sheetal, go wait outside with Ajoba, I will be back in fifteen minutes . . . People tell me that that girl is like a reincarnation. I was friends with their mother. She told me that she looked at my daughter as her own. But then she left the village soon after and hasn't returned since.'

'What can you tell me about that day?'

'It's only been six years, but it seems as if it all happened many decades ago. I still remember Anisha's face. That moon-like face peeking through the door and asking me what I was preparing for lunch, even though she knew that lunch was always the same. Sometimes she brought along tiffin, but often she simply ate the food I prepared because she liked that food and she didn't like her lunch.'

'What did she do with the tiffin then?'

'Who knows? It was always stale.'

'Did she eat in school that day?'

'No. She was . . . going out.'

'You saw her?'

'I did. It has troubled me ever since. I don't sleep at night, thinking: I really should have asked her where she was going. I should have shown more concern. But I knew Anisha. She wanted freedom. She craved freedom more than anything else. It was because of the situation at their home. Their father died due to some illness, and all those years . . . the sisters were neglected. You think they are surrounded by people, you think they have so many people at home, but they were actually very lonely, those sisters. They didn't have any friends. Only Priyanka had a good friend outside that circle.'

'Yes, Janhavi.'

'Janhavi. That child was devastated when she heard about it. No one told her anything concretely, and for the longest time she thought . . . she really did hope her friend would return. They were innocent children, and I still see a lot of them, their classmates, but I can't ask them if they think about the sisters. I don't think they do. No one here really thinks about the sisters, you must have seen that for yourself.'

'They have other things to do.'

'But how can you forget the deaths of three young children? Three innocent little souls?'

'I don't know what to say. I have felt the same way for the past six years. But I don't know. Maybe we forget the dead who don't directly matter to us. And maybe we, too, forget them all too quickly. I don't know.'

'Yes. Maybe I am more affected because of my guilt. I should have told Anisha not to go anywhere that day. I should have told her to run straight back to school. She was my responsibility, after all. But I valued her attention, for some reason. Anisha had a way of doing that. She didn't pay attention to a lot of people, always in her own world, but when she did pay attention, she made you feel as if you were a part of her world, as if you were special. That's how I felt. So I let her be. I let her feel as if I was an accomplice in her adventures, someone who silently encouraged her. I was stupid.'

'And what about the other two?'

'They just followed her. What else could they do? They didn't have it in them to think for themselves.'

'Do you blame Anisha for this? I have heard a lot of people say that. That the eldest sister led them to their deaths.'

'That is nonsense. They were raped and they were killed and everyone was outraged for a couple of days. But I will tell you, most of the men here would do it if they were told you would never be caught or arrested or whatever. They would do it. Rape is just a . . . it's just a crime for them. They don't really care about whether it goes against a woman and her freedom. It's just a crime, so you take away the punishment and the police and then it simply turns into a game—a game you can play because you want to and a game you don't play because you don't want to.'

'I know many of my friends who would probably do it too.'

'Then you should not keep such company.'

'What did Anisha say to you, that day when you met her?'

'She said they were going somewhere because their mother was calling them. She was with her sisters.'

'What time was this?'

'I don't remember. But school time. The worst part is that I knew she was bluffing, but I didn't stop her.'

'So . . . you were the one who heard about hurda?'

'No, that was Janhavi. I . . . Janhavi didn't want to say anything. She told it to me and I wrote it in that note.'

'That was the biggest lead.'

'I don't know about that. But it didn't lead anywhere. Now they are saying the sisters died in an accident or that they . . . killed themselves. Either way, I should have stopped them.'

Santosh Ranmukhe, Witness

(Excerpts from an interview transcript. Interview conducted on 5 March 2019.)

'It is difficult for me now. I hope you understand.'

'Take your time. I just need to know what happened. How did you stumble upon the bodies? That's it. It doesn't have to be about anything else.'

'I have . . . it has taken me a lot of time to get over it. I don't know if I can . . .'

'Take your time, Santosh.'

'At that time I was coming back from Ahneri—'

'That late?'

'I went to Ahneri for a marriage, but I forgot about a meeting I had with a businessman from Pune that day. On 15 February. The police have checked this. Anant Dada Pawar, the businessman's name. I am still in touch with him. I was supposed to meet him, but I completely forgot and went to the marriage. The meeting was scheduled for 8 a.m., and I needed to seal it because business wasn't going well. I needed some support, I needed my dung cakes to have outside exposure, so that I could expand the business and draw in more money. I had my children's school fees and other expenses to take care of, and things weren't going well. So I woke up very early on that day and decided to hitch a ride back. Some trucks are always going that way, and luckily I was picked up by one almost immediately after I reached the highway. It wasn't much of a distance, but I had to go home and prepare some papers. The temple-side area, I don't know it very well. I am not a very outgoing person, and whenever I do go outside, I go in a shared rickshaw or on a bike, I don't walk. But that day the truck left me by the highway and I started walking into the village from the temple side. Dawn was just breaking, I remember, and I was a little thirsty. So I spotted the well as I walked and decided to stop by the well and draw some water. The walk to the well was really difficult because of the rains the previous night. It had stopped raining by then, of course, and I was thinking of giving up on this well and trying at the next when I almost slipped and fell. But I found my balance and for some reason continued walking. That is how Parmeshwar intended it, maybe. He wanted me to find those little girls . . . and that's how it happened.'

'Can you describe it a little more? That moment. When you saw the bodies.'

'No. I have tried to forget it for a long time. I can't.'

'Okay. Fair enough. What happened then?'

'I was scared, and I screamed and I went running to the village. I bumped into Tatya. Tatya Khandle, the social worker, the right-hand man of that MLA. I don't remember his name. He came to the village after that once, I remember. So I bumped into Tatya—Ghotya his name is. That MLA's. I am sorry. I told Tatya about the bodies. I was scared. I didn't know what I was saying. Bobdich valli hoti. I couldn't even speak properly. I wasn't aware of what I was saying, quite frankly. Let alone recall it now. I don't know what I told Tatya. I didn't understand what I was saying. I thought I was going to have a heart attack. I just told Tatya and Tatya said he will call the police, calm down, bhau, don't worry, and I said okay, I will go home then, and I went home and I lay down. I didn't think about my meeting, or about anything else, I just slept. It . . . I don't know why I did that. When I woke up, it was already all over the place, but the police, I remember, were clueless. They asked me about this two or three days later, when everything had died down a little. That's what happened. They recorded my statement and then they left me.'

'Did they ask about Tatya?'

'Ask what?'

'About you meeting Tatya? Did they say anything about that?'

'No. I don't think so. No. I don't remember.'

'Did you tell them that you bumped into Tatya?'

'No. You don't take Tatya's name that easily around here. He was a bigshot. In fact, he got my business up and running here in this village, like everybody else's. With a little influence, a little money. You know, those things. So people don't—You have to understand these little things. If you saw Tatya or met Tatya in uncomfortable places or at uncomfortable hours, you kept mum and carried on with your life. You didn't say anything about it.'

'Achha.'

'Haan. That's how it is. And I didn't say a word about Tatya and Tatya never said anything to me about that day. The police took some statements and then for some time they kept bothering me about this and that, but eventually no one was really concerned. And that was it, as far as I am concerned.'

Bhushan

Bhushan loved the feeling of those pomegranate-red rain bugs scuttling across his palm and settling on his fingertips. Janhavi hated those bugs, but then she hated all insects: she never painted or sketched bugs. Always obsessed with her squirrels and her sparrows. Not that Bhushan didn't like squirrels or sparrows, but there was more to the natural world.

Bhushan didn't really hate anything or anyone. It was true that he didn't like the company of people in general, but he didn't hate them. And of course there were exceptions: he loved his parents, he loved Janhavi—his only friend—and sometimes he thought he loved his brother Ravi, even though Ravi ignored him most of the time. In a lot of ways they were poles apart. Ravi liked his cricket and his cars, and he dreamt of opening his own car shop one day. Preferably in a city. Bhushan, on the other hand, wanted nothing to do with any village, town or city: he wanted to live with his birds and his insects and his animals. Preferably inside a forest. Away from all this.

Janhavi wanted something similar. She was elder to him by two years, and their friendship had started spontaneously one day when Janhavi was sitting by the temple, writing something in her notebook, and Bhushan was trying to get Lukhya, one of the stray dogs, to sit down. 'Bas, Lukhya, ne bas!' Janhavi ended up laughing at Bhushan's futile attempts, and then she had tried to sketch them, Lukhya and Bhushan. Bhushan loved that sketch: it was as if she had clicked a photograph! At least that's how he had felt then.

Now Bhushan and Janhavi were inseparable. They didn't talk much, but they liked each other's company. Sometimes Janhavi would start talking about something that had happened in her class, or something that her mother had said to her, and Bhushan would listen and nod, even though he didn't always understand what she was telling him. Like that day when she told him that she couldn't stop sketching the paddy fields and wells and her friend Priyanka standing by those wells. Bhushan remembered Priyanka faintly. Or rather he remembered the three sisters, and he remembered that time when he had told the police uncle about Mullah Chacha and had received a Dairy Milk in return. Those were confusing days . . . there were so many people in the village and so many policemen.

The policemen scared Bhushan: they had taken away his brother Ravi and Ravi had returned home crying in pain. When Baba asked him where exactly it hurt, he pointed at his back and at his bum, but Bhushan couldn't see any scars or marks there. It must have hurt from the inside, but there was no doubt that the pain was real. Ravi had cried for days and nights after that, refusing to go to school or for that matter step out of the house at all. Bhushan didn't feel comfortable thinking about those days, so whenever Janhavi spoke to him about Priyanka, he kept mum and looked into the distance, trying to think about something else instead.

Janhavi continued to babble as Bhushan watched the rain bugs move across his palms and jump down on the ground. She was telling him about this journalist who was asking about the three sisters. Bhushan tried not to pay attention to her as she kept asking him whether he was listening.

'Bhushan . . . Bhushan, what did I say? Do you understand what I am saying? Priyanka . . . he is here to solve that case. He is here to tell us who killed my friend.'

'*I* am your friend,' Bhushan said, sitting down beside Janhavi now and laying down his arm so that the rain bugs rushed out and disappeared into the bushes.

'Yes, but so is Priyanka. He said: Who do you think killed her? I want him punished. I really want him punished.'

Bhushan sighed and closed his eyes. Why did Janhavi have to talk about her friend? That friend had brought nothing but misery in his house. And in this village. Why did they have to die?

'He is going to everyone and asking. He will find out. Surely he will find out.'

'Is he from the police?' Bhushan asked because if he was from the police, he should warn Ravi and tell him to stay away, skip school, hide somewhere for the time being.

'I don't think so. He is a journalist.'

'TV wala?'

'I don't think so. But he is going to solve this case, you will see.'

'But if he is not from the police, how can he solve a case?'

'He is from Mumbai.'

'Mumbai?'

'Yes. Do you know where Mumbai is, Bhushan?'

'No.'

'Well, he is from Mumbai. Very far away.'

'But he is not from the police?'

'I don't think so.'

Bhushan was about to ask another question, but then he spotted something jumping in the bushes and he forgot everything about Priyanka and the police and the journalist. He peered at the spot where he had seen movement and there! He saw it again. Away he went after it.

Ganpat Lawane

(Excerpts from an interview transcript. Interview conducted on 26 February 2019.)

'Haan, bhau, you ask me whatever you want to ask.'

'I am here to talk about the three sisters' case.'

'Haan, bhau, I know. Word gets around.'

'So how did you know Tatya Khandle?'

'Haan, bhau, I was his right-hand man. Ganpat Lawane my name is. Ask anyone around here who Ganpat Lawane is and they will shit their pants.'

'Can you tell me a little bit about Tatya? Who was he, what did he do. All those things.'

'Haan, bhau, even Tatya couldn't tell you about himself, what do you expect? Tatya Bhau was Tatya Bhau. Ask anyone around here who Tatya Khandle was and they will shit their pants.'

'That day, when Santosh Ranmukhe found the bodies, he met Tatya. What was Tatya doing outside at that time?'

'Bhau, I would like it if you watch your tone, bhau. I am helping out. I want to help out. But you watch your tone. What was he doing? Haan, bhau, we all were outside. We all were searching for the girls. That night was very bad. I was quite young then. I was scared. I am not ashamed to say that. But when the community is in trouble, you have to stand up. That's what Tatya Bhau did. He stood up for his friend. Ajoba was Tatya Bhau's friend, did you know that? Always drank together when they were young. Tatya Bhau was rooted to this soil, bhau, he was a man of this land. These people loved him. These people worshipped him. That's what I want for myself.'

'So you were a part of the search party.'

'Haan, bhau. We were searching all night. Ask anyone and they will tell you. Ask anyone what Ganpat Lawane was doing that night and they will tell you.'

'Were you all drunk?'

'No. I mean I wasn't.'

'Then Tatya was?'

'I told you to mind your language, bhau, I told you. Or I will pull that tongue out and feed it to the dogs while it's still attached, bhau, I am telling you. You talk any rubbish about me, I am okay. No problem, dada. But don't say all this about Tatya Bhau. Tatya Bhau never drank. In his youth he did, but then he stopped. He never stopped anyone from drinking, but he never drank himself. Remember that.'

'Then the others were drunk? The others who were with you, in the search party?'

'Maybe. Maybe not. I don't remember.'

'Can you tell me a little bit about your search? Whatever you can remember.'

'Haan, bhau, we did a little bit here and there. We had returned from the police station. That Inspector was not much of a man. He saw us and he began to shit his pants. He had his gun out and all. But Tatya said nothing doing. Let them kill us, nothing doing. Whatever happens, we are going to help that Ajoba and we are going to fuck that guy. I don't remember his name but I remember he died the way he deserved to die. Getting killed by some bitch in the—'

'I am sorry. Are you talking about PI Dighole? Sanjay Dighole?'

'Haan, bhau. Dighole. That bastard was all—'

'Wasn't he killed by someone from the Aangle family? Some Mama?'

'Arey, bhau, that is all bullshit, I am telling you. Some bitch from the family killed him because he was molesting her. Or because she had been fucking him. Or because he had been fucking her. I don't know what their exact scene was, but some bitch killed him, that I know, bhau. For sure. But a woman of the Aangle family killing a man—people are bound to ask: What the fuck were the men of the family doing then, bhau? I will tell you about the Aangles. Fuckers are getting anal for the zilla parishad all of a sudden.

Why? They were never interested in politics, always interested in politicians. Now they are interested in politics. Why? They are expanding their business na, bhau, that is why. They are already into illegal liquor. Very bad quality. Now they want to enter the sand-mining business. Very lucrative, brings in money in crores, I have heard. Bhau, they are just fucking with me. Now that Tatya Bhau is gone, they are just fucking with me. I am telling you. You write about them. Leave this, write about them. Bastards have a lot of dirt under their nails. Just go and cut their nails and you will find three books to write. Not one, three.'

'Right now I just need to focus on this. Can you tell me what you mean when you say that you searched for the girls? Some details. I mean, can you be a little more specific?'

'Arey, bhau, even about this case. Even about this case you can go and ask the Aangles and I would like to see them answer. I remember what had happened at that time. At that time that Bawankule had raided—'

'Who is Bawankule?'

'Ratnakar Bawankule from the Excise Department. He had raided three of their factories. Somewhere in the khopchi. Bawankule knew about the factories, bhau. They had been there for years. But the Aangles suddenly had some problem with him and they stopped paying bribes or something like that. So the Excise Department started raiding. And, bhau, they arrested these women and teenagers and small children who were used to smuggle liquor to Nagpur. Bhau, that Aangle got frustrated. He told the press about a party in the zilla parishad office. That chutiya Charan Mudruk. That chutiya had a nice party in his chambers from morning to night. All money for the midday meal scheme, they used it up for the party. Mast videshi daaru na, bhau. But Aangle made a scene out of it, one year after that party, bhau. Imagine this—'

'No, but what about the case? The three sisters' case?'

'Arey, I am coming to that na, bhau. Have some patience. What was I saying? Behenchod, I forgot. This is the problem with you journalist people, behenchod, no patience. Haan, bhau, so that Aangle . . . Aangle started doing things to divert attention. Haan, that's what. He started doing things to divert attention from his factories. He started pointing fingers. But it wasn't enough. So he had the three girls killed. So that the matter would be sorted once and for all na, bhau. He thought killing young girls would attract national attention na, bhau. Rape and murder, you imagine. Arey, what you imagine, you were here na then. You are the reason he did this. You meaning the press and the politicians and all that. Mast juicy story and everyone picked it up and he was let off. That's what happened. No one cared about Aangle anymore. And Aangle continued with his business. Now he wants to enter the sand-mining business and fuck with me in the zilla parishad. That is what is happening, you write about that.'

Godambe

(Excerpts from an interview transcript. Interview conducted on 26 February 2019.)

'I know about the Aangles, Chutranshu, of course I know about them. What do you think? I have been reporting in this area for the past fifteen years, behenchod. Fifteen years I spent here. Nothing else, just reporting.'

'What have they got to do with the case?'

'They have a lot to do with a lot of cases. Dighole's, for example.'

'With the three sisters' case?'

'As far as I know, nothing. Why would the Aangles have anything to do with the three sisters' case?'

'Someone told me that they murdered the sisters to divert attention.'

'Divert attention from what? Their women fucking other men? Their women being the whores that they always wanted to be?'

'No. Some illegal liquor business. Raid by the Excise Department.'

'Are you moving around with a lot of Tatya's men, chutiya? Because if you are, you are going to get nowhere. First of all, there is nowhere to get to. If you ask me, you are wasting your time. Like you always have. And you are wasting your life. Because those girls killed themselves. Not because they wanted to, but because they were reckless and they slipped and they got killed. That's all there is to it, behenchod. You get it fixed in your head and focus on real things.'

Inspector Deshmukh

(Excerpts from an interview transcript. Interview conducted on 25 February 2019.)

'I don't remember much about the case. But I agreed because madam said I should tell you whatever I know. But what I know is minimal. Really minimal. Because that mother wanted the case to go straight to the CBI. She didn't trust us. She accused us of involvement with the local people. What local people, behenchod? Excuse me. I don't know what she was talking about. We did our work diligently. Dighole was incompetent, I am willing to say this on record. Om shanti to him, but he was incompetent and he did not act on time. Death shouldn't blind us to a person's mistakes. And his mistake was that he was too lazy. I know because that's how he was perceived in the police force here. Anyway, he was useless, Om shanti to him, but he was useless and we had to do his job. We did our job, and we faced the mother and her accusations. I mean—can I speak off the record?'

'Sure.'

'The mother was a mystery to everyone. She washed her house after her husband's death, as if there was some infection or all those memories needed to be washed off. She was called a witch. Now I don't believe in this business of witches and all, but I have seen some very twisted things happen in my time. Outside dargahs and all. They tie a black thread and they convert you to their Sufi Islam sect and then they try to do some jantar mantar and take your kidney out. There are these babas, Baba Taj and Baba Chhabisvi, who do these things. They do some jantar mantar and the next thing you know you are without a kidney or an eye. Do you know that sect? What was that song? Dama dam mast kalandar. Haan, that sect. They pluck your eyes out, you know that? These people are all savages. They were savages and they are savages. That's all there is to it. And this woman, this mother, she was influenced by some of them, I have heard—'

'Who told you this?'

'Arey, what you want my khabris now? Would you reveal your sources if I ask you to tell them to me so that we can compare notes? What sort of journalist are you, bhau?'

'Tell me what else you know, Inspector Saheb.'

'Haan, so this man, Kader, Kader Muhammad, we caught this man. He is from Rajasthan. That presents multiple possibilities. He is an illegal migrant from Pakistan. Because he doesn't have any identification documents. No papers. And now get this—his sons live in Kolkata and the Gulf. Imagine this, behenchod: he called them to send him some money and they disowned him. They disowned their father. They said: Do what you want to do with him, we don't give a shit. And they really didn't give a shit. Now you tell me, you are a Hindu, would you do something like that to your parents?'

'No.'

'Why? Because of our culture, dada. Our culture is not like that. Theirs is a foreign culture, that's why.'

'But did this Kader Muhammad meet the sisters?'

'I don't know about that. This Kader, so he was from Rajasthan. Tonk, in Rajasthan. Some village or town. And he used to come here to sell blankets for thirty years. For thirty years that's what he did, sold blankets. And gave chocolates to children. And people say he gave a chocolate to one of the sisters. Imagine that. Can you believe it? Selling behenchod blankets for thirty years, that's what he did. We caught him by the collar and fucked that guy. We investigated the shit out of him.'

'Where is he now?'

'Jail, bhau, jail. He is a terrorist. Out and out. Him and his friend. Nazir Ansari. It's very clear.'

'Did you get any proof?'

'What proof?'

'That he is a terrorist.'

'Isn't his name enough? No, but we had caught a terror module in Bhandara. They were planning something big—'

'In Bhandara?'

'No, behenchod. What are they going to do in Bhandara? Blow up paddy fields? No, they were involved with some module in Pune. We arrested thirty bastards. Including this Kader. They were planning something for Pune and Mumbai and Madhya Pradesh. All these termites.'

'What did you find out then?'

'I don't know, bhau. The case was transferred to the Maharashtra ATS. Now it's there. You ask the ATS what the progress is.'

'Okay, but what about this case? The three sisters?'

'Arey, leave the fucking three sisters. I am telling you, that terror case is bigger and juicier. You will get a lot more stuff there. I am telling you.'

'How could they find no one after all these years?' the grandfather of the sisters asks me. 'No one?'

He looks genuinely bewildered. We are sitting inside what was once the sisters' home. They used to live here, the seven of them. The three sisters, the grandparents and the parents. Their father worked at the nearby car factory as a mechanic and made a decent living. But then he got sick, and as he began descending into the depths of his disease, the family's fortunes started to dwindle. The father passed away in 2011, but the exact nature of his disease was still a matter of speculation in 2013.

'I mean, no one? There are so many suspects here. They caught a lot of people, I am told. But it was as if it was some other person's granddaughters, not mine, because I was never really kept informed. I only got to know things through people and through newspaper articles,' the grandfather says.

He is sitting on a chair while I am sitting on a rickety stool that the sisters used to climb on to display the cardboard trophies they won in their in-house dancing competitions.

And that is what the grandfather focuses on: the imaginative abilities of the three sisters. They were very innovative in their games, he says. 'They would hold dance competitions and they would ask me to judge them. And they always made trophies cut out of cardboard. The trophies always used to look real. They paid attention to what they did: dance, craft, singing, playing. Everything.'

It is quiet and peaceful outside. Nobody visits this house anymore, the grandfather says. His daughter-in-law has shifted to another town a couple of hours by road, for a job. The grandmother of the sisters died in 2015. Ajoba, as he is called around here, spends his time chanting mantras and, he says, 'talking with my granddaughters'.

'They speak to me in my dreams and I answer them when I wake up,' he says. This is a claim that cannot be verified, of course, but I nudge him to tell me more about what they say, his granddaughters. Do they tell him about the killer?

'No, they don't. I told you to stop asking such questions,' he snaps, before calming down. 'It was such a terrible tragedy,' he says after a brief pause in which he seemed to be gathering his thoughts, 'but no one seems to think so anymore. Now I am just a lonely grandfather to girls who are dead. They don't even say murdered these days, because they don't think the girls were murdered.' The grandfather stares into the distance, trying to control his voice.

What he says is true. Around Murwani, where the girls grew up, played and lived all their lives, no one seems to remember the incident, and those who do remember think that it was an accident and not a murder. The people here don't look scarred by the memories of those murders, they simply don't know what to do with that knowledge anymore. Take Shashikant Kerkar, a schoolteacher at Murwani Vidya Sadan, where the sisters used to attend classes: 'It's an old thing,' Kerkar says in Marathi. 'People have moved on.' When I ask him to describe the girls' faces, if he remembered them, he is quick to accept that he doesn't. 'What were their names again? Priyanka, Sangeeta and . . .?'

The new principal of the school remembers the incident in 'vivid detail' but says that he doesn't dwell on it. 'Life goes on, and anyway, that was an accident. What are you going to do about it now? We increased the security measures, of course. And nothing has happened ever since.'

It is in such an atmosphere of indifference that the grandfather is hanging on to his memories and his tales. He says there is nothing else to his life now. 'My granddaughters were my life. I blame myself sometimes, and I apologize to them every day. Every single day. Because I should have been more careful. I should have cared about them more. I should have been the one to keep an eye out for them, being the only male in the house. But I didn't. It was my mistake.'

Sometimes Ajoba calls himself the killer, but everyone in Murwani is in agreement that, to quote a local shopkeeper, 'The man is a gone case.' He certainly has been deeply affected by the incident and by the fact that no one seems to be concerned about it anymore—which is perhaps why people tolerate him and sometimes sympathize with him.

'Well, his granddaughters were killed. What do you expect?' says Ranjita Sugandha, who heads a Women Development Centre in the area and is an activist for the Rashtriya Ekta Gathan. 'I don't believe in the accident theory,' she says, adding that she is 'fully in support' of the family, whatever remains of it. 'I believe that the girls were raped and killed by a person named Kader Muhammad,' she claims, although no one really knows who the person is. He was among the blanket-sellers who used to visit the area from Rajasthan to do business, and had been involved in the trade for thirty years. Now he is in jail, but for a different reason: Kader Muhammad has been accused of terrorism, and of plotting 'secessionist and terrorist activities' and procuring funding from Pakistan, Bangladesh and Dubai.

'He is a terrorist, a rapist and a murderer,' Ranjita declares. Kader's 'terror case' is still being investigated by the Maharashtra ATS and there has been no conclusion yet to the case of the three sisters.

'We have been writing letters to the SP to get this case moving and not assume anything just yet. We have been requesting for a more thorough investigation with Kader Muhammad as the prime suspect. But the police don't seem to be interested,' Ranjita says, in effect criticizing an administration led by the party she is a member of.

'That doesn't matter,' she says when I point that out to her. 'Justice,' she says, 'is far more important than politics.'

Shanti Borkute

(Excerpts from an interview transcript. Interview conducted on 7 March 2019.)

'The sisters came to live with us after the death of their father. I am their aunt, their mother's sister, and my name is Shanti. I didn't care much for my sister, and I still don't, but the siblings were innocent.

I didn't have anything against them. Why hold grudges against children? My sister is a vile woman. She used to abuse me and my husband and our children when her husband was alive. About this thing or that. Property and money. That's all she cared about and I think she still does. I don't think she loved her daughters as much as she says she does, but who knows? She might have changed. I don't have any contact with her, and I want it to remain that way.

'The reason I agreed to talk to you was because I felt bad about what happened with the three girls. They died in a horrific manner—when I heard about it I cried the entire day. And now, even in their death, they don't have any dignity. I liked the girls. I can't say I didn't. Their financial position was poor, and our financial position is better, as you can see, but of course that's because they didn't have a father. No earning member as such. It was all very sad, so when they came to our house, I decided that the least I could do was let them have some fun. I had an argument with my husband about this. He didn't want them to stay for more than three days. But I said let them stay for a week. Let them compose themselves. They are helpless, those poor things. My husband wasn't convinced, but when he saw them he relented. He told me that he felt pity for them. I lucked out with my husband, I am telling you. He takes such good care of me, my children. Doesn't even drink. Doesn't smoke. Works at his shop and his cow-dung business diligently. I lucked out, as I said, but not everyone is as fortunate, and my husband recognized that. He spoke to them and he told them not to worry, think of this as your home, think of these children as your siblings. That's what he said.

'The girls were scared and shy. The one week they were here, in Sanjegaon, they kept to themselves. I was alarmed to see them that way, because they never left each other's side. That Anisha took care of them, and I am told she always did. But I am not sure. Because she was also a thief. She stole things from our house. Small things. Earrings that we had brought from Mumbai; my son's sketch pens; a ring, which was fake but still; a glass paperweight . . . other such things. Nothing very serious, but she had it in her to steal, and to steal moreover from people who were trying to give her some peace, some solace. Imagine that. And that middle sister, what was her name?'

'Sanchita.'

'Yes, Sanchita. That middle sister would keep a watch while Anisha went around trying to find things to steal. I know because that's what I saw. It so happened that my husband pointed out that things were getting stolen. At first it was his comb which was stolen, but he thought he had misplaced it somewhere, so he didn't really bother about it. After he came home one evening, he went to have his evening bath. When he stepped out, he found that his watch was missing. He had kept it on the bedside table when he went in, it was there, he kept repeating. Then he remembered the missing comb and said things are getting stolen. He didn't say the sisters are stealing things, he is too decent to say such things, but he said that things are getting stolen. That's it. I decided to keep an eye on the sisters. So one day when they thought no one was watching—but I, their aunt, was—the two sisters went inside the house and into *our* room and began to open drawers. Actually, Anisha opened the drawers while Sanchita just hung around outside the door, keeping watch. I watched them from the kitchen. I think they were too stupid to realize that I was in the kitchen. Too stupid or too careless.

'They couldn't find anything, so they walked back outside to play with the stones. Only the three of them, those sisters. They never included my daughter or my son in their games, I don't know why. The youngest one, what was her name?'

'Priyanka.'

'Priyanka was very bright, I remember. She played and laughed with my children sometimes. She was a normal girl who wanted normal things. But the other two . . . that Anisha was a brute. She led them to their deaths, that's what I think, personally speaking. But of course it's sad, it's sad what happened to them and I cried the whole day when I heard about it. The next day we went there, me and my husband, to Murwani, for the funeral. But there was no funeral, of course, because the police were doing their thing. I left all our differences aside and I went and held my sister's hands. She wasn't crying, but I wasn't surprised because she hardly ever cried. Even when our mother died, long ago, when we were children. And then our father died, also when we were quite young. She never cried. And she wasn't crying then, simply sitting and staring, as if the deaths had happened to someone else and she was merely a relative of the family. Not a mother whose daughters had been . . . but that's how she is. And I went and told her not to worry, that everything would be all right, and she looked at me and she said: No, of course not. Nothing is going to be all right. That's when I saw she was holding a scrapbook with photos of some actresses . . . and I felt sad and I felt pity and a sudden surge of love for my sister. You know how it happens when you look at a person and you know that they are suffering and no matter what you think about them, you feel sad for them, for the condition they are in? That is how it happened with me then. But then it passed and we came back home and that was that. I haven't seen her since and I haven't spoken to her since. We didn't want to get involved in that jatra. My husband said we have to keep our distance. Nothing doing. Even today he is not happy about this interview. But I keep thinking about the girls, sometimes, when I am alone in the kitchen or alone in the hall watching TV and some song in which one of the actresses from the scrapbook is dancing . . . And I think about their fate. What happened to them? They were children, you know, they were just innocent girls without a father, and they really deserved better. That's what I want to say, essentially.'

Narayani Bawane

Narayani Bawane had seen the journalist around. Almost everyone in Murwani knew about him by the time he approached her for an interview. He didn't say much by way of an introduction: just that he was a journalist who was writing a book about the three sisters. Then he started explaining the case to Narayani, and she had to cut him off.

'I know the case. I knew the three sisters,' she said, or rather whispered. He apologized and smiled sadly, or so Narayani thought it was: a sad smile. 'It seems as if nobody remembers them,' he said.

No, Narayani thought, nobody *wants* to remember them.

But the man looked sincere; someone who wanted to listen, someone who was willing to listen. Narayani had never really spoken about the three sisters, particularly about Anisha, to anyone after those days. No journalist had approached her and neither had any police official. The only journalist she had really cared about had abandoned her. She did see Godambe around once or twice, but she never bothered to talk to him after what he had told her. Then Godambe had stopped coming, and Narayani had her own difficulties to face: a single mother without a husband caring for a daughter without her father. She had been shunned by everyone but her family. She was told to leave the school, since of course she wasn't the best example to the students. But in a way everyone had accepted what happened with her, because everyone thought: What else can you expect from those people and their women?

It was Tatya who helped her find her feet. Tatya and those women from the Rashtriya Ekta Gathan. Or rather one woman called Ranjita, who was starting a papad manufacturing service called the Murwani Mahila Udyog with Tatya's help. REG wanted the local business to integrate more people from the Dalit and tribal communities, and she was the perfect fit. 'That way you can also feel included in our Hindu fold, be a part of it,' Ranjita had told her. 'Now don't go and convert to those Jesus-wale and Buddha-wale. And if you do, don't come here,' she had added.

So Narayani had continued to live on the edge of the village, with her daughter, her father—her mother had passed away in 2016—and, sometimes, her guilt. She didn't feel guilty these days, not as much as she used to, but of course she did think about Anisha and the sisters once in a while—on some days, often—because she believed that she could have prevented their deaths. She could have prevented that tragedy.

She had resigned herself to living in Murwani, living with her past, trying to build a future for herself and her daughter. But then this journalist had arrived, she had spoken to him, and then someone had told her—or she had heard someone say something along those lines—that the journalist had been here before. In 2013, after the death of the sisters. That he had come here from Mumbai. And that he had returned to write a book or an article or something, but he had been here before. Which is when she realized why his face and his voice had seemed so familiar.

Avdhut Patambe

(Excerpts from an interview transcript. Interview conducted on 5 March 2019.)

'There. That is the memorial.'

'I am sorry about his death.'

'He was twenty-four. Who dies at twenty-four? What is the meaning of death at twenty-four? I don't understand. You write about this. I was told there is a journalist coming to write about the problems in this village, you—'

'Actually I am here to write about the three sisters.'

'You write about this. My brother Ashok Patambe. Ashok Patambe, you write it down. I want his name to be printed. I want the government to know that he died because of them.'

'How did he die?'

'He was killed by a tiger. He was with us in the afternoon, eating his lunch and then cleaning his teeth with a pin. That's how I remember him. He always cleaned his teeth with a pin. We told him it's dangerous but he never listened to us. Never listened to us. All his life he did what he wanted, and now I remember him like that: cleaning his teeth with a pin. In the afternoon he was with us, we had our regular nap and then he woke up and went to the farm for the fodder to feed the cows. Look there, do you see that? That's where our cowshed is. Very healthy cows. But the tiger ignored the cows and came straight for my brother. Who would have thought? Ashok didn't return for a long time. We were not bothered because we thought he must have met someone, he must have gone somewhere. Something always comes up when one goes out to the field. But three hours passed and still no sign of Ashok. So we went looking for him. There it was, his sickle in the field. Nothing but his sickle. We found his body a few metres away, but that was later. We searched the village, we raised an alarm. The police asked us to come back the next day if we didn't find him. But we found him that night, mauled, half-eaten. The police said this had nothing to do with them, this was the forest officials' area. The forest officials said we had warned the villagers about the tiger—'

'I saw the warning posters. Tiger in vicinity.'

'And who cares about warning posters? People like you. From outside. What are we going to do about those posters, you tell me? This was our farm. This was Ashok's farm. The forest department says they'll give us some compensation, but they want some papers about the ownership of the farm that we don't have. I want you to write about this.'

'When did this happen?'

'Last year.'

'And have there been any other tiger attacks in the area since?'

'I don't know. I have been trying to get the compensation. All I know is that we are yet to get the promised compensation. Who is going to return Ashok to us? What happened to the tiger? Did they kill it? Who knows? No one knows anything in this village.'

The Tramp

(Excerpts from an interview transcript. Interview conducted on 25 March 2019.)

'I was a tramp then and I am a tramp now, but I heard that you were interviewing people who were in the village at that time and who know something about the murder of the three sisters. I was a tramp then and I am a tramp now so no one took me seriously then and no one takes me seriously now. But I thought I must tell you what I saw because I have been telling people what I saw for the past six years and no one here believes me. Of course, now I have stopped telling it to people and now I have stopped believing what I saw. But when someone said that there is a young man here who is trying to talk to people about those sisters, it all came back to me and suddenly I started believing in what I saw. But maybe not. Can you decide that for me?

'So what happened was that I was a tramp then and I am a tramp now, and at that time it was particularly cold and I had wrapped myself up in my shawl and I didn't have much to eat but the dogs around me were hungry. I was surrounded by stray dogs. Kallu, Shikya, Bokya, Waghmare, Gavatphool. Now Kallu and Bokya are dead. Waghmare went somewhere and never returned. Gavatphool, the bitch, and Shikya are my only companions. But at that time we were six. Me and my five dogs, who were hungry. I was a little less hungry because I had some food at the hurda party in the evening. A little bit of food, nice meat of something I couldn't recognize, and a little bit of beer and a little bit of hurda and then I had walked back into the village and sat quietly in my corner with my blanket. But Kallu, Shikya, Bokya, Waghmare and Gavatphool were still hungry because the hurda party people did not give them anything. So I was thinking—'

'Who were the hurda party people?'

'They were some men and some young boys. Very hatte katte and all, I remember, which was not surprising because they were eating a lot and they were drinking a lot and they were smoking something . . . and they passed me the smoke and I smoked it, thinking it's a bidi. But it wasn't a bidi. At least not the kind of bidi I am used to smoking. And when I asked them whether it was a bidi, they started laughing and one of them said: Yes, it's a bidi. Have another drag. Have another drag. A long drag. Have a long drag. I remember his voice and I remember his face, because he seemed to be the eldest of the lot. And he said: Come on, sit with us, we are having fun—'

'What time was this?'

'I don't remember. I think it was around five in the evening. And then—'

'What day was this?'

'That day. The day it happened. That evening the sisters . . . Those sisters were killed on that day. That day.'

'Go on. Did you tell this to the police?'

'I told this to the police but I was a tramp then and I am a tramp now so no one believed me.'

'Go on.'

'No one believed me and they said you talk to your dogs. You fuck your dogs. That bitch is your fucking randi. And you, you dog-fucker, expect us to believe you? They told me never to show my face again and I never showed my face again.'

'Who told you not to show your face again?'

'The police. I went to the police station and the first thing I got was a slap from the Constable outside, who was mulling his tobacco. Then I told him my story. Then he said go tell this to saheb. But saheb slapped me thrice and told me to shut the fuck up. When I shut up, he told me to start speaking my piece. When I began speaking, he slapped me again and told me to wash my face and particularly my mouth, because I smell like a mortuary. When I asked him where I could wash my face and my mouth, he told me to shut the fuck up and start talking. I got confused. So I did what I generally do when I don't know what to do: I kept quiet. And that's when the saheb slapped me for the seventh time. He said: Get the fuck out of here if you don't have anything to say. I am repeating it word for word, because I want to be truthful. He said: Get the fuck out of here if you don't have anything to say. And as I was about to get the fuck out, I realized that I did have something to say to the saheb. So I turned around and I began to speak. I told him about the hurda party and I told him that there were six men and I told him that those six men had offered me meat and some beer and some bidis and then I came back to my spot and sat with my blanket wrapped around me, trying to think of how my dogs were going to get their food that day. So then I decided to just go and ask those fair fellows of the hurda party for some spare food. Anything would do, I wanted to tell them. It's for my children. Especially Gavatphool, because she had been sick and she had been whimpering and telling me that she was hungry. So I walked back to the fields, beyond that temple, near that well, and when I walked back, in total darkness, I heard whispers and I heard someone say: You hold the legs, I'll hold the hands. And I heard someone say: Where are we going? And someone else began to sing some song, and someone else said—I remember this—someone else said: We should have kept them longer, I am thirsty.

So I thought they were done with the party and were now heading back, but their exchange was strange. Whose legs and hands were they holding? I didn't think about it much at that time and I started searching for food at other places in the village. Because I was hungry, too, I was very hungry and I even thought: Fuck these dogs, I want my food. But then I slapped myself twice because I shouldn't think such things about my children. They are my children, those dogs. So when I heard about the three sisters in the well, I thought about my dogs, what would I do if something like that happens to Gavatphool or to Waghmare or to Shikya? And then what I had heard began playing in my mind quite suddenly and I said: I must tell this to the police. About the hands and the legs. But no one believed me because I was a tramp and I am a tramp. They called me a dog-fucker but I am not a dog-fucker, I never was. I love my dogs, they are my children. Do you fuck your children?'

Inspector Deshmukh

(Excerpts from an interview transcript. Interview conducted on 25 March 2019.)

'Arey, that dog-fucker knows shit. All this is off the record, haan. That tramp, that fucking tramp made a whole lot of mess. Imagine this. He came to Dighole, then he came to me and we both kicked him on his gaand, like he deserved to be kicked. Imagine that. And not just us. Okay, you don't believe us, you think we are some incompetent chutiyas from a small town who don't know how policegiri works, okay. But even SP Madam asked him questions he couldn't answer. He told her that he heard all this on 15 August, Independence Day. He says he was born in 1947—15 August 1947, which is why he remembers the date. This hurda party, he said, happened on 15 August. So she said: Okay, fine, 15 August, tell us who all were there? You know what he tells madam? He says: You were there, I saw you, and I saw this man—he pointed at me—and I saw Amitabh Bachchan. Now you tell me, behenchod. We are getting kicked on our asses every fucking hour there and this dog-fucker is bullshitting us. You tell us if we were wrong in slapping that guy. Don't listen to him, he will mess up your head and he will enjoy doing it too. That fucker knows what he is saying and what he is doing, he just wants to screw with us.'

Reportage

I ask Ajoba whether he visits his granddaughters' graves. He opens his mouth to speak but then decides against it.

'There was only one grave,' he says after long minutes of silence. He draws a rectangle in the air. 'They fitted all three of them inside that.'

A single rectangle.

'Do you visit them often?'

Ajoba is looking outside—we are sitting right where he said they were sitting or sleeping when they found out about the girls—and he is scratching his beard. He turns his gaze towards me, slowly, and stares at me for what seems like an eternity.

'I don't need to,' he says.

'Why?'

'Because they are here with me. With us. Right now.'

I feel a chill run down my spine.

After about a minute of silence, he gets up and walks to the kitchen. He rummages through something and pulls out a white jute bag, the kind used for storing cement and rubble on construction sites. He walks back to the chair and starts taking out the contents. Three dolls, a plastic cup shaped like a wine cup, a duster, a violet teacup and a pink kettle, a grey bus trying hard to look authentic, a toy gas cylinder and a red scarecrow. The dolls are more or less identical: one of them has her hair tied up in a blue bandanna, another one has plain, straight hair and the third is bald. Ajoba picks up the doll with the blue bandanna and says: 'My name is Anisha.'

I say, instinctively, as if I am expected to: 'Hello, Anisha, I am Chitranshu.'

Ajoba then holds up the bald doll and moves it such that it seems as if the doll is nodding her head, although the doll itself has no such function, cheap as it is. I notice then that its neck has cracked, so that allows the grandfather to make her head nod.

'My name is Sanchita,' the grandfather says, without changing his voice.

'Hello, Sanchita. My name is Chitranshu.'

Ajoba picks up the third doll with the plain, straight hair, hands it to me and says, 'My name is Priyanka and I want you to protect me.'

I don't know what to say. I look at Ajoba and I feel a hollow in my stomach. The hollowness of anxiety. I hold the doll carefully, as if the doll actually is Priyanka, although now that I think about it, it may as well be her body. Priyanka's delicate body, as fragile as this doll; her life as cheap as the price of this doll. I hold the doll gently by her legs and bring it before my eyes. 'I will try my best, Priyanka,' I say to the doll, without looking into the doll's eyes.

Ajoba clears his throat and takes the doll back. He places the dolls side by side and touches the one representing Sanchita: 'I loved watching TV. I couldn't watch it for a long time, and I can't watch it now, but at that time I loved watching TV. I liked the teleshopping network especially. I loved dancing too. I taught my Ajoba how to dance. Do you remember, Ajoba? Tell dada about that.'

Ajoba stops talking and starts nodding. 'Yes, I remember,' he says, smiling sadly. 'She taught me how to dance. She held my hands and just started dancing. I have never danced, perhaps once or twice very long ago during some weddings. But Sanchita . . . She was the only one who cared about what I was doing, where I was going, how I was doing. She was quiet otherwise, but when it came to me she was always talking and in a mood to chat. I don't know why. Maybe she saw her Ajoba's sadness. I didn't get any love. Not from my wife, not from my son, not from my daughter-in-law. Just my granddaughters.'

Then he picks up Priyanka's doll and says, 'Don't say that, Ajoba. Everyone loves you.'

Then he starts sobbing.

API Sangere

(Now Police Inspector Sangere, posted in Sakoli. Excerpts from an interview transcript. Interview conducted on 17 March 2019.)

'Do you know anything about Dighole's murder?'

'He was murdered.'

'Arey, Sangere Saheb. Come on. You know things but you are not—Look, all this is off the record. I won't print your name. You have nothing to worry about.'

'You speak na with Deshmukh Saheb. You speak to him na, off the record.'

'I am speaking to Deshmukh Saheb. But I also want your version of events.'

'I don't have any version.'

'Sangere Saheb. Come on. Godambe referred me to you. Tell me about that guy, Kader Muhammad. I know you were there and I know you interrogated him.'

'Arey, you talk then na with Godambe. I have nothing to do with the case. I am posted in Sakoli now.'

'I know you are posted in Sakoli. But you were in Murwani then and you worked with Dighole and Deshmukh both. You know—'

'Arey, you speak na then with Karamble. Constable Karamble. He worked na with them.'

'Karamble. Can you give me his number?'

'No. I am in Sakoli now.'

'Just share his number.'

'I don't have.'

'Arey, Sangere Sir, just his number . . . Listen. That Kader case—'

'Haan. Okay. Please. Thank you.'

Raju Bokle

(Excerpts from an interview transcript. Interview conducted on 28 February 2019.)

'My name is Raju Bokle and I sell cigarettes at two spots. Near the police chowki and near the petrol pump. The petrol-pump-wala shop is for the petrol-pump-wala people and the highway people, and the chowki-wala is for the local people and the police people. But this is now. Six years ago I had one little shop which was called Bokle Paanwala, and it was run by me, Raju Bokle, the one and only paanwala in Murwani. I sold Goa, I sold Bombay, I sold Hyderabadi. I sell Nagpuri kharra and I sell local kharra. Every kind of tobacco. I have contacts in Nagpur, Pune, Mumbai and Bhandara. But Bhandara contacts everyone here has. Bombay not everyone does and Guwahati no one does, so that increases Raju Bokle's demand. My father, Sadanand Hirve Bokle—may his soul attain sadgati—he started this business here many years ago. He started this business of paan when he was twenty. When he was fifteen he ran off to Varanasi. But a Bokle cannot survive in Varanasi. A Bokle has to be here, in Murwani, in Maharashtra, because a Bokle cannot survive anywhere else. That's what I know and that's what my father knew. My father learnt the business of paan while he was in Uttar Pradesh and when he lived in Bengal and when he visited Assam. He travelled a lot around there, sleeping on roads, shitting on railway tracks. He had eleven siblings, so nobody noticed that he was gone for a long while, and when they did, they didn't care. My father, Sadanand Hirve Bokle. I have many siblings too, it's just that I don't know them, kay? Ha, did you understand? I was talking about my illegitimate brothers and sisters in UP and Bengal and Assam, kay? But anyway, he came back here and he set up the paan business by the blessings of Kalyanji, Rabindranath Kalyanji, a small-time businessman in Varanasi who funded the first Bokle shop. When I opened my second shop—'

'When did you open your second shop?'

'In 2016. Three years ago. When I was opening it—'

'What has the second shop got to do with the murders?'

'I personally went to UP to—what murders?'

'The three sisters.'

'Who three—oh that. Oh yes. Those sisters. Arey, no, bhau, I don't want to talk about them. It's too dangerous to talk about them.'

'Why? Why is it dangerous?'

'Why is it dangerous, kay bholya. I have heard the stories. About people talking about the three sisters and then dying in accidents, getting blisters all over their bodies, going impotent. Did you speak to Sujay

Borkar? No, of course you didn't. Because you can't. Borkar was the police patil here. He used to be at Bokle Paanwala twenty-four hours of the day. Twenty-four. He came and he sat and he chit-chatted. This and that and that and this and again this and that. He used to talk too much and he used to talk too loudly. He said it was his work to talk and gather information. Bocha. After the murder he started talking about the sisters to everyone. This happened, that happened. One time he said the sisters slipped and fell due to the rains. Because the ground had become slippery. Then he said no that's not possible. That's not what happened. Then he said Tatya's men killed them. Then he said they killed themselves. Because of all their lafdis at home—'

'What lafdis?'

'Arey, the usual problems. That Aajibai was a psycho, that mother is a psycho, that grandfather is a poor asshole with nothing to do and no one to go to. What do you expect? And that father died because of some chetuk I have heard. Some soul-eating and soul-drinking business that many people say the mother did to the father. You know how the witches suck souls so that they can make themselves immortal? Those caste people have it particularly—'

'Which caste do you belong to?'

'Same caste, bhau, but our gotra is different, and in any case our lifestyle is different than theirs. Our lifestyle is a little more advanced and open. But same caste, which is why I know what the women in this caste can do. It's hereditary, they say, this soul-sucking business, that's why our caste women live for more years than other caste women. You observe. What caste are you?'

'Brahmin.'

'But what kind of Brahmin? Konkanastha?'

'Konkanastha.'

'Haan. So now you go back and ask your Aaji or you ask your mother or father or Ajoba. They will tell you why they never ventured into these people's areas. There's history. They used to suck souls, the women of our caste. Especially of the Brahmins because the Brahmins were Pandits who were the kattar traditional enemies of the lower castes. You ask me. I know all this. The Pandits used to trap the evil souls in their kalash and wait until the souls turned to ashes and then the ashes were thrown into the Ganga. That's how it happened. Arey, but we were talking about something else.'

'Sujay Borkar.'

'Haan, Borkar, that poor chutiya. He got trapped in all this. I'll tell you what happened. Sujay Borkar was the police patil and everybody was asking him whether he had any clue about what happened, who did this, whether there was any confirmation and this and that. All the villagers used to give him a lot of bhav, rao, so one day what happened was that Borkar said: Tatya's men did it. He told this to me, rao, to me and several other people. The police found the beer bottles, he said, and the police were going to send them for forensics. But the night they were going to send the bottles to the forensics, Tatya Khandle arranged a jungi hurda party for them. Understand? At some farmhouse, rao. Aangle's farmhouse perhaps. I don't know. But Tatya organized a mast jangi party, and all the officers got drunk at the party and Tatya replaced the beer bottles. That's what Borkar said before he began to talk about the sisters. The sisters were like this, the sisters were like that. Especially about the eldest one. Seven or eight months after that, I think, it was that year, the year of the sisters' murder, I remember it very well, he was wandering somewhere around that temple. That temple where the sisters were killed. And he came back to the village running. Now others asked him: What happened, Borkar Saheb? What happened? But our Borkar Saheb couldn't speak. Our Borkar Saheb was bleeding from his mouth. Just bleeding. Nothing, just blood splattered everywhere. He was taken to the hospital and the doctor refused to treat him, because the doctor said this is the sisters' curse, bhau. His tongue was gone. Gone. Ask Raju Bokle. Raju Bokle saw it, I saw the large gap there, in his mouth. No tongue. And you know what? I saw this with my own eyes. The dogs here, those dogs that run around with the tramps, they were eating a fresh piece of meat the day after. Black meat. What meat? You figure it out.'

'But all that was after the murders. What about before that? You saw the sisters at the petrol pump.'

'Haan, that. I saw the eldest one leaning against one of the pillars of the petrol pump. She was wearing a sexy dress, with the . . . it was a good dress. She looked se—she looked good. Pretty. I went there to deliver something. I delivered it. I tried to find her while returning but by then she was gone. I don't know where or which way, bhau. Raju Bokle only says what he sees.'

'So you saw her at the petrol pump. Did you tell this to the police?'

'Haan, many times. But what are they going to do with that? They found the clothes and the beer bottles and the berries and they couldn't find anything. So many clues people found here. Footprints and all. So many clues here and there, scattered. So many people saying this and that. But the police didn't find anything.'

'Did you have any prior contact with the sisters?'

'No, bhau. I do my work and I observe and I keep quiet. What is it to me who does what?'

'Achha, but why did you go to the petrol pump?'

'I told you. Delivery.'

'What delivery? Paan?'

'No, the other stuff. The good stuff. Ganja.'

'Who did you sell it to?'

'Now, bhau, I don't remember his name. I remember only my name, and that too on good days, kay? Raju Bokle. But some very young guy at the petrol pump smoked that stuff. He put it in his bidi and smoked it. He told me that way he doesn't even realize when his shift gets over, it's that smooth. And at that time I sold it cheap, because I got it cheap from Varanasi. But not many people bought that stuff here, so the dhanda was actually thanda. Only that petrol pump guy.'

'Does he still work there? At the petrol pump?'

'Na, bhau. He left soon after that accident.'

'Which accident?'

'That three sisters accident, rao. He left after that.'

'Did the police interrogate him?'

'Why would the police interrogate him?'

'Do you still sell ganja then?'

'Haan, but I changed my dealer. This one comes from Andhra Pradesh. The boys here these days have that shauk. Mahakal, Mahakal, Mahakal, they keep saying.

Jai Mahakal! I don't smoke it myself, but they tell me it's good quality stuff.'

'You have some right now?'

'Haan, ahe na. But not here, at the shop.'

'Good quality, na? How much for a bag?'

'A bag, bhau? Aai zavli. Let's go to the shop first, smoke a cigarette, relax. We will talk there.'

Chorus

'Of course the girl had a boyfriend. What do you think? They were always loaded with money, those sisters, and that Anisha, of course she had a boyfriend. What do you think?'

'Hmm. I had heard of a boy in the neighbouring village. Hmm. Some boy she used to meet on the highway. And in the fields. Hmm.'

'I am not sure, bhau. I am new to this village. I have only heard stories. What stories? Haan, that the sisters were rich and all that. I never saw the sisters, to be honest. I don't even know how they looked. But I have heard stories about them.'

'This is something that I have never told anyone. But I think now nobody cares anyway. That eldest sister had a boyfriend in the neighbouring village. But she also roamed around with other boys. Especially from the rich families. She used to target them. She used to see that these boys are from rich farmer families, with land and all, and she used to target them. She would roam around on their bikes and she would get money from them for her dolls and her bags. I have heard this, but not a lot of people know about this because she used to go to the neighbouring villages. Go there during the day, roam around in the market and the fields—God knows what they did there—and then come back by evening. I have seen her myself, coming back in the evening from somewhere outside the village. That's how she was. My friend Gopu Lakhane from Sawri has seen her with a boy there. Sawri, it's two hours from here by bus. Imagine, bhau. Fourteen years old and whoring herself around . . .'

'There was some talk of romance with local boys. That eldest sister. She had some lafdis with the boys here, but I was never interested in all that. Who has the time to discuss all those things?'

'I remember when they disappeared, those days, there was talk about how the girls had new bags. Shiny new bags. Nobody had proper bags here. Everyone carried their tiffin and their books in a cloth bag. At least everyone who went to their school. Murwani Vidya Sadan. Convent-school people had bags, sometimes, but not Murwani Vidya Sadan students. But those sisters had bags. Now how did the sisters get those bags? They were poor. Very poor. Not even proper light in their house. But they had those proper bags. And a TV. Their mother worked in the factory kitchen. Factory kitchen. And then they have all these expensive things. Imagine that. Someone must have been giving them money, na. Something was not right. Either the eldest sister or the mother . . .'

The Mother

(Excerpts from an interview transcript. Interview conducted on 28 February 2019.)

'I want you to recreate that day for me, if you can. As much as you can remember.'

'Which day?'

'The day the sisters disappeared.'

'You mean my daughters.'

'I am sorry, yes, your daughters.'

'It's been so long. So many years have passed. But I will try. You are going to write about this?'

'Yes.'

'Okay. I will try . . . I was the first one to wake up that day. That used to be my life: wake up early and start planning for the day ahead. Wake up early and start living a life that was dedicated to the lives of others. That is how it was. Normally it was Aaji who would wake up before me, but that day she hadn't, for some reason, I don't remember. I would wake Ajoba up after I had prepared the tea and the chapatis. He would sit up, but he wouldn't open his eyes. He had his rituals. Always muttering some prayer, always talking to his God. Once he was done with all that, he would get up and go and brush his teeth and wash his face and gargle thrice outside our house. Then he would walk in and ask for his chapatis. He would roll the chapatis and dip them in the tea, one by one. That was his breakfast. Usually he preferred silence in the mornings, because he said that the mornings are when God observes and God judges. Which is probably why he never complained about the breakfast. He ate whatever I managed to prepare. Never complained. Nothing. Not even a whimper. But Aaji expected something new every day. But who had that kind of money? Ajoba understood that; Ajoba never complained.

'We had one kholi and one kitchen and that was our home. All of us slept together in that kholi, stretching out our two mattresses in the kitchen. Me and my three daughters and then Aaji and Ajoba. The girls always wanted to sleep next to Ajoba because he whispered stories into their ears, but Aaji didn't like that, so they had stopped insisting. We went to sleep at around ten and woke up at around five. That's how it was.

'That day I woke up at around four-thirty and slept for fifteen more minutes before getting up and starting with my usual morning rituals. Take the bucket outside, fetch water from the well, prepare tea and chapatis, wake up the girls, prepare them for school. That day I remember Ajoba had clipped their nails. I remember that. He had woken up and he had had his tea and then he had woken the girls up and the first thing Aaji remarked was that their nails were too long, they should be clipped. I don't know how important all this is, but that is what I remember. Aaji had asked Ajoba to cut the girls' nails. Why would she ask for their nails to be clipped? I don't know. She had never paid any attention to the girls . . . But as I was saying, Ajoba clipped their nails and I prepared their lunch. I had given them something that was left over from the previous night's dinner, that's how it usually went, fresh chapatis and whatever was left from the previous night's dinner. But that day Anisha was adamant that I make something fresh. Now what fresh thing do you want? She wanted dal, rice and pickle. I don't know, usually I would have slapped her there and then and told her to eat whatever I was giving and thank me for it instead. But that day I relented. I decided to give her whatever she wanted, I didn't slap her. I prepared the dal and I packed her some rice I had kept aside for dinner. The pickle we already had. All this took some time, so Anisha told my younger ones, Sanchita and Priyanka, to start walking and she would follow. It was getting late, so I packed all this up quickly, rice and dal and pickle, and told Anisha to share it with her sisters and sent her away. That's the last I saw them.'

'What happened after that?'

Reportage

It was a normal day: that's how the grandfather and the mother put it. A normal day when the girls woke up at six-thirty in the morning and freshened up. After they had their daily tea and chapatis—Anisha would eat the most, three chapatis, while Priyanka, the youngest, would eat two, and Sanchita would eat just one; 'She had a very bad appetite. She could go without food or water for eight or nine hours, without a whimper,' says the grandfather—the grandfather clipped their nails. Interestingly, it was Aaji who had pointed out that their nails needed to be clipped. This, their mother alleges, is 'proof' of the grandmother's involvement in the alleged murder.

When their mother says this, I ask her why she thinks the grandmother would want them killed. The reasons vary: 'Because she hated the fact that she had granddaughters and not grandsons.' 'Because she hated the fact that their ancestral property would be divided up among outside families once the sisters were married.' 'Because she wanted to keep the property and she wanted it to go to her brother's family, because her brother had grandsons.'

I am not sure how valid those theories are. At any rate, the theories stand if and only if it is proven that the sisters were murdered. That, as we know, is a matter still shrouded in mystery.

But back to the day. The nails were clipped, the girls were readied. The mother used to help the girls get ready until about two years prior, when Anisha was handed over the responsibility. 'She didn't exactly enjoy it,' the mother says, 'but she was dedicated to her sisters, so she did it. She scolded them a lot more than I did, but I didn't mind that. I thought they needed discipline.'

That day the girls were ready before time. It took them five to ten minutes to reach the school. Anisha came into the kitchen to pick up their tiffins at around seven-ten. That's when she found out that the tiffin was chapati and leftover drumsticks. Nothing doing, said Anisha, we want rice and dal and pickle. The mother says that she had expected this. 'Anisha hated leftover food,' she says. 'I tried as much as I could to prepare food in the morning, but with my own work to take care of, it was difficult to juggle everything. I had to prepare lunch for Aaji and Ajoba as well. But I relented, because I thought the girls deserve to have a good lunch at least. I don't know why I thought that way on that particular day, because usually I would have slapped Anisha and told her to be on her way.'

The mother, teary-eyed, says that she is glad that she relented. 'Perhaps there was something that was telling me that I should fulfil their last wish.'

The mother quickly cooked the dal and packed it along with the rice that she had prepared for dinner and some pickle. It was a full meal, a meal that Anisha had finished eating by the time of her disappearance, but Priyanka and Sanchita had not. When I ask the mother, carefully, whether she thinks the girls died hungry, she nods her head slowly. 'Six years and I still get up in the morning thinking I have to prepare lunch for my daughters. And I still think about that day when the little ones did not eat and died on an empty stomach.'

The girls trotted outside their house, as usual, and walked towards the school. Their mother saw them take their usual route and went inside the house and forgot all about it. She admits that she often forgot about the girls and what they were doing and where they were during the course of the day. 'It's a natural thing,' she says. 'You get entangled in your daily chores, going to work, working, you don't really think about your children constantly.' I am not a parent, so I wouldn't know, but a lot of parents here in the city echoed the mother's opinion. They don't often think about the children once they are off to school. It's the grind of daily life, and nothing to feel guilty about, a friend—a parent of two girls—says.

But Anisha never reached school. Her bag was found, later, during the search, inside a granary on the way to the school. This is where the police suspect Anisha changed out of her uniform. The land adjoining the granary belongs to the Aangles, and the family has been questioned about why the granary was kept unlocked. According to the Aangles, it was an oversight on the part of the man appointed to look after it. But according to the locals, it was always kept open, so there was nothing really unusual about that.

'These things attain importance when something like a murder happens, but such things are very common in villages such as ours,' a local who did not wish to be named told me.

It is almost certain that Anisha changed into her 'shiny clothes', as the police and the locals have called them, inside the granary. Were the girls in on it and knew what Anisha was about to do? Was all this planned by the sisters beforehand? We will never know. But there is speculation, of course. The mother says that the youngest one, Priyanka, was not easy to convince when it came to bunking school or leaving the school at half-day. She was dedicated to her studies and did not exactly like Anisha's actions. Sanchita, on the other hand, was the 'dumb one', according to her mother.

'Sanchita was always tagging along with Anisha, so even if she disagreed with something that Anisha did, she wouldn't open her mouth and would just go along. I know that's what happened with Sanchita.'

Ajoba, however, disagrees. He has always been of the opinion that Sanchita was the brightest, and he says he is ready to 'bet anything' that Sanchita would have protested had she had any inkling of what was going to happen. 'It is true Priyanka was the most disciplined, but Sanchita wasn't dumb,' Ajoba says, protectively.

At any rate, Sanchita and Priyanka reached school. The classes started at seven-thirty. For the next four and a half hours, Priyanka and Sanchita were in their respective classes inside the Murwani Vidya Sadan school, while Anisha, a shopkeeper in front of the school said, came to his shop to ask for a 'rubber band, a couple of chocolates and a cello tape'. The shopkeeper told this to the police, and the police, for a couple of days, went around the town with sniffer dogs in search of a rubber band, but no rubber band or cello tape were found. It's strange, says a Constable present during the investigation, where did these things go? No one knows.

But it isn't clear what exactly it was that Anisha did during those hours when she had bunked school, and it's difficult to determine, because Anisha had bunked school before and in the past instances she did various things, including roaming around the fields adjoining the well in which her body was eventually found. We can only guess. She might have been roaming around on that side, the temple side, around the well, or she could have been on the exact opposite side of the village, on the petrol pump side, beyond which a couple of roadside stalls dot the highway. These stalls sell Chinese bhel, Chinese rice, pulao and noodles, and the owner of one of the food stalls—called Sandesh Hot Chinese—says that he had served Chinese bhel and pulao to Anisha a number of times during school hours.

'I never asked her whether she was bunking school or whether she had a holiday. That is not my job.' But he contradicts himself a little while later when he says that he 'raised concerns' about her habit of bunking school 'a number of times'.

'I never asked, but I knew,' he says when confronted.

In any case, according to Raju Bokle, a cigarette-seller in the village, he saw Anisha wearing a green top and jeans and leaning against one of the pillars of the petrol pump 'sometime between one-thirty and two-thirty' in the afternoon. This is not corroborated by any other witness, but the police have recorded Bokle's statement. So it would be fair to say that Anisha was, until two-thirty, alone, but that would be wrong, or at least strange, because according to police records, Anisha had picked up her sisters from their respective classes at around twelve noon. What did the sisters do in between time? And what was Anisha doing alone at the petrol pump two and a half hours after picking up her sisters?

'That's one of the gaps we have been unable to fill,' a police source who was involved in the case told me. The period between twelve and two-thirty, then, remains blank. Those who manned the Chinese bhel and pulao stalls told the police that the sisters did not visit the area that day. Another shopkeeper, from the temple side, says that the sisters did come to his shop to buy three Gems packets. This was around 12.30 p.m. 'I can never forget that sentence,' says the shopkeeper. '"Kaka, Gems packet dya na teen." That's what she said.'

At twelve-thirty, then, the sisters were around the temple area. But then they disappeared again, and only Anisha showed up, this time around the petrol pump, which is a good half-an-hour to forty-five-minute walk from the shop where the sisters were last seen together.

Piecing together the day after this point is difficult, because there are too many theories. One of the 'anonymous tips' that the police received from one of the 'white boxes' that they had put up outside the girls' school informed them that Priyanka had said something about 'hurda' before leaving with Anisha. The same tip, a source said, claimed that Anisha said she was called by their 'Mummy'. Now, there are contradictory claims about who was called Mummy inside the Gudadhe household: the grandmother or the mother.

'They told me someone had given them a tip. Anisha had told someone that they were called by Mummy and they were going for a hurda party. Who is Mummy? I am not Mummy, I am their mother, their Aai. They always called me Aai and they always called their grandmother Mummy. So you figure it out. And Mummy, as it happens, was out of the house for a good two hours . . .' says the mother. But the mother's claims regarding what she was called at home—Mummy or Aai—are contradicted by the grandfather, who says that she was called both Mummy and Aai, while the grandmother was only called Aai.

'We thought the tip had solved the problem,' the police source said, 'but it only added to the confusion.'

Because whom to believe? The mother and the grandmother were interrogated for 'five hours every day for a week' according to another police official. But the mother says that she was grilled for 'three hours' for 'three whole days'. Which, she says, is a lot more than the grandmother, who was only interrogated for an 'hour or so' on the day the bodies were found. They had alibis, but they also had 'convincing arguments against each other'.

'But we didn't have the freedom to pursue the case as we wanted to,' a senior police official on the investigating team says. 'For one thing, it took an inordinate amount of time to establish whether the sisters were indeed raped and then murdered or simply murdered and then tossed into the well. If it was a case of simple murder, then the ambit of the investigation would have obviously widened and the mother and the grandmother would have been the prime suspects. But for the longest time everyone had simply assumed, based on the post-mortem, that the girls were raped, so the suspicion fell more on men than women.'

The bit about the hurda party, or the word 'hurda', however, is an interesting detail that has so far been missed or ignored. Hurda parties are common in the area, and they were once very popular. A report in the *Indian Express* says that in the eighties, families would light fires and roast hurda, or jowar cobs, in the open during chilly winter nights. These days, say the villagers, the parties are not as exciting an affair as they used to be, but they still retain their allure. On the afternoon and evening of that 14 February, however, there was no hurda party, at least as far as the villagers who were questioned are concerned.

And yet, there was.

Ganpat Lawane is a local community worker with political aspirations. He is young, he rides a Bullet and he has the swagger and the confidence required to 'manage' his team of young and old 'social workers'. He considers the Late Tatya Khandle—an influential figure in the area and another political aspirant who was killed by a heart attack about a year ago—his mentor.

This was the same Tatya Khandle who had taken the initiative to search for the girls and had pressured the police into filing an FIR.

Lawane says that he doesn't remember that day particularly well, but there could have been a hurda party organized by Tatya's men in that area during that time.

'Potti worked when there was work and partied when it was time for a party,' Lawane says. 'Potti' is the local slang for young boys. He says he is not at all defensive about the whole thing, because they had let the police know about the parties, and the police had even cross-examined all those who could have been present at the party. No one is sure who was, however, because the party, according to Lawane, 'began when no one remembered anything and ended when no one remembered anything'. Whatever that may mean, one can deduce that the party had been full of revelry. The police say that they focused the entirety of their attention on these people for a long time, but nothing came of it.

'Besides,' says a police source quoted earlier, 'it wasn't a hurda party. There was no hurda there.'

Lawane was with Tatya at that time, touring the neighbouring fields for a 'business deal'. The shopkeeper near the temple side, quoted earlier, told me that he had seen Lawane walk towards the temple at around 12.30 p.m., when Anisha must have been at the petrol pump. What does that mean, I ask the shopkeeper, and he just shrugs. 'Not just that,' he says, 'that day I saw Tatya converse with both that old woman and with the mother, as well as with those blanket-sellers from Rajasthan.'

But, of course, the shopkeeper's words cannot be believed, not in the least because he never told this to the police. It's an unwritten rule here, many tell me during the course of my interviews, you never out Tatya on anything, even if it was something as harmless as spotting him near a well or a temple.

'Tatya Khandle was an influential and dangerous man, but more than that he was a helpful man,' says a local source, 'so nobody wanted to go up against him. He had deep pockets and he was always willing to dig in deeper for a friend. Look at how he supported Ajoba after that incident. Stood by him and helped him in the investigation. That's how Tatya was.'

The lane that twists and turns towards the village panchayat is named Tatya Khandle Marg, and there is a memorial built with money contributed by the villagers right outside the Gram Panchayat. Why is there no memorial for the girls? 'What did the girls do for the village?' Lawane snaps. Then he smiles. 'Don't get me wrong, bhau. Whatever happened to them was tragic and wrong. But there is a difference, na.'

So the hurda party. What came of it, apart from a couple of beer bottles? Nothing. After chasing the men around, trying to find evidence against them, for about a fortnight, the police seemed to have given up. Was it due to Tatya, seeing as he was such a connected figure? No one is willing to admit anything. Everyone's lips are sealed. But Lawane offers an explanation: 'Tatya was the first one to gather his men around and start a search, not the police. Who intimidated the police into filing an FIR? Why would Tatya do something like that if his men were involved or if he was involved? Think, bhau.'

In fact, it was Tatya who had found their bodies in the well. Or so goes the story. Actually, however, a local businessman had found the bodies and bumped into Tatya while he was panicking and rushing into the village. Tatya was a part of the search party, as was Lawane. They had told Santosh, the businessman, to go home and rest while they handled what was to come next, since what was to come next was not going to be easy. Tatya seems to have been everywhere that day, I point out to Lawane, who merely laughs.

'Tatya was everywhere every day,' he says. 'You can ask anyone.'

This is true. Tatya *was* sort of a social butterfly, and his vocation demanded it. Moreover, he was a bachelor with a 'lot of time for social work'. He 'mentored' youngsters like Lawane in 'community service'. And he had 'sons' and 'daughters' across the length and breadth of the tehsil, according to Lawane, so there is nothing 'surprising or suspicious' about the fact that Tatya was everywhere that day.

'That's probably just coincidence,' one of the police sources says.

Well, then, what happened? After Anisha was spotted at the petrol pump by Raju Bokle, no one saw the girls ever again, not alive, at least. The case halts there. After that, it's open season. But people are divided into two or three camps. Some of them, including senior police officials, believe that Kader Muhammad, the blanket-seller who was known as Mullah Chacha around Murwani, lured the girls, raped them and then killed them. Muhammad had been coming to the village for the past thirty years, and he was a familiar face in the town. Many did not believe the police when they detained Mullah Chacha for questioning, but what changed their opinion was the allegation that someone had seen Muhammad offer a chocolate to a girl. But even there it is unclear whether it was one of the sisters or some other girl who had nothing to do with the case. Now Kader languishes in jail, waiting for the ATS to finish their investigation in a terror case in which he is a suspect.

Then there are those who believe that the sisters had decided to host a party for themselves, but their little adventure had turned into a misadventure—that one of the sisters had slipped and fallen into the well and the other two had jumped in to save her. Ajoba, during one of our chats, mentioned that Priyanka had once, as a child, crawled up to a well and tried to peep inside. Her father had spotted her in time and pulled her back. 'Otherwise she would have drowned,' Ajoba told me. He had been making a point about Priyanka's curiosity, but the anecdote struck me as prophetic when people told me how one of the sisters could have tried to peep inside the well and could have slipped.

Still others claim that the sisters, fed up with their situation at home, had been driven to suicide. And then there are those tales of black magic and human sacrifice and tales of lust and even—believe it or not—aliens who abducted the sisters or killed them in disguise. The last angle fascinated me the most, but the one before seems more pragmatic. With a fourteen-year-old out and about on Valentine's Day, didn't the police think about Anisha's love life? Didn't the police pursue that angle, of a tale of love and lust gone horribly wrong?

'We did, for a little while,' says the police source quoted earlier. 'But nothing really came of it.'

Godambe

(Excerpts from an interview. Interview conducted on 2 April 2019.)

'I told you na, randichya, this is not going to end well for you. The good thing is that it ended merely with nothing in your hand. Did you get your murderer? Did you get the closure for your fucking book? This could have been far worse. That Lawane is a dangerous man, and the people here are sensitive. I don't understand why you wanted to pursue that case. What did you come up with anyway? A diary full of notes and thirty-three pages of a book that doesn't go anywhere. Write another feature story instead. Write about that Kader Khan guy. Or whatever his name is. Who is going to be interested in three sisters who were murdered six years ago? Who cares? I am far more experienced, you should have listened to me. Now I am helping a journalist write about the farmers and their crises here. Their crises and the land–human–animal conflict and all that. You wasted all these months, I could have helped you with the land–human–animal conflict. I could have helped you with anything but those three little sisters, but you were acting as if your worthless piece-of-shit life depended on it. I don't understand. You even called Sangere up. He is calling me and telling me to stick it where I shit because you told him that I referred you to him. Behenchod, who told you to say that, chutiya? Randi saala, you want to fuck with yourself, go ahead and do it, but don't pull me into it . . .'

Chitranshu Chitale

Chitranshu had really liked that woman. Narayani Bawane. She had a cooing, sweet voice and there was life in those eyes. If you were an empathetic person, you could see, instantly, that the woman had suffered. She was a lonely woman, and there was an interesting story there: a Mahar who had refused to convert. That way she was an outcast within her own community, and then also with all those upper-caste assholes.

She was with the Rashtriya Ekta Gathan, and Chitranshu didn't like those assholes either—a set of upper-caste men who pretended to care about tribals and Dalits because they wanted a farcical, imagined Hindu unity. What a joke. But of course Narayani had nothing to do with the politics of REG. She was only trying to make a living, and who could blame her if some organization came to her and offered help and monetary benefits?

Chitranshu liked Narayani. So when she told him that she would like to meet him again, he was happy. Perhaps she had a few more anecdotes, and Chitranshu could do with those. All that he had gathered about the sisters had left him with an incomplete picture of their lives. He wanted a fuller profile, a richer profile with enough depth. He wanted people to *feel* for those three sisters, and he wanted people to understand the gravity of their deaths. That was the only way to shake them out of their boots, out of their comfort zones. This is the reality of rural India, wake up and take off those globalized aviators for God's sake.

The only problem was making eye contact. Yes, of all the problems that he could have faced, eye contact was perhaps the gravest here, Chitranshu thought. He had lost his ability to engage fully with female interviewees or find a comfortable space with them ever since he was accused of harassment. *Sexual* harassment. Most people didn't believe in those accusations. Who would? Chitranshu was a harmless man, for the most part. And out-of-office parties . . . he never *did* anything, but who doesn't want sex? He had asked Rujuta, that intern, whether she wanted to take him back to her place, and when she had said no, she wasn't interested, he did not insist. Okay, maybe once or twice. That wasn't as bad. And when did touching a girl's waist become sexual harassment all of a sudden? He touched a lot of waists, and no one had been bothered about that. Shouldn't a man try for sex in this world anymore? It wasn't as if he had pushed her on the bed and made out with her forcefully. I mean, come to places like Murwani, Chitranshu thought, and compare the kind of things that women have to face here with your MeToo movement, you will understand how frivolous most of your concerns are. Next thing you know, they will start accusing you of sexual harassment just because you are jerking off to girls.

The complaint against him had gone nowhere, so apparently Rujuta quit journalism. Well, good for her, Chitranshu thought, one needs to build tough skin to be in this game. But who was he to speak? He had ended up quitting too. For different reasons, though. He would like to believe that his reasons were more ethical.

Whichever way one saw it, at the end of it all, Chitranshu had ended up losing his confidence. He could no longer speak to women properly. What if they accused him of leering at them, looking at them in a certain way, and labelled that as harassment? That fed into his style of interviewing. He could no longer look them in the eye confidently and ask them questions about their lives, about their troubles, about the things they faced as women day in and day out.

For some reason after that whole MeToo thing, Chitranshu felt as if he had lost the legitimacy to ask women about the problems they faced. Chitranshu believed that as far as he was concerned, that movement had been responsible for his inability to ask questions, to do his job properly. There might be some heft to the other accusations, and all the best to those who had taken the legal route, but this was ridiculous: Rujuta's meaningless and useless accusations had left him with a perennial fear of talking to women. Is that what they wanted, those women?

He wanted to get comfortable with Narayani. He wanted to listen to her story, and he wanted to profile her in depth in his book. He had decided to make her a major character, to present her as the strong woman of the hinterlands, someone who could stand up for herself without launching any movement and making Twitter threads about it.

Narayani Bawane

(Excerpts from an interview. Interview conducted on 2 April 2019.)

'Is it okay if I refer to you as Narayani?'

'I don't care what you call me.'

'Okay . . . Well, why did you want to meet me again? I am done with your interview, actually.'

'I wanted . . . What else have you got? Did you manage to find out who killed them?'

'No. Why is everybody asking me that? I am not a detective. I am a journalist. I am trying to write a book about the forgotten sisters.'

'Nobody has forgotten the sisters.'

'A lot of people have. You told me that yourself. That people have moved on.'

'A lot of people haven't moved on. I told you my story. What are you going to write in that book? Are you going to write about the sisters or are you going to find out who the killer is?'

'Like I said, I am not a detective. I would—'

'But you want to find the killer.'

'Yes, Narayani, ideally that should have been the . . . I mean, it's not exactly my job to hunt for killers. But you know as well as I do that nobody is bothered about who the killer is here.'

'And you think you can come here from your Mumbai and find out the killer for us. Solve this mystery for us.'

'What has Mumbai got to do with this?'

'Aren't you from Mumbai?'

'Yes, but—'

'So why did you come here?'

'How many times should I repeat this? To write about the three sisters. About this incident.'

'Why?'

'I am not sure why you are asking me all this. The others—'

'The others are simply fooling around with you. They probably know who killed the girls, and they couldn't care less. They probably sit and drink with the killers every night. But you . . . you come here and you say you want to write a book about these three sisters. Why?'

'Because . . . you must know that I came here, six years ago, when the incident happened, right? I came here to report on the story. But when I went back, I thought it was inadequate. The plight of these sisters never left me. It was always with—'

'It must take a lot of time to come here, no? From Mumbai to Murwani.'

'It does.'

'But not six years. Not that much.'

'I am not sure what you mean. Narayani, look—'

'Did you know that they were raped at that time, the sisters?'

'Of course. It was all over the—'

'And what about the woman *you* raped?'

'I am sorry?'

'What about the woman you raped that night?'

'What are you talking about?'

'Do you know Arvind Godambe?'

'I am—Godambe . . . Yes. He is just a passing—'

'Do you know Arvind Godambe?'

'Yes. I know him. But I am not—'

'Then you know what I am talking about. How do you live with yourself after what you did? Do you even know what you did? Did you enjoy it? Did you boast about it to your friends in Mumbai? Fucking bastard. And then you have the gall to come back here and talk to people about how sad you are about the three sisters and how they were raped and how no one was arrested for the gruesome crime and how you are going to make everyone remember that and make everyone feel guilty about that. *You*. Fucking bastard.'

Ganpat Lawane

(Excerpts from an interview. Interview conducted on 1 April 2019.)

'Haan, bhau, this is exactly where our Tatya Bhau died. This is exactly where. You are standing there. Many people came. I was the first one to see him go. I was right here, where I am standing. I saw the life leave his eyes. The soul leave his body. It was one of the most tragic things I have ever seen. I cried, bhau, of course I cried. Why don't you write about our Tatya Bhau and his social service?'

'Can you just tell me a little bit more about that night? How did you . . . Just tell me more about the night.'

'Arey, bhau, you are just . . . it was nothing. It is nothing. You are going on and on about the night, bhau, we don't remember what we ate for dinner last night.'

'Whatever you can remember.'

'Haan, bhau, ask that randi na, what is his name? Aangle re. What is his name? Sadashiv. Haan. Sadashiv. Ask him what happened that night.'

'Why Sadashiv? What has he got to do with this?'

'Arey, he told potte let's get some pavvas and have a grand hurda party—'

'But isn't Sadashiv from the Aangle family?'

'Haan, bhau, so the potte—'

'How come he drank with these people?'

'—wanted to—*these* people meaning?'

'I mean . . . you know, your people.'

'Lukkhe samjato kay be tu amhala? We are useless people or what just because we are social workers? You are also sitting with me, na. You are useless or what?'

'That's not what I meant. You continue—'

'At least that Sadashiv never discriminated. He never said you are poor people, I am a rich person.'

'I am sure. That's not what I meant—'

'Sadashiv. That way, bhau, I will tell you he is a decent man. Just that the fucker can't fuck his wife. Or any wife for that matter. And—'

'Tell me about that day.'

'Arey, haan na bhau. I am coming to that. Sadashiv is a decent fellow, but he likes to drink. And you can't blame him for that, if you ask me. He likes to drink with everyone, but nobody drinks at his house daily. So he came and drank with us. But that day the boys wanted to sleep. They were exhausted, the boys. But that chutiya would not hear of it. He wants what he wants. He is a faggot, by the way, bailya. You know how their hands are, always ladylike. I don't . . . this is what Fawdya told me—'

'Fawdya?'

'—he said the boys kept grabbing Sadashiv's cock. They gathered around in the afternoon and they kept grabbing his cock. Fawdya said they were trying to check whether it works and it did work. Everyone knew he was a weird little gaandu, that Aangle. Imagine, the Aangles have an impotent son. He is married to that sexy woman: if I were Aangle I would fuck her from behind, around, above, below everywhere every single day. I don't know how he got that meat, but he did, and that's that. But that Sadashiv . . . haan, Fawdya said the boys kept grabbing his cock and he kept pushing them away. And someone said during the party: Fuck me, I want to fuck you. Some person from here only. Or maybe from Punjab or Chhattisgarh or something. Maybe one of the truck drivers. Haan, bhau, some of those people, or someone from the village, I am not sure, bhau. So someone said: Fuck me, and Sadashiv got angry. He began shouting: I am not a faggot, I am not a faggot, I can fuck, I can fuck. I don't know why he did that, because everyone knew he was a faggot and he can't fuck. The entire village knew. But everyone started laughing. Finally someone said: Why don't you prove it?'

'Then?'

'Then that chutiya tried to prove it. But he couldn't, that's what Fawdya said.'

'What do you mean he tried to prove it?'

'I don't know, bhau, that's what Fawdya said. That he tried to prove it. After that everyone blanked out.'

'Who is this Fawdya? Can I get his contact?'

'Arey, what contact. He disappeared long ago.'

'Then someone else from that day? That party? Someone?'

'Everyone disappeared, bhau. I don't know where they are. Chhattisgarh, Jharkhand, Odisha, Bengal, UP, Kashmir. They keep moving about, those people. You ask na, that Aangle guy, try grabbing his cock, he will get a massive hard-on looking at a city man. I am telling you.'

Inspector Deshmukh

(Excerpts from an interview transcript. Interview conducted on 2 April 2019.)

'What are you talking about?'

'He said so himself. They asked Sadashiv Aangle to prove it. What does "prove it" mean? He tried to rape the sisters.'

'Go and talk to Sadashiv then. I have other things to do.'

'You have to investigate this. This is what we know: even the tramp said he was at a party and he heard—'

'Yes, that fucker said that I was at that party too, and so was SP Madam. Let's crack open the case and get someone to interrogate *me*, behenchod. The CBI refused to touch the case and the CID said it's an accident, but crime reporter Chitranshu Chitale has solved it. I will recommend you for a medal, don't worry.'

'Deshmukh Saheb—'

'Look, don't waste my time. Tell this to SP Madam or write about it or do whatever you want to with it, but that case is closed. Kader Muhammad lured the sisters into his Love Jihad racket but that horny fucker ended up fucking them himself. That was that. When the ATS reaches a conclusion about that terror module case, we can see about this. National security is more important, na.'

Anjali Shukla, IPS

(Excerpts from an interview transcript. Interview conducted on 3 April 2019.)

'Is that sufficient evidence?'

'No. But, madam, the—'

'Can I be frank, Chitranshu? There are a thousand such cases languishing in every part of the country. There might be a murderer, there might not be a murderer. There might be a rapist, there might not be a rapist. Who knows what happens in the back of the beyond? We can try our best, but that is the best that we can do, you know? A year or so after the sisters' case, I remember I read about the flight that had disappeared. I don't remember which flight it was, but it was a big case—'

'The Malaysian Airlines?'

'Yes, the Malaysian Airlines. One of my friends' uncle was on that flight. She was devastated. There is still no closure for her. But that is not the point. The point is that the world is yet to find that flight or any of its debris or remnants. It was a flight, an entire flight, for God's sake. But it disappeared and the world has moved on. It was shocking when it happened, but the world has moved on. I consoled myself with that news. If a flight can just vanish without a trace, how practical is it to hope for justice in a small village of a small tehsil in an ignored district in a country such as India? It isn't prudent. Such cases will languish, hard as it is to believe. There is nothing else to it. Don't break your heart over it.'

Reportage

The Aangles don't seem as reprehensible as they are made out to be. They are an influential family, but they don't perhaps yield as much influence in the public imagination as, say, Tatya Khandle. That affects their image, but I don't think they are concerned about their image as much as they are concerned about the continued expansion of their businesses, which, according to the eldest of the Aangles, Ashok, is already 'spread out'. They deal in rice crop, they deal in sugarcane crop, they deal in clothes and they deal in tobacco. But where does the real money come from, I ask half-jokingly. The talk of the town is different, Ashok Saheb, I say, but Ashok simply shrugs it off.

'In a business, there are things that you don't want to do but have to. And people like you always prefer to focus on those things,' he says, nonchalantly and in chaste English.

Ashok says he is the only one from the family who will meet me, since the Aangles are a close-knit clan with strict rules regarding any sort of media interaction. Ashok, the man who handles most of the business, is also the family's spokesperson. I tell him that I am not working on a book about rural business, as he had initially thought I was, but about the murder of three sisters six years ago. He says he knows, word gets around, but he wanted to meet me to 'establish contact'.

'Most people don't like journalists, but I do. I think you people risk your life and your sanity to really look into and explain what matters, and that is admirable. I never say no to meeting a journalist if I can help it.'

'Then we can talk about the sisters freely, I hope,' I say.

'Freely, yes, certainly. But not reliably because I had nothing to do with the case, and I still don't know much about it. You see, we live in the village, but our lives are very removed from it.'

Ashok Aangle is protective of the family reputation. He is careful in what he chooses to say, and very smart. He makes banal and widely known and reported news, like the fact that there are illegal liquor distilleries cropping up all around the area, sound like exclusive information. But most of what he says is not even useful. I try to gently nudge the conversation back to the sisters, but Ashok repeats that he had nothing to do with the sisters. He wasn't even here at that time, he came back two days later.

'When your Mama killed Dighole?'

Ashok is not taken by surprise, and he looks into my eyes and nods confidently, as if he had anticipated exactly this question. He is prepared.

'Yes. I was injured, did you know that? Dighole hurled a rock at my forehead. You can still see the scar here, can you see it?'

I can't, but I nod my head. 'Yes,' I say, 'clearly evident.'

'I don't condone what Mama did to him, of course,' Ashok says. 'But Dighole was drunk and he started creating a scene. Which is fine. But then he started abusing the women of the house. And our Mama is a little sensitive about those things . . .'

We are sitting inside a gazebo in a garden in the backyard of the Aangle house. It is a duplex bungalow crammed with over two dozen people, but there is ample space around it: the backyard, and then in the back of the backyard, the paddy fields.

'I personally believed Dighole was a superior detective mind. Too bad, what happened to him,' Ashok says.

'He was certainly intelligent.'

'You met him?'

'Once. When we were quite drunk.'

Ashok smiles and nods and looks into the distance. He starts telling me about his other business, the sugarcane business, and its history, and then how they are related to the Vikhe-Patils and the Chavans. He ends one anecdote—about a prominent politician in Maharashtra, so I note it down promptly—and is about to meander to something else when I apologize to him and ask him whether he knows the talk about his brother.

'What do they talk about my brother?' he asks me, his smile intact.

'That . . . That your brother is a faggot. I am sorry to use that word, but that's what they mean.'

There is complete silence from Ashok, until he opens his mouth to say something but then his lips dissolve into a smile again. 'My brother has a five-year-old kid. Shantanu. That is all I would like to say about this matter.'

'Fair enough,' I say. 'Can I at least talk to him?'

'Who?'

'Your brother. Sadashiv.'

'He shifted to the US. Minnesota. Our uncle has a dairy business there, Sadashiv looks after that because uncle wanted to return to the village and retire . . . Sadashiv rarely comes to India these days. Business is expanding,' Ashok says, giving me a bright Colgate smile.

Ashok's wife brings tea and Ashok introduces us. He tells his wife that I am here to write 'negative things about the family' but then assures her that 'nothing will happen to him'—meaning me. Then I get a lot of Aangle family history, their origins and their rise out of poverty and their commitment to the land that is Maharashtra and to the country that is India. Ashok tells me about new projects and business expansion plans, and he tells me that even though he can comfortably shift base to Nagpur or Mumbai, he prefers the simplicity of village life. He talks a lot, much of it bullshit, and I keep listening. I don't end up asking him about that night, that party, and what Lawane had told me. It's a practically useless visit, but Ashok has certainly managed to 'establish contact'.

Chitranshu Chitale

Dear Chitranshu,

Thank you for sending us your manuscript. We found the concept interesting, but at this point we think the book lacks the research and therefore authenticity required for a gripping true crime narrative. Moreover, there is no conclusion, practical or thematic. We would like to discuss further if and when you find something more interesting that would authenticate the story.

Thank you,

Vandana Gopi
Noble Publishing House

What is a good story, Chitranshu wondered, and what is an authentic story? And does a good story have to be necessarily authentic? And would an authentic story necessarily be a good story? Chitranshu didn't know the answers, of course, he didn't. All he knew was that once upon a time there were three sisters, and they died, and some believed that they were killed, and others believed that it was a tragic accident, and many believed it was probably suicide. Life went on.

Heading back home from the annual Sunderabai Hall book sale, sitting by the window—a lucky win, for once—Chitranshu pulled out his notebook and held the tip of his pen over a blank page for a few seconds. Then he started writing.

Quick Reads

Hurda by Chitranshu Chitale

Chitranshu Chitale, crime reporter turned novelist, has drawn on his previous experience to write this tense and taut thriller about the murder of three sisters in rural Maharashtra. The novel begins with a typical premise, tracing the steps of the eldest sister on the day of the murder, and draws you into the story. It's a readable book, with a number of well-drawn characters jostling inside a pacey plot. A traditional whodunnit which is both accessible and thought-provoking, it asks the usual murder mystery questions: who and why. Chitale answers these questions satisfactorily while building a good profile of the sisters and their world. A quick but gripping read. Recommended.

Acknowledgements

It is astounding, when one really thinks of it, how many people have helped make us whoever we are through their generosity, kindness, wisdom and advice. I would like to thank, first of all, my family—parents, grandparents, my brother, my uncle and my aunt—for being the pillars of support that they have always been.

I was fortunate to have been selected as one of the South Asia Speaks fellows in 2021. My mentor, Prayaag Akbar, was an incredible support. A brilliant writer and a discerning reader, he helped me gain back the confidence I had lost in myself and in my writing. SAS and the mentorship and encouragement from Prayaag and founder Sonia Faleiro have been of immense help throughout this journey. Thank you.

Without my agent Kanishka Gupta, *Hurda* would have probably remained just a Microsoft Word document. I thank him for his confidence in the manuscript, and his vital reassurances through the process of submission and publication.

R. Sivapriya at Bloomsbury helped shape this book into what it is today. I thank her for her advice and suggestions about the manuscript, for putting faith in a debut writer with hardly any writing out there and for tolerating my impatience.

Thank you, also, to the many sources I consulted while writing this book. You spoke to me in confidence—

now I hope I have written the book that I promised you I would write.

Then there are those friends and beta readers who have always been my greatest cheerleaders: Pranav Nair and the people at Gopalkrishna, Joanna George, Sahil M. Parsekar, Omkar Gokhale, Aryan Sathe, Advait Ubhayakar, Aakriti Handa, Tanya Khandelwal and all the people at D. Thank you.

About the Author

Atharva Pandit is based in Mumbai. His writings have appeared in The Wire and the *Economic and Political Weekly*, among other publications. He was the 2021 South Asia Speaks fellow for fiction. *Hurda* is his debut novel.